in the time we lost

Carrie Hope Fletcher

in the time we lost

sphere

SPHERE

First published in Great Britain in 2019 by Sphere
This paperback edition published by Sphere in 2020

1 3 5 7 9 10 8 6 4 2

A CIP catalogue record for this book is available from the British Library.

ISBN 978-0-7515-7127-1

Typeset in Sabon by M Rules
Printed and bound in Great Britain by Clays Ltd, Elcograf S.p.A.

Papers used by Sphere are from well-managed forests
and other responsible sources.

Sphere
An imprint of
Little, Brown Book Group
Carmelite House
50 Victoria Embankment
London EC4Y 0DZ

An Hachette UK Company
www.hachette.co.uk

www.littlebrown.co.uk

To those haunted by what ifs: life's too short to spend it wondering what could have been. Go for it.

Prologue

A Wedding

July 14th 2018

The clouds burst open like eggs being cracked for a cake. The rain came tumbling down onto her silver shoes as Luna Lark hoicked up her dress and swung her feet out of the car.

'Did anyone bring a brolly?' she laughed, looking up expectantly at her one and only bridesmaid.

'Sorry.' Lottie bit her lip, shielding her face with her silver clutch bag. 'It was sunny when we left! I checked the weather on my phone and everything!' Automatically, Lottie moved the clutch bag from over her own head to hover over Luna's as she got out of the car. Luna's peculiar naturally white hair fishtailed its way down her back and her blue eyes glistened as she looked up at the church.

'Well ...' Down the pathway to the doors of the church, she could see her fiancé's brother and best man, Stephen, waiting for them. 'It's not far. I'll just have to make a mad dash for it!' Luna bundled up the skirt of her second-hand dress into her arms, pushed herself to standing and teetered down the cobbled pathway as quickly as she could. She giggled and shivered as the rain splashed her bare shoulders but it only lasted for a few seconds before she was safe under the archway next to Stephen. Stephen was short and wiry, not unlike his younger brother except Noel was taller and knew how to hold himself. Stephen, however, had all the charisma of a spider and, in the eight years that she'd been dating his brother, he had never warmed to Luna. That was just Stephen, though, she had always thought. He was distant and cold, yet strategic and pragmatic and he was always the one to call in a crisis. Stephen and Noel's mother had once described Stephen as a 'a funny fish' and Luna couldn't think of a better way to describe him. Now that he was to be her brother-in-law, she was ready to embrace his quirks and his chilly nature, once and for all.

'Luna ...' he started.

'I know, I know, I'm a little late but you know me and driving. I must have made that poor driver go at about five miles per hour. I think the traffic behind us thought we were a hearse!' She wiped her dress down as best she could. 'How do I look?' She twirled.

'Beautiful, Luna,' said Lottie as she joined them,

wobbling slightly as one of her heels got trapped between the uneven paving stones.

'Luna ...' Stephen tried again.

'Oh, your mum would be weeping right now if she were here!' Lottie sobbed and lifted her bouquet to hide the sudden onslaught of tears.

'I think Dad would be the one sobbing!' Luna smiled but felt a lump fill her throat. 'And Jeremy would just be laughing at them both.'

'They're all watching. Up there.' Lottie pointed to the darkening clouds above them. 'I just know it,' she sniffed.

'Yes, this rain is probably J's doing!' Luna peeked her head out from under the archway and lifted her gaze to the sky just as a large drop of rain splashed right between her eyes and slid down the bridge of her nose. 'Thanks, bro!' she laughed, giving the sky a thumbs-up.

'*Luna*, are you even listening to me?' Stephen huffed.

'Yes, *Stephen*, but you've not said anything. I know I'm a little late but I honestly couldn't have gotten here any faster. You know what I'm like!'

Once upon a time Luna had been an avid driver; knowing her getaway vehicle was always parked just outside was liberating. She'd drive anywhere and everywhere she possibly could, feeling cramped and nauseous in the passenger seat if anyone else ever insisted that they should be behind the wheel. Once upon a time, she probably would have wanted to drive herself to her own wedding. She'd scroll through songs on her iPod whilst driving, she'd answer text messages, even apply her lipstick in the rear-view mirror without a second's thought. She'd heard of the horrors of being complacent when driving, of course she had. Who hadn't! But ... she was a *good* driver! It would never happen to her! And she was right. It didn't. It happened to her family.

She was eighteen years old and had been staying over at her boyfriend's house when she had received the call. As the result of someone else's arrogance behind the wheel, her mother, father and brother had been killed in a crash that totalled both vehicles. The other driver had been on the phone, and didn't pause for even a split second before darting across a busy road. The speeding vehicle had hit the rear of her parents' car, sending it spinning into the front garden of someone else's house. Luckily the owners had been upstairs asleep when it happened, but had they been in their living room watching TV there might well have been more fatalities to add to an already too-long list. The car had been crushed entirely, like a giant had tried to turn it into an accordion. Her mum and dad, she was told, were killed instantly upon impact but her brother had held on just long enough for her to be able to say goodbye. Ultimately, he had died of his injuries in hospital.

'But ... I'm such a *good* driver,' sobbed the defendant in court but no amount of tears or apologies would reverse that one fateful, fatal night. The night that had robbed Luna of her entire immediate family.

Luna mourned and tried her hardest to continue

through life but it was difficult when she felt like she had nothing good to latch onto, no light at the end of a seemingly million-mile-long tunnel. Her mother's twin brothers came and stayed for a while, their jolly nature helping to brighten her up as much as they were able and together they sorted out all the outstanding family affairs whilst sharing stories long into whiskey-fuelled nights. Stories that Luna had never heard. Wild tales of her parents' past that they probably would have trusted her with when she was older than just eighteen but would now never be able to tell her themselves.

'You know your mum used to smoke?' Uncle Bryce said, sloshing more brown liquid into Luna's glass.

'You're *kidding*,' she sputtered.

'Oh yeah! Like a chimney!' Uncle Bill bellowed.

'She could do all the tricks, too. Smoke rings, that French inhale thing ...' Bryce swirled his fingers through the air.

'Like Frenchie in *Grease*?' Luna asked.

'Isn't that what Dave from next door used to call her?'

'Yeah! That's why!' Bill sipped his drink.

'*Sure* it is!' Luna and Bryce howled and Bill couldn't help but spray his whiskey into the air. Luna couldn't have been more grateful for their company. However, as soon as they left, the weight of it all came plummeting down around her and she felt like she had very little in life to look forward to any more. So when her boyfriend Noel proposed, it felt like fate had intervened – and Luna was a big believer in fate. A 'hopeless romantic', as they say. She'd read every vaguely romantic novel the library carried by the time she was sixteen so it was no wonder that she now wrote them herself. She could dream up a romance between two unlikely lovers in moments and have the first draft of a novel done and dusted in six months. Although Noel had proposed a little half-heartedly, didn't have a ring and most certainly wouldn't have wanted to get his clean, pressed trousers dirty by getting down on one knee, Luna was still thrilled. With a job writing romantic fiction, she couldn't wait to start a dream life with her new husband and leave all the horror behind her. If anyone deserved a little bit of happiness it was Luna. A new life, a new husband and one day a new house and children

... now, she felt like she had everything to live for.

'*Luna* ... he's not here,' Stephen blurted.

'Who's not here?' Luna's smile was still plastered on her face.

'*Noel*.' Stephen wiped his forehead with a flat hand. 'Noel's not here.'

'Well, why not?' she laughed, tapping an imaginary watch on her wrist. Something twinged in her gut: she wasn't sure if it was panic or one of the bones in her second-hand dress poking through the fabric.

'The traffic that side of town was a bit dodgy when I checked it out this morning.' Lottie reached out for Luna's shoulder. 'He'll be here soon!'

'It wasn't the *traffic*.' Stephen shot Lottie a look under his untamed eyebrows.

'He's never late.' Luna adjusted her veil.

'He's not *late*,' Stephen said, shooting Luna the same look.

'Well, then *where* is he?' Lottie demanded. Stephen sighed. '*Well?*'

'He's . . . not coming.' Stephen shrugged and with that, Luna's ivory bubble burst . . . as did Lottie's temper.

'*What do you mean he's not coming?!*'

'He's just not quite . . . ready.' Stephen shrugged again.

'That little *shit!* Urgh, I could just KILL him! I always knew he was a total weirdo – sorry, Luna – he was always acting aloof and he was a right arse at your birthday party! This is just the arrogant icing on a very gigantic cake made up of his bullshit! A bullshit cake! And I actually can't believe that he would just . . .' Lottie wandered out into the rain to take out her anger with her clutch bag on the hydrangea trees that lined the path.

'Luna, I'm sorry. He said to tell you he thought he was ready but he isn't. He's sorry, too.' Stephen tilted his head and she wanted to punch the only-ever-so-slightly apologetic look off his face.

'Let me speak to him.' She could feel the sob rise in her throat.

'He's asked you not to call.' Stephen checked his phone again, a message very clear on his screen.

'Call? You mean he won't even see me?'

7

'I'm sorry.' He didn't look up as he swiped to the right and tapped out a response.

'You keep saying that.'

'Because I am.' He shrugged again.

'Is that him?' Luna leant over his arm but Stephen quickly returned his phone to his inside jacket pocket.

'I'm sorry.' He squeezed the top of her white lace-clad arm but Luna pulled out of his grip. Stephen rolled his eyes and had Luna not felt so elegant and demure in her dress, she was sure she would have hit him. He stepped out into the now-pouring shower and left Luna outside the church. A church filled with family and friends, waiting for a wedding that would never happen.

One

A Year Later

Louise? No. I knew a girl at school called Louise. Always used to chew with her mouth open. Billy? Too jovial. Robyn? With a Y? I suppose, but Starbucks would never get it right.

The world through the window was a miserable blue-tinged grey, the glass becoming increasingly spattered with rain the further north of Britain Luna rode. She was sure the man with his incessant snoring opposite her at their cramped train table, still clutching a map of Scotland in his hands as he snoozed, had missed his stop. John o'Groats was the last stop in Scotland before the tracks lurched out across the sea to their final destination:

Ondingside. However, unable to bring herself to be the bearer of bad news, she sat quietly looking out of the window and let him, at the very least, have a peaceful sleep. Her phone buzzed and the name LOTTIE flashed up with a picture of the two of them, their arms wrapped around each other so tightly you couldn't see whose belonged to whom. The contents of Luna's stomach rose into her throat but she swallowed and turned the phone screen down onto the table.

I've always liked the name Persephone. Percy for short. Hardly less conspicuous than my real name, though, I guess. Plus, it means I wouldn't be able to name my child that ... but to have a child, I'd quite like a boyfriend to have that child with and the last one ran away ...

Luna glanced down briefly at her new open notebook in which she'd written the date, a few potential names and doodled maybe a hundred crescent moons in the top left-hand corner. She flipped backwards a page where the vague beginnings of her new novel haphazardly appeared on the page, making little sense and giving her even less inspiration. The beginning of a novel was always the hardest for Luna. She'd written five books thus far and every time she was faced with the glaring blank page of a new notebook or her laptop, it was almost as if she couldn't remember how she'd written novels before or how she could possibly write one again. Usually she had some vague central idea that she could write around but this time, she had zip. Once she made a start and got the ball rolling she knew she'd be okay but first she needed to figure out how exactly to roll the ball, and with deadlines looming in the near future, there was the undeniable flutter of panic in her stomach. Her notebook was as empty as her head.

A tragic love story in which one of them dies on the way to the church and the other is left waiting at the altar ... no.

A funny love story in which an unlikely couple bond over their mutual love of stamp collecting but then one of them gets left at the altar and ... nope.

A dystopian love story in which the population of Earth is shipped off to another planet where our heroine falls for someone of an alien species but when it comes to vowing to spend the rest of their lives together, the alien does a runner .... Okay, Luna, you need to stop.

All her ideas led back to her failed relationship but as Lottie had kept reminding her: 'You weren't technically left at the altar, so that idea needs to die. What is it they say? Write what you know? And you don't know what it's like to be left at the altar. Because you weren't. It was just ... I dunno ... a near scrape with a dead-end future. Write about ... I dunno ... having a weird name. OR ME! Write about *me*!' No one would want to read about her failed almost-marriage or all the tragedy that came before as much as she wouldn't want to write about it. However, her creative juices had dried up and no other ideas would flow.

She closed the notebook and told herself that starting tomorrow wouldn't be the worst thing in the world. One more evening of leaving her notebook's pages empty wasn't going to tip the scales. She reached for her coffee cup and the raised semi-circle of shiny, white skin on the back of her right hand glistened in the harsh train lighting.

'You'd think, as an author, I'd at the very least be able to pick a better name for myself than Luna,' she muttered. She had been called Luna because of her crescent-moon-shaped birthmark on the back of her right hand, on the fleshy bit between her thumb and forefinger. It was light and shimmered like a stretch mark but hadn't faded over the years. In fact, it only seemed to shine brighter.

'Nah, it's got nothing to do with that mark!' her brother used to jibe. 'It's because you're so dim and nowhere near as bright as the *son*!' he'd laugh, gesturing to himself triumphantly.

'Well, we were either going to call you Luna ...' her mother would smile, 'or Croissant.'

Once upon a time, she had loved her name. Luna Lark. Night and day. It held weight and had meaning. 'With a name like that,' people would say, 'you could be a ...' and they'd insert all manner of exciting jobs. News reporter, actress, astronaut ...! As a child, her schoolmates would relish calling out to her in the play-ground, like the word had magical powers. In a way, it did. It conjured up a friend, every time. Everyone wanted to be *Luna's* friend. The mother of one of Luna's class-mates had thought that her daughter had made Luna up as an imaginary friend, not once considering a person could actually have such a unique name. Said mother had had quite a shock when her daughter brought home an actual child, for whom she hadn't prepared dinner, on the assumption that imaginary friends didn't need feeding. Even Luna's parents seemed to swoon when they called her down for tea. Far from the hippies one would expect, her mother was a midwife, who'd heard women call their children far more extravagant and ridiculous things than 'Luna', and her father worked from home as a children's author, who would name his *characters* far more extravagant and ridiculous things than 'Luna', too. Luna and her father would spend hours on sun loungers in the garden, under blankets in the pitch black of night, looking upwards for meteor showers or the International Space Station as it flew close enough to be seen. Whilst the bats dove for moths above them, he'd tell her stories of 'Luna the Space Explorer' and her alien friends who sailed on waves made of stars.

'I think my love for outer space and the extraterrestrial became imprinted onto you, Luna. Quite literally,' her father would say, taking her hand and kissing her crescent scar. 'How lucky am I to have captured my very own little moonbeam.'

Moonbeam was his special nickname for her and had been ever since she was born. She loved it almost as much as she loved her official name. That was until people started saying it differently.

Luna, I'm so sorry.

That's Luna. Poor Luna.

Are you all right, Luna?

Everything will be okay, Luna.

Luna. Luna. Luna.

The pity made her feel sick. The lilt in everyone's voices and the sadness in their eyes made her want to shut her doors, bar her windows and never return to the outside world again. There was little satisfaction to be had from someone saying your name when no one ever said it with anything but sorrow. Luna had heard her own name said so many times in such a way that she'd rather be called Snoopy or Mickey Mouse or Velma Dinkley if it made people sound different when they spoke to her. Anything but Luna. She felt like she had become a creature that was able to suck the joy out of any room just by being present. She could be having one of her few and far between 'okay days' and yet she could sense the discomfort radiating from the people she knew when she passed them by. No one knew how to even be around her any more, let alone speak to her.

I don't need a new name, she thought. *If anyone asks, I'm Miss Lark and that's that. No one needs to be on a first name basis, anyway. No one needs to get that close.*

The train pulled into the station. Luna had thrown everything into her backpack, retrieved her case from the

14

rack and was on the platform before the sleeping man had even been able to ask where he was. Luna pushed her bright orange ticket through the slot and stepped into the station. WELCOME TO ONDINGSIDE! was emblazoned across the exit but the sign was rusty and looked like it was one strong gust away from falling on the heads of travellers and so had very much lost the merry sentiment of 'welcome'.

'Home sweet home,' she muttered, her breath swirling into the air in front of her.

'Need any help, Miss?' a man asked as she walked underneath the dodgy sign. He pushed off his cab and flicked the last of his cigarette to the curb, smoke still dripping from his mouth as he spoke.

'I need to get to Nobody's Inn?' She showed him the map on her phone. He nodded and opened the boot. 'I . . . I've been there before,' she added.

'Then you'll know it's not far from here,' he said, giving her a hint of a smile. "Bout a four-pound journey.' She nodded back and climbed in the back of the cab.

Luna always lied and said she'd already visited whatever her destination, in order to avoid cabbies mounting up their fare by driving round in circles and ripping her off. This time, however, Luna wasn't fibbing. Not only had she visited Ondingside before but she'd also stayed in Nobody's Inn and every time her circumstances seemed more dire than the last.

'Could you drive a little slower, please?' Luna said

15

when her stomach somersaulted as the car lurched around a roundabout, the right-hand-side tyres almost tipping off the tarmac. The driver grunted his response, although he still seemed to be taking the narrow country bends at an alarming pace, but before Luna could complain again, the familiar sight of a pub flashed past her window. The Green Arrow.

'Urghh.' She groaned at her stomach but more at the memory now swimming in a cider-soaked haze in her head.

A year ago, Luna had washed up in Ondingside with a 'barely used' wedding dress in her suitcase to sell and an empty ring finger. What had meant to be a romantic trip for two had turned into a very lonely and very non-refundable solo getaway. When Luna had suggested going somewhere neither of them had ever been before, she had expected somewhere abroad. Her heart had sunk when she'd been presented with British train tickets but Luna told herself off for not being more specific and knew that Noel would have picked it as the cheapest option. Nothing, however, could have deflated her excitement. 'I'm happy anywhere as long as I'm with you!' she'd said, with hearts in her eyes. Noel grunted in reply.

Luna should have noticed that his enthusiasm wasn't only lacking towards the trip but also towards their relationship. She definitely realised far too late that she *wasn't* happy anywhere as long as she was with Noel because being anywhere with Noel usually meant she was worried he would be snippy with their waiter for forgetting to bring tap water to the table or be constantly watching her bank account with a furrowed brow because he was overly frugal with his own money and so never contributed to even the food in the fridge, let alone the bills for the house. She was always tense when he was close and often curating her real thoughts and feelings to avoid an argument that usually happened anyway. Even his justification for jilting her had been as weak and cowardly as his actions were. In his feeble and formal email, he'd used classic phrases such as 'It's not you, it's me' and 'I just don't think I'm mature enough yet' and 'Maybe in another world it would have been different'. She knew it would have been Stephen pushing him to explain and tie up loose ends, not a genuine apology. There wasn't even the word *sorry* in sight. So, when she was sitting in what would have been *their* room, alone, she didn't feel sad that he wasn't there, but sad that she didn't feel sad he wasn't there. Luna wanted her fairytale happy-ever-after more than she had wanted Noel, which meant she'd put up with Noel in order to get it. It wasn't right and she knew that now. She just wished she'd been stronger and let go of him sooner. Being alone was better than being with someone for the sake of it and so being alone was exactly what she would do. Lottie had offered to come with her so that they could turn it into a 'drink-until-we-forget-what-he-looked-like' trip but Luna insisted that she needed to clear her head, not cloud it, and that alcohol would be the last thing she turned to for pain relief from her aching heart. This was why Luna never told Lottie what happened on her first trip to Ondingside the year before her permanent move there and why Luna would *never* tell Lottie what actually happened …

Two

What Actually Happened

July 15th 2018

The Nobody's Inn looked very pub-like from the outside. It was small. So small, in fact, that Luna wondered how many rooms there could possibly be in order for it to classify as an inn. It was quaint, shabby and looked Tudor-built although whether that was authentic, Luna wasn't sure. It seemed to be the only building for miles, plonked on a little hill overlooking the sea. The warm yellow light pouring out of its windows looked heaven-sent to Luna after the long journey, but the inn's landlady had been over-familiar when she'd checked in. She'd asked too many questions and never seemed to wait for an answer. However, now she was gone, Luna wished she hadn't left at all, as the silence was crushing.

Her room in the inn was nowhere near as shabby as its exterior, but for such a small room, it was filled with far too much furniture. A bed, two bedside tables, a wardrobe and a coffee table by an armchair. Luna felt she was constantly having to dodge sharp wooden corners as she opened up her case and started to unpack. She hung up her second-hand wedding dress on the outside of the wardrobe and sat on the edge of the bed, staring at it, with its worn lace sleeves and slightly off-white colour, not from design, but age. It had been given to her by her mother's sister, Auntie Judith, and a family friend had made the alterations as best she could but there was little to be done except make it the right size to fit Luna and repair the beading that had come away. Luna had only worn it for only half a day, and the beads that didn't need repairing at the time were now hanging from their threads and the lace had become a little fuzzy. Lottie had tried to bundle Luna back in the car after Stephen had broken the news that her husband-to-be was actually her husband-*not*-to-be but Luna couldn't bear to sit still in such a confined space feeling trapped and suffocated. So, she'd taken off her heels and her veil, thrown them in the car on the passenger seat and walked home in the rain. She wrangled with her emotions all the way back. The feeling of frustration that Noel had embarrassed her in front of everyone they knew punched the feeling of relief that she wouldn't have to spend the rest of her life with Noel in the face. The opposing feelings rolled over and over in her gut until she couldn't make head or tail of which feeling was worse.

Luna hoped the first wedding her beautiful dress had seen had been happier and more successful and hoped it would forgive her for putting it through such humiliation. Looking at the dress now, Luna felt that she should have known. It was a mess – as her marriage would have been had Noel actually gone through with it.

Luna had been besotted with the *idea* of what they could have been and not what they actually were. What they actually were was two lost souls who hadn't *chosen* each other but *found* each other and latched on for dear life when they thought they might drown. They were exactly what the other needed at the time but most certainly not what they wanted. Not for forever, anyway. Luna wished she'd been the one to realise it first. She certainly wouldn't have waited until their wedding day to throw in the towel, but nothing could be done now except to repair the damage as best she could. Although Stephen was, and always would be, an arse, at least he'd forced Noel to front any outstanding costs from the wedding.

'Too bloody right!' Lottie had yelled at her down the phone. 'The wedding didn't happen because of him so it's only right that the eight-foot-long bill doesn't happen to you!'

The only thing Luna had to deal with was the

embarrassment, which was why she was currently in Nobody's Inn, on an island no one really knew existed that had a population of 383. Luna planned to start writing her new novel and read all the books that other people had written that she had packed in her suitcase. A week of reading and writing mingled with a little sulking and very little else. She'd not even planned to leave Nobody's Inn if she could help it. Food was served downstairs and she was ravenous after that six-hour train journey and so that was exactly where she would start.

'Kitchen's closed on Sundays, darling. No hot food, just a selection of sandwiches, but in all honesty, they're not our finest cuisine. You're better off trying the Green Arrow for hot food. It's only down the road and their fish pie is to die for! Y'know, I'd never had fish pie before I'd tried it there and as soon as I did, it just had to go on the menu here! They don't just do fish pie though, there's so much to choose from on that menu and . . .'

Luna slowly backed towards the door and slipped out. She could hear the landlady still talking as she got to the edge of the drive and she google-mapped 'the Green Arrow'.

The word 'bustling' didn't quite cover it. Luna walked for fifteen minutes down country pathways, passing cows and sheep in field after field until the buzz of a hundred conversations broke through the rustle of the trees. The people of Ondingside spilled out into the street and the chalkboard sign outside the pub told Luna why.

Beers sloshed over the edges of full pint glasses outside as punters scanned through lists of famous books and authors on their phones, holding them skywards for even just a glimmer of better reception. Luna collided with a man and just dodged the tidal wave of ale as it tumbled from his glass.

'It's only half six . . . ' she mumbled as she ducked into the heaving pub. The noise inside was almost unbearable as a man with a mic tried to speak over everyone, shouting into it, making the speakers crackle.

'Hello everyone! I'm Beau, your host with the most for the evening!' He paused for laughter. None came. 'Tough crowd. The drunker you are, the funnier I am, so keep drinking, lads!' The host caught Luna's eye for a moment. 'And ladies!' He picked up his own beer and raised it in Luna's direction. Luna pretended she hadn't seen and made her way to the bar.

The clientele looked regular. They all took their – presumably usual – seats as they filed in and everyone seemed to know everyone. There was even an elderly gentleman who felt so at home that he'd fallen asleep in the corner behind a table adorned with six empty pint glasses.

'Are you still serving food?' Luna asked the bartender

as he was about to serve someone who had arrived after her.

'WHA?' shouted the bartender, cupping his hand behind his ear.

'Are you still serving food?!' She mimed putting something into her mouth and biting.

'FOOD?' he yelled and Luna nodded, her stomach growling so hard now that she was sure he could hear it over the rabble. He pointed to a sign.

TONIGHT THE GREEN ARROW IS ONLY
OPEN TO QUIZ TEAM MEMBERS.
FOOD AND DRINK SERVED TO YOU
KNOW-IT-ALLS UNTIL MIDNIGHT.

She reached into her jeans pocket, pulled out a pound coin and held it out to him. He pointed to yet another sign.

NO SINGLE PUB QUIZ PLAYERS.
TEAMS OF TWO OR MORE. BUDDY UP!

Luna's heart sank. She didn't much like the idea of giving up and having to search for food somewhere else and passing all the people on the way out that she'd already passed on the way in was an embarrassment she wasn't keen on feeling. Just as the barman was about to walk away she reached across the bar and tapped his arm.

'I'M WITH HIM!' she yelled, pointing to the elderly

man asleep in the corner. The barman held up two fingers at her but before she could feel upset she realised he meant for her to pay for her new quiz teammate too. Considering the gentleman was unwillingly taking part in her fiendish plan to get fed, it was only fair. She shrugged and rooted around in her coat pocket for another pound.

'FISH PIE AND A … A … A PINT OF CIDER, PLEASE.' Luna very rarely drank. It wasn't that she didn't enjoy the taste of alcohol or really even the way it made her feel when she was nearing her limit. It was quite simply the fear of being sick and she had her best friend Lottie very much to blame for that. On Luna's eighteenth birthday, her dad had hired a limousine for herself, Lottie and a few other friends to take them into central London where they would have dinner at a restaurant in Covent Garden. Lottie had come over during the afternoon to get ready with her, and brought a water bottle that she had previously filled with cheap and nasty vodka. She let Luna take a swig not knowing it wasn't water and she sprayed it across her room as it began to burn its way down her throat. They laughed and Lottie clapped her hands as Luna drank her way through the bottle as the evening drew near. Just before they left, Luna's mum invited all of her friends into the kitchen to open a bottle of champagne and proudly poured her what her parents thought was her first drink as an eighteen-year-old. Luna blamed her slight wobble on not being steady in the heels Lottie had forced her to wear and downed her glass of bubbly.

'Why don't you have one for the road, Luny?'

Luna winked and sucked in her cheeks, trying not to smile as her mum poured her another, looking delighted as she drank. By the time they teetered out to the limo, Luna felt waves of nausea crash over her. Once the car started moving, Luna thought she was going to be okay ... until she knew she absolutely was not.

'Hey!' Lottie shrieked as Luna emptied out her handbag onto her lap. 'What are you—?' Luna wasn't able to empty everything out in time before she vomited into the handbag. 'PULL OVER!' Lottie yelled as she banged her fist against the partition between them and the driver. Luna, humiliated, left her handbag in a bush, couldn't bring herself to eat much at the swanky restaurant and begged her friends not to tell her parents when they got home. From that point onwards, Luna never drank more than one drink, no matter what the occasion.

Luna wasn't sure if it was the jaunty pub atmosphere that had made her fancy something a little stronger than her usual lemonade, or whether she was giving in to the mild air of peer pressure she would feel were she the sole person in the pub without an alcoholic beverage. Either way, it was the meal she couldn't wait for, it didn't matter what she washed it down with.

Sheepishly, she sat opposite the sleeping man. Even if she hadn't picked him to be her lucky teammate, it was the only free seat in the house due to his lack of conversation. And his snoring. And his smell. Luna was just starting to think that maybe it wasn't her best idea when a plate was placed in front of her upon which sat a little separate dish of steaming fish pie surrounded by a sea of chips. Luna dug in and immediately burnt her mouth on the sauce underneath the pastry but it was oh-so worth it.

'Remember to chew,' said a voice above her. 'We don't want you choking to death before the quiz begins. It's not like he's gonna have many of the answers.' Luna looked up and a trickle of gravy rolled down her chin. It was the quiz host.

'I'm Beau, the Quizmaster,' he beamed. Up close, Luna noticed how jolly he looked. If a 'Santa Claus: The Early Years' film was ever made, he'd be Luna's first pick for the title role. His round face had only soft edges and his big brown eyes were endlessly kind. 'Team name?' He bobbed his clipboard.

'It's just me.' Luna shrugged.

'And who are you?'

'Just me.' Luna turned back to her pie, hoping that answered his question.

'And what's *your* team name?' Much to her dismay, Beau pulled out the other rickety chair from under the table, swivelled it around and straddled it, his slight beer belly moulding against the wooden bars. 'S'cuse me, sir!' he said to the sleeping man who snored loudly back in reply.

'Do I have to have one?' Luna dug out another little piece of pie to avoid his focused stare.

'Come on, everyone's got a silly quiz name. That's arguably the best bit of a quiz! See them over there?' He pointed to a rowdy bunch of about six young guys all dressed in cricket gear, their overly long kneepads still strapped to their gangly legs, all sitting swivelled to the side to avoid taking each other's eyes out. 'Quizz On My Face,' he chuckled.

'Lovely.' Luna stuffed the forkful of pie into her mouth whilst his gaze was elsewhere.

'And that lot over in that corner?' He gestured with his pen to four women, all laughing raucously over their glasses of red wine. 'Quiz-Team Aguilera.'

Luna swallowed and swigged from her cider. 'Funny.' She attempted a smile but a burp gurgled in her throat, causing her to grimace.

'So what will it be?' He poised his pen over the clipboard.

'Just me.'

'That's your team name? "Just Me".'

'I suppose it is, yes.' She nodded.

'Well, all right then. But just to warn you, bad team names don't get much appreciation at the Green Arrow.' He poised his pen above the clipboard once more but Luna shrugged.

'I'm mainly just here for the pie, anyway.'

'Yes, I can tell. Although considering how much of it is around your mouth, I'm surprised you're not still starving,' he chortled. 'Well, don't say I didn't warn you.

Oh, and good luck. You know much about books?' Beau pulled a sheet of paper out from underneath the list of punny team names and tucked it under her dinner plate.

'A little.' She couldn't help smirking underneath the hand that was wiping the sauce from her upper lip. Beau narrowed his eyes at her and then disappeared amongst the gathering quiz teams, leaving Luna to finish her pie in a slightly less monstrous way.

As far as pies went, it wasn't too shabby but Luna was more surprised to find how well the cider was going down. She had never really been one for casual drinking, never finding a 'usual' or anything that tasted better than it made her feel, but this cider was sweet with a sharp little kick in the back of her throat that had left her with a warmth in the centre of her stomach that seemed be spreading outwards. She downed the dregs and as the bar was quietening down as people took their seats for the nearing quiz, the barman caught her eye and wiggled an imaginary glass in his hands with a raised eyebrow. Luna wiggled her own glass back in response.

'Okay!' Beau shouted down the mic. The speakers squeaked, everyone clutched their ears and some of Quiz-Team Aguilera screamed.

'Nice one, Beau!' yelled one of the erotically charged gentlemen from the unfortunately named quiz team. His team made a noise Luna had only ever heard football crowds make on the telly when her brother had watched it religiously.

29

'All right, settle down everyone! I know it's boring but I do have to start off by stating the rules.' The pub groaned. 'I know, I know, but there's only two! One: mobile phones have to be turned off now.' Another groan. 'My eagle-eyed friends here at the Green Arrow and I will be keeping a lookout. If we catch anyone sneakily googling under the table, you and your entire team will be *disqualified*! Even if you're just texting the other half, any phone usage will get you into trouble. Two: the answer on the Quizmaster's sheet, the Quizmaster being yours truly ...' – he paused again for applause that never came so he coughed to cover up the sad silence – 'is final, even if it turns out to be wrong!'

Luna took a long gulp from her fresh, bubbling glass and eyed up the sheet Beau had given her. It had four sections to it, each containing six blank spaces. *Authors of Yesterday, Books of Today, General Knowledge* and a picture round. The picture round had images of front covers, their titles smudged over, and a little box underneath to presumably guess the name and author. Luna fiddled in the pocket of her coat on the back of her chair for a pen and when she found one, started filling them in.

Wuthering Heights, The Casual Vacancy, Fifty Shades of Grey, Breaking Dawn, Game of Thrones and *Juliet, Naked*. Luna folded up the bottom half of her paper and put down her pen with schoolgirl pride. Beau caught her eye and she could actually feel the corner of her lips lift, just a little.

'Okay, ladies and gentlemen! Let's get started!'

The first round of questions was simple and Luna had all the answers. Jane Austen, J. R. R. Tolkien, Mary Ann Evans (George Eliot), George R. R. Martin and George Orwell. The second round had Luna's brain fighting through a cider-induced haze to drudge up names such as *The Serpent of Essex, The Miniaturist* and *A Horse Walks into a Bar* but Luna was certain she wasn't wrong. At the very least, she knew she was more clued up than everyone else in the bar despite her inexperience with alcohol starting to show.

'Okay, kids! Third round, final question! Are you ready?' Beau rumbled down the mic.

'WHEEEYYYYY!' replied the pub.

'Who said "Elementary, my dear Watson"?'

'Got it!' shouted a man at the table next to Luna's, brandishing his team's answer sheet.

'We've nailed this, girls!' Quiz-Team Aguilera sloppily high-fived each other and geed each other up into a sudden frenzy of cackling. Luna looked down at her answer sheet.

It's not Sherlock Holmes. Everyone thinks it is. But it's not. It's P.G. Wodehouse ... but the answer on the quizmaster's sheet is final ... and I don't know if he'd know that.

She glanced over at Beau, who happened to be casting an eye in her direction.

He knows. I know he knows.

31

'Okay, ladies and gents. Time to hand your papers in. Now, as much as we love you all, we can't trust you not to cheat your answers. So we'll be doing the marking and we'll be back with you for the scores in fifteen minutes!' Luna quickly scrawled down *P.G. Wodehouse* and couldn't help but try to find Beau's gaze as she handed over her crumpled, slightly damp sheet of answers to one of the female bar staff.

'Another?' she asked.

'Yeah, go on.' And to Luna's surprise she reached out and touched the girl's arm.

Fifteen minutes for Beau was painful. Filing through dissolving sheets of paper that stank of beer and gravy and the further down the page he got, the writing became increasingly illegible, the answers more daft.

According to The Quizzard of Oz, the UK's richest author was 'That one who wrote about that boy with the cut on his head'. Beau sighed. He was strangely inclined to give them the point just because he knew who they meant. However, he wasn't *that* generous and had very strict rules when it came to his beloved pub quiz. Beau always found that being far more sober than everyone else in such close proximity was a fresh kind of hell he could only bear to put himself through once a week. When he was behind the bar, at least there was a large barrier but the quiz put him right in the midst of the drunken rowdiness and he could practically hear the rapidly depleting brain cells. It would be worth the extra cash he received on top of his measly weekly wage when the winner was finally announced.

Luna was on her third pint of cider. Between the night with her uncles after her family had died and this unprecedented drunken haze she now found herself in after being left on her wedding day, a worry flashed in Luna's mind that this was the beginning of some kind of coping mechanism. The warmth flushing through her body felt glorious, like she'd been submerged fully clothed into a bubble bath and the cloud she felt like her head was in didn't seem to fog up her judgement like she thought it might, but instead brought a strange sense of clarity. Luna felt very peaceful.

'Okay, you lot ... it's time!' The whole pub went silent, as if Beau had turned its volume down. 'Considering their speciality is Musical Theatre they've definitely *brought it home* ... in third place it's Les Quizerables!' The bar gave them a hearty cheer as a couple in their mid-forties went up to receive a box of Quality Street.

'In second place, it's our usuals You're a Quizzard, Harry! Well done, lads!' A group of four only-just-eighteen-year-old boys high-fived each other and went up to receive one free drink token each then headed straight to the bar, their empty wallets not letting them wait to redeem them. Quiz-Team Aguilera collectively rolled their eyes.

'All right, boys, settle down. Okay, now for our winner. Usually, I'm up here saying "It was so close! There were barely any points in it!" ... but this time, ladies and gentlemen, someone very clearly came out on top. Not only has our champion of the night won by twelve whole points, but it's the first time in the history of the Green Arrow that someone has got *every single* question correct.'

Luna felt a little bubble start in her gut and rise into her mouth.

'Now, she's new here and so doesn't quite have a grasp on the team name element yet but even though she might not have the name she definitely has all the answers ...'

'You're joking.' Luna's stomach flipped.

'This week's winner is ... Just Me!' Beau started clapping but had to reluctantly desist when no one else joined in.

'What?'

'Just me?'

'Are you saying you're the winner?'

'No, no, the name of the team that won is Just Me.'

'That would be me.' Luna stumbled out from her little corner and around the bar to where Beau stood on his small square platform.

'I thought people weren't allowed to enter on their own!' One of the gentlemen from Quizz On My Face tried to stand but his knee pads just wouldn't let him.

'I wasn't on my own! He's part of my team too.' Luna gestured back to the sleeping man who was now barely visible as he'd slipped so far under the table in his drunken state. 'He fell asleep quite early on but ... still.'

'Well, that's not fair!' A brunette from Quiz-Team Aguilera stood and hit her knee on the underside of the table but tried to pass it off as rage at the unfairness of the quiz.

'Lacey. Lacey. Lacey!' one of her teammates called to her wobbling friend. As she stood, she knocked the table and spilt nearly everyone's drinks. She continued to wobble herself as well as the table whilst her team tried to mop up the mess and save their belongings.

'Hey, look now. She's followed the rules.' Beau said down the mic. 'He's part of her team and he paid ... right?' He looked hopefully at Luna.

'Yup.' She hiccupped and gave him two thumbs up.

'Exactly! And considering she didn't have much, if any, help from her team, she still managed to beat all of you lot by *twelve whole points*! Even if she'd had a team of seven, it doesn't change the fact that this lady here had all of the answers. I think she very much deserves first prize!'

'I don't. Who does she think she is? I've never seen her around here before,' said the brunette, picking up her wine and downing the last of it whilst looking Luna directly in the eyes.

'No, me neither!' said the man from Les Quizerables.

'There's no rule that says only regulars at the Green Arrow can enter.'

'Well, there should be! I enter this quiz every week, *Beau*!' Lacey lost her balance and sank back down onto her bench seat.

'And every week, *Lacey*, your team writes down the name "Donald Trump" to at least three of the questions in the hope that one day he'll be an answer.'

'Hey, look! She didn't get all of the answers right!' Lewis had snuck behind Beau and rifled through the sheets to find Just Me's answers. 'She said "Elementary, My Dear Watson" was said by Woody Allen!'

'No, I didn't.' Luna shook her head and stumbled backwards into the bar.

'Yes, you did.' Lewis brandished the paper but Beau took his wrist and lowered it to his eye level.

'That says P.G. Wodehouse.'

'No, it . . . ' Beau flipped the glasses from his head onto the bridge of his nose in one flick of his finger. 'Oh . . . yes it does.'

'But everyone knows Sherlock Holmes said that!' squeaked Lacey, standing once again.

'Yes, but Sir Arthur Conan Doyle wrote Sherlock Holmes so really it was him who said it,' said the woman from Les Quizerables.

'That's what everyone . . .' Luna swallowed, her mouth suddenly filling with saliva, ' . . . thinks. But Sherlock actually never said it and it never appears in any of Carthur Donan Noyles books.' She swayed.

'Arthur Conan Doyle,' Beau whispered in her ear.

'That's what I said!' she hissed back but wobbled backwards again. He gently placed a hand on the small of her back to steady her. It was meant to be a kind, friendly gesture but Luna's body responded in a way she certainly didn't expect. All the alcohol-infused warmth in her body rushed to the small of her back and the apples of her cheeks flushed so red and so hot she thought they might catch fire. Her stomach started to churn.

'I told you the answers on the Quizmaster's sheet are the correct answers even if they turn out to be wrong and my sheet, if Lewis can vouch for me, says P. G. Wodehouse.'

Luna fought down another ball of gas.

'So whether you like it or not, this lovely, albeit slightly pissed lady, is our grand winner!' Beau took her hand and raised it in the air and picked up his pint with the other and raised it in a toast-like fashion. 'Anything you'd like to say, Just Me?' he asked.

'I . . .' The pie in her stomach churned. 'Well, I . . .' She felt another burp rising in her throat. 'Um . . .' Except it wasn't a burp it was . . .

'Bluuurghhhhhh.' Luna bent forwards and vomited into the only container that was readily available: Beau's half full pint of beer. It overflowed over his hand and onto the floor with a gruesome splatter. The quiz teams groaned and gasped together and despite most of them already being at a safe distance, they all leaned away. Quiz-Team Aguilera got up and teetered outside on their stilettos but not before showing Luna their disgusted, scrunched-up faces.

'I'm so sorry,' Luna mumbled, wiping her mouth on her sleeve.

'Oh, it's fine. Not the worst thing to have happened to me in this pub!' Beau laughed, cautiously putting the very full glass down on the bar and gratefully taking a napkin from the barman.

Luna ran back to her table and picked up her coat. 'Use the prize money to cover my bill,' she said. 'Whatever's left is yours.'

'Don't go. C'mon. No need to be embarrassed! Sit down for a bit.'

'No, thank you. I need to get some air.' Luna pushed through the doors and out past the smoking women who cackled as she jogged past them, back towards the safety of her room at the inn.

Beau watched her go, desperately wanting to call after her. 'What was her name?' he asked the barman, who shrugged back at him with a mild grunt. 'Great, thanks.'

Beau thought about racing out into the darkness to search for her but Ondingside was small. 'Well, if she's not staying here she'll be at Nobody's Inn. I'll check there in the morning.'

Luna, on the other hand, had different plans. She raced back the way she had come, although it took her fifteen minutes longer than it should have done owing to her drunken state, and as soon as she got back to the inn, she scrambled up the stairs two at a time, ignoring the landlady's pressing questions, and crawled under the covers where she hoped the embarrassment wouldn't find her. In her haze, she was asleep within moments.

Thanks to her thumping head she was awoken in the early hours of the morning, just as the sun was starting to rise. Fuzzy-mouthed and fuzzy-brained, she quickly started to pack up what little she had already unpacked. She scribbled on a page in her notebook, ripped it out and threaded it onto the hook of the coat hanger of her wedding dress. Luna stepped back and took one last look at it before she let go of it for ever. Of course, she wanted to get married again, but not in a tainted dress and hopefully, next time not in one that was second-hand. Next time, things would be different. Next time ...

Three

Back to Reality

July 15th 2019

'Welcome, my lovely! My sweetpea! My angel! Welcome back to Nobody's Inn. A second visit! It's so rare people visit twice and I am so pleased you've made it!'

Luna's legs were stiff and clicked at the knees as she stretched them out of the cab. Although the inn looked a little worse for wear, its owner, Pearl McArthur, looked as spritely as ever. Her grey hair had been pulled back away from her red dapple cheeks and swooped into a messy bun on the back of her head that was held in place with what looked like a chopstick from a Chinese take-away. Her skin was wrinkled like a Sphynx cat but her misty grey eyes were mischievously sparkling through the tiniest pair of glasses that were precariously perched on the tip of her nose. She wore a long and baggy grey jumper, jodhpurs and burgundy wellington boots. Before Luna knew it, she was enveloped in knitwear. 'How was the journey? Not too long? I hate trains. Not my thing. All those people and smells! Did you get caught in the rain?' Luna took a breath to answer as Mrs McArthur finally let her go but the lady continued. 'It was here about an hour ago and disappeared as quickly as it came! You can never predict the weather these days! Are you hungry? I made shepherd's pie earlier this evening. Do you like shepherd's pie? I've never met anyone who doesn't but it's always good to ask. Lots of vegetarians lurking out there now.' Mrs McArthur had popped open the boot of the taxi without hesitation and was dragging Luna's blue suitcase out as if she'd done it a million times before and with strange ease for seemingly such an elderly woman. 'It's still warm from earlier on today so I won't even have to heat it up for you in the microwave. Things always go soggy in the microwave, don't you think?'

She disappeared through the open door to the inn with the luggage and, wide-eyed, Luna shook her foggy head and snatched up her rucksack from the passenger seat, paid the cabbie and, with an inaudible 'thank you', scampered inside. 'It was just a single room this time, was it? No one else coming to stay with you? Not that there's a problem with that at all! A girl on her own against the world will probably get more done if my late husband was anything to go by! Such a layabout, he was, although I loved him more than anything . . .'

Mrs McArthur rolled Luna's case up to the bottom of the stairs and left it there whilst she hurried past the reception desk and into the empty bar area to their left, still chattering to herself. Luna wondered if it made any difference to her whether Luna was able to hear her or not. She figured not as Mrs McArthur disappeared into the kitchen, her voice only a faint murmur.

Inside, the inn's dark red painted walls were dingy and peeling and Luna had lost count of the cobwebs, not only hanging in every corner of the high ceiling but in every corner of the many gold gilt frames and coating every inappropriately extravagant sconce. There was a strong draught whistling through one of the various cracks in the inn's structure, and Luna wondered how strong a breeze it would take to topple the whole building. It certainly felt like the sort of place thriller stories began. Luna thought she was currently at the part in the plot just before everything takes a turn for the terrifying, when she's handed the key to room thirteen and told to lock her doors at night because the ghost of someone who once died there still roams the halls. *It's a shame I write romantic fiction,* she thought. *If only I had a penchant for the paranormal.*

Mrs McArthur was still chattering and clattering about the kitchen, so Luna took a closer look at the frames on the walls. Luna was certain they hadn't been there the year before but then, last year, Luna had been either in a hurry or drunk when she'd rushed through the lobby so she couldn't be sure. There were at least a hundred frames downstairs in the reception and through the bar alone. As she walked to her case at the bottom of the stairs, just a glance told her that the frames continued all the way up to the next floor. Faded and yellowing newspaper cuttings from decades gone by depicted the Inn's greatest achievements over its years in business.

ISN'T IT AMAZ-INN!
IT'S THE OLDEST INN IN BRITAIN!

BEST FISH 'N' CHIPS INN TOWN!
MISS-INN IMPOSSIBLE?

TOM CRUISE LOOK-A-LIKE
SPOTTED IN ONDINGSIDE!

Most of the clippings showed Mrs McArthur and her husband standing out front, their arms around each other, grinning down the lens with chests puffed out. Dotted between the cuttings were old black and white photographs, depicting, Luna presumed, people of note who had stayed here, none of whom she recognised. Some were perched in the bar with drinks in their hands, heads thrown back in laughter, some were jangling their room keys for the camera and others stood out front with their suitcases. Some photographs were a little more current, Luna realised when she spotted the elderly Mrs McArthur herself beside someone who really did resemble Tom Cruise, if Tom Cruise were seventy and severely tattooed. *Easy mistake to make when you're desperate for business,* she thought.

'. . . And I knew we couldn't keep going on the way we were going so, in the end, I just got rid! Kicked him out on his behind and kept this place for myself! It was my father's before mine and his father's before his and so on and so forth. Places like this are best kept in the family. Anyway . . . single room?' Mrs McArthur re-emerged from the kitchen with a tray covered in tin foil and an already open bottle of cider. She slipped behind the reception desk and started flipping through the sign-in book.

'Yes. Please. Thank you,' Luna croaked.

'Good, aren't they?' Mrs McArthur nodded at the walls. 'Been saving all those clippings my whole life and one day I thought, what good are they doing in a box under my bed when they could be on display! I wondered if maybe it was arrogant to show off your achievements but then I thought, what good are friends if they can't cheer with you when you win, eh?' Mrs McArthur paused for maybe the first time since Luna had arrived and all Luna could think to do was nod.

'No one joining you later on?' Mrs McArthur slid her

finger down the page and then across when she found Luna's name.

'No,' she said.

'I don't charge extra for two people in one room, y'know!' Mrs McArthur chuckled.

'Just a single room. Please.' Luna's clenched her jaw.

'Not a double, just in case?'

'I'm alone!' Luna snapped back. Mrs McArthur coughed and averted her gaze from Luna's wringing hands. 'It'll just be me staying here. Just like last time. No one else. I've come here alone and that won't be changing.' Luna thought about smiling but those signals didn't reach her face.

'Not to worry. Single room it is. Here's your key.' Mrs McArthur turned away and for a moment, seemed to do nothing except take a deep breath. Luna took that moment to do the same. She heard a rattle and Mrs McArthur turned back to her to plonk her key onto the desk. It was brass and relatively small in comparison to the great, whopping keyring it was attached to. The long rectangle plaque made of overly polished dark wood bore the word NOBODY engraved in bold gold capitals. As she took the key, Luna briefly smiled.

'People kept forgetting to give the keys back at the end of their stay. We don't have those newfangled replaceable plastic key cards. Just good old-fashioned sturdy keys. I figured no one was going to accidentally walk away with these bloody great things, are they?' Mrs McArthur laughed. 'This way.' She deftly whipped up the tray and pushed it into Luna's hands. Had Luna not taken it straight away, it would have clattered to the ground as Mrs McArthur was upon her case in milliseconds and hoisting it up the stairs.

The room was almost identical to her last, except now with the addition of a travel kettle on the table along with a mug filled with complimentary teabags and tubes of sugar. The curtains had also been upgraded to a plush velvet that would block out all the morning light for the leisurely lie-ins Luna loved so much and for just a moment, she thanked whoever was listening that her job as an author allowed her best quality work to come from her bed whilst dressed in her pyjamas.

'I have to ask, my dear,' Mrs McArthur laid Luna's case down in the corner of the room and stood straight with a puff, 'what brings you to Ondingside for a second time?'

'What do you mean?' Luna put her rucksack down on the edge of the bed and opened it.

'Well, the last time you were here you left that lovely dress behind. It can't have been giving you any pleasant memories and you were alone then and you're still alone now.'

Luna winced at Mrs McArthur's blunt delivery. 'I just need somewhere quiet.'

'It's certainly that. Well, when you've had your fill of boredom I'm sure London will be waiting for you when you decide to go home.'

'This is my home now,' Luna said.

'Excuse me?'

'I'm staying here until I can find somewhere more permanent.'

'You're staying? For good?' Mrs McArthur would have clutched her pearls were she wearing any. Luna simply looked at her, hoping her silence was confirmation enough. Mrs McArthur sighed.

'All I'm trying to say is ... why here? A town where there's not even four hundred people, in the middle of nowhere important, where there's only really a post office, a doctor's, a bookshop ...'

'A bookshop?' Luna looked up from her bag.

'A *second-hand* bookshop. Don't for a second think we get anything new in this town. Well, except for you, I suppose. There's *nothing* here, Luna. The most exciting event of the year is the play the island's school puts on just before the summer holidays. The whole island goes. This year it's *The Wizard of Oz*.' Mrs McArthur sat herself down on the end of Luna's bed, seemingly without a second thought as to how odd it may be to make yourself so comfortable in the room of a paying customer. Luna went back to rummaging for nothing in her bag. 'This town is perfect for someone like me who has never known anything other than a humdrum life at the very edge of civilisation but for someone like you ... someone young and spritely, to come from the big wide world out there to a tiny little place like this ...' She shook her head and all the wrinkles in her face became deeper for a moment. 'Forgive me for prying, Miss Lark, but I can't imagine what must have happened to you in order for you to actually *choose* to live somewhere like Ondingside.'

Little did Mrs McArthur know, it was perfect for someone like Luna. For someone who was done with grief, mourning and other people's pity, done with embarrassment at the hands of ridiculous men who couldn't decide what they wanted until it was almost too late, done with too many people knowing who she was and why she was sad. A tiny town where no one knew who she was and she had no reason to tell them was perfection.

'I just need a bit of peace and quiet. Somewhere to find order and purpose. Ondingside seemed like a better place than any.' Luna laid down her case and opened it up, hoping the comfortable Mrs McArthur would take the hint.

'Well, then. I'll leave you to it. Hope the pie's okay. Oh! I almost forgot!' Mrs McArthur clapped her hands together. 'A little birdie told me that you like cider!' Luna stood up straight. 'So, I thought it might go nicely with your pi—'

'Who told you that?' Luna snapped.

'B-beau.' Mrs McArthur's shoulders fell and her hands found her pockets. 'When he was at the Green Arrow. He came looking for you the day after you left last year. Seemed you made quite the impression.' Mrs McArthur's eyes twinkled over the rim of her glasses.

'I don't know what kind of idle gossip you've heard but I'm not really much of a drinker,' Luna snapped and the instant the words had whipped out of her mouth and slapped Mrs McArthur in the face, turning her expression from mischief to melancholy in a moment, she wished she could erase the last minute.

'Oh, I'm ever so sorry,' said Mrs McArthur contritely. 'I didn't mean to—'

'No ... no. *I'm* sorry.' Luna shook her head. In this new life that she'd envisioned, no one knew her business but that didn't mean people wouldn't be curious. It was human nature to pry and ask questions. Luna knew she would never be able to put a stop to people's intrigue, but the boundaries would be set in how much she was willing to divulge. She didn't want attention but that didn't mean she had to be rude in order to fend it off and it certainly didn't feel right to snap at someone who was just trying to be kind. 'I just ... ' She sighed. 'I embarrassed myself a little ... well, a lot ... in front of Beau last year and I still haven't really forgiven myself for it. Would you mind if we kept that between us? I want to start afresh here and the last thing I need is lingering embarrassing stories.'

'Oh, my love, your secret is safe with me. I'll take the cider back downstairs with me and—'

'Actually ... ' Luna couldn't help but smile and the twinkle returned to the elderly woman's eyes.

'Enjoy your evening.' Just as the door almost clicked back into place, Mrs McArthur flung it open again. 'By the way, *The Wizard of Oz* is on tomorrow night at five p.m. Might be a good idea to come. Get you integrated into the community.'

'I'm not an ex-con!'

Mrs McArthur smiled in spite of Luna's obvious reluctance. 'Just ... think about it.' And finally she closed the door.

Luna couldn't be bothered to unpack and so only rummaged around for her pyjamas and her clear plastic toiletry bag. She sat in bed and ate the shepherd's pie, which was rather wonderful, even when cool, and the cider was exactly what she needed to put her in a woozy, sleepy state for her first night in a strange room. She plugged in her phone next to the bed and noted the six missed calls from Lottie.

'Ugh ... I'll call her tomorrow,' she vowed and set her alarm for 10 a.m. 'Just a little lie in.' Luna reached down by the side of her bed, into her backpack and pulled out her notebook.

Today, she wrote, marks the end of one chapter and the beginning of another. For me. Definitely not for my book. My book is currently at a dead end. Hopefully these new pages in my own life will inspire a lot of literal pages for me ... and my especially worried editor.

Luna hadn't been keeping a journal for long. If she was being honest, it wasn't really a journal at all and more a sentence or two at the end of each page in her notebook. She was shying away from the idea of keeping a diary so as to avoid feeling like her thirteen-year-old self again. Reading back her diary entries from her teenage years made her cringe hard and she was sure she would be doing the same with these scribblings in a decade or so. Luna had tried hard to get her life back on track in the year since the almost-wedding but it seemed that there was nothing she could do to shake everyone's pity. She tried going to yoga three times a week but the poses were too hard. She tried baking but ended up with more cake than she and Lottie could eat on their own (and no one else was coming to visit ...). Gardening wasn't her bag and the only sports that didn't require joining a team of some kind were squash and golf. Golf wasn't her bag either and the one and only time she attempted squash she ended up with a black eye. Luna decided therapy would be a good idea. She had so much left in her head from the loss of her family and she desperately wanted an impartial party to talk to about Noel. As brilliant as Lottie was at trashing her ex, Luna felt she needed someone who was unbiased. She was also hoping that there would be something she could do that would make her feel more at peace with everyone's judgement, considering she knew she couldn't control anyone else's actions and reactions but her own. She'd been struggling with her writing as a result of the fog of feelings in her head and was distraught to find that her therapist suggested journalling as a way to deal with her stress and anxiety. Luna also hoped that the mere action of writing would get her creative juices flowing again and open some kind of literary floodgate but she'd had no luck on that front as of yet. Still, she held out hope.

As she turned out the light, Luna realised she hadn't pulled the curtains shut. She scrambled out from under the covers and just as she grabbed the curtains in her hands, she noticed the view. Her room was at the back of the inn where her window looked out over the sand and the sea. The grass rolled down a little hill and stopped abruptly where it turned to sand and the more Luna looked at it the more she longed to feel it under her bare feet. The waves silently pushed and pulled, turning from black to white as they foamed onto the shore. Above, hanging in the sky like a ball on a string, looking proudly down upon it all, was the moon, not quite full.

Luna had a habit of waving at the moon ever since her father had told her a story: when she was born, she was actually a twin but the other sister had to be sent up to the sky to watch over her. It had always been just a story but in the years that had passed she wondered if there had been truth to it. Had she, for the briefest amount of time, been a twin? Had her father told her that story to try and soften the awful truth of losing a child? Or had he just tried to make sure Luna never felt alone in the world and that if she ever felt scared or lonely, all she had to do was look up? Luna supposed it didn't matter now. She would wave all the same and she'd feel comforted knowing the moon was watching over her as she slept in this strange new town.

Luna opened her eyes and saw nothing but white. She blinked rapidly but her eyes were definitely open. She was just unable to see anything more than the sheet of snow falling in front of her. She lifted a hand in front of her face and saw a vague shadowy outline but nothing more. Luna called out but her voice echoed into a great expanse of emptiness. She took a step forward and her bare foot crunched the snow beneath but she felt no cold and her foot left no mark. Wrapping her arms around her naked body, she trudged onwards. The flakes whipped at her face and she fought against her long hair dragging in the wind behind her shoulders. The ache in her chest and her heavy limbs made each step more difficult but at least the frost wasn't biting as she thought it might. Her voice carried out through the blizzard but there was no one around to hear her and so no one came. Luna forged on alone.

Four

Day One

July 16th 2019

Just after midnight, a dog sniffed along the bottom of a garden fence. He could smell his prey and hear its heart-beat not yards away. He started to dig, his paws pulling up clumps of mud, grass and flowers until his muzzle could fit underneath the wooden panels, then his head and then his front paws. He dug and scratched until finally, the Jack Russell was in next door's garden. He sniffed along the ground, the scent in his nose stronger than he could bear. He crept around in the dark until he spotted two bright eyes and before his prey even had a moment to breathe its last breath, it was no more.

The dog clambered back under the fence, through the

flap in the back door and trotted mud all the way up the stairs to sleep at the foot of his master's bed, pleased with his impressive catch and kill. The body of the rabbit would lie in the grass until morning, waiting to be found by a tearful father, not sure how he would tell his little girl that Bruce the Bunny was dead.

Getting out of bed had never been Luna's strong suit. Her alarm would always jolt her out of unconsciousness and she'd spend the next twenty minutes resenting it for waking her and the world and its social norms for demanding that she must get up and mustn't stay in her pyjamas in bed all day eating peanut butter with a teaspoon straight from the jar. Sadly, the life Luna wished she could live wasn't the life that was going to make her feel fulfilled or successful in any way, shape or form and she knew it. However, Luna felt those twenty minutes of resentful scrolling through social media were important for her own self-care, so allowed herself that at the very least.

Luna was expecting the shower in her room to leave a lot to be desired. However, Mrs McArthur had certainly kept such an old place in good shape. The water stayed hot for the duration of her lengthy shower and there were even miniature complimentary shower gel and hair care products that Luna made full use of. She stepped over the edge of the bath, wiped down the mirror with the end of the giant white towel she'd wrapped herself in and stared into the glass. She knew that it was her own reflection in the mirror, of course, but the person staring back at her wasn't who she imagined when she thought of herself. When she was forced to think of what she looked like, she thought of the eighteen-year-old Luna, fresh-faced with plump cheeks, wide blue eyes and her hair neatly plaited, not a strand out of place. The reality in the mirror was always a shock to Luna in comparison to the memory. She was merely a ghost of that girl in her head. Now, the skin under her eyes was constantly dark and slightly puffy, her face was gaunt and pale and her eyes were glassy and unfocused. Time, it seemed, had stopped in her mind when her family had died. She still felt like the eighteen-year-old she once was, so it felt uncomfortable to see that time hadn't been kind. Who she was now wasn't who she wanted to be and the hardest person to present that to was herself. Luna breathed and her reflection blurred into non-existence as the mirror fogged once more. Once her teeth were brushed, her hair was dry and fishtailed and she was dressed, Luna opened the curtains and cracked the window to let her room fill with the crisp sea air for when she got back.

'I hope that coat's nice and thick. It's starting to get nippy out there, Miss Lark,' Mrs McArthur chirruped as Luna appeared at the top of the stairs, freezing for a moment at the sound of her voice.

'It's only July!' Luna said with a stifled yawn.

'Can't deny that chill in the air!' Mrs McArthur called as she disappeared through the door to the kitchen. Luna had thought the air had a bite to it when she'd opened the window in her room but hadn't given a moment's thought to how odd that was for a July summer's day.

'Scotland's *always* cold.' Luna shrugged, opened the door and shuffled out into the chill.

Google Maps wasn't being entirely helpful. Luna stood outside the inn for ten minutes watching the little blue arrow as it swung this way and that. With a huff, Luna decided to walk down to the beach and follow it along until she saw some kind of civilisation. The wind had certainly picked up and made its way into the collar of Luna's thin pale-blue coat, like icy hands around her neck. She pulled it around her but it wasn't a coat designed for warmth as much as it was for calm and mild summer evenings. The black sea was thrashing against the white of the sky and Luna didn't dare go near the edge of the water as she could feel the cold spray against her face from quite a distance. Any closer and she feared she'd be drenched by the time she met any of the 383 people living in Ondingside. The wind whistled past her so loudly she didn't hear the sound of the Jack Russell's feet slapping against the wet sand as it bounded over to her until it was darting between her legs and circling her, kicking up sand over her shoes.

'You lost?'

Luna spun around, her boots sinking a little as she turned. An elderly man stood above her on the little grassy knoll, holding a green tennis ball in one hand and leaning on a cane with the other. His dog ran back to him and bounced at his feet, waiting for the game to begin.

'No! No, no. Just ... wandering.' She pointed towards the other end of the beach.

'Well if you *wander* up there and along that little road here for about ten minutes, you'll *wander* into town,' he snipped, then threw the ball. The Jack Russell flew down the beach after it in a blur of black, ginger and white and leapt into the air as it bounced. Luna felt a little tinge of embarrassment fire into her cheeks but she shook it off and let it dissipate on the strong breeze.

'Bloody dog,' the man whispered as he trudged closer.

'Seems sweet,' Luna said as the little dog waddled back, tail wagging, and dropped the ball for another turn.

'Sweet to us, maybe, but he wasn't so sweet to next door's rabbit last night.'

'Ah,' Luna said, suddenly drawn to look at the Jack Russell's little pointed teeth.

'Welles here has put me in a rather difficult situation.' The old man sniffed hard. 'Come on, boy.' He huffed and tipped his flat cap to Luna.

She looked down the beach, which inarguably didn't seem to lead anywhere so she took the man's advice, climbed back over the knoll and headed in the opposite direction.

'Well, this isn't half bad.' Luna shivered as she approached a little roundabout surrounded by shops. As Mrs McArthur had said, Luna spotted the Post Office sign to her left and what looked like a newly renovated building directly opposite which bore the sign ONDINGSIDE MEDICAL PRACTICE with the NHS logo in the right-hand corner. However, there was not a person in sight. Luna couldn't see the bookshop yet which had piqued her interest the most but she knew the island was so small that it wouldn't be long before it appeared.

'Mornin'!' A man with a walking stick tipped his flat cap at her as he hobbled past. Luna mouthed a 'Morning' back but the sound didn't quite make it out. Growing up in London meant you were taught to never talk to strangers, even if they were being polite. In fact, in Luna's experience Londoners had perfected the art of Resting Bitch Face to avoid unwanted social interaction whether it was polite or not. On their list of skills was also how to inconspicuously cross roads to avoid charity workers, how to huff at people who didn't know how to use the Tube ticket barriers – or which side to stand on the escalators – without them realising you're huffing, and how to expertly dodge between tourists taking photos in Piccadilly Circus and still make your destination on time. Saying anything to strangers wasn't Luna's strong suit, let alone polite greetings, but she didn't feel as strongly opposed to a 'Good Morning' here or there as long as it didn't lead to a conversation in which she'd have to reveal anything about herself.

'Just find the bookshop. That's all you need to do in town today. Find the bookshop ...' Luna clacked her tongue about in her mouth, 'and maybe some coffee.'

Luna was a self confessed 'coffee snob'. Starbucks and Costa just wouldn't cut it when it came to her sacred morning drink and it was one thing on which Luna wouldn't budge.

'A Costa flat white comes in a latte-sized cup! That's *not* a flat white!' she'd argue. Luna liked supporting independent businesses as opposed to chains and always felt the products came with a little extra love, but she also had a beautiful coffee machine of her own, currently in a storage unit back in London, which she'd have to get delivered when she finally found a permanent residence in Ondingside. She bought only the best beans and relished the whirring and clunking noise it made when she fired it up. Luna couldn't write without a coffee steaming away on her desk, its sharp aroma chasing away the fuzz in her head. Luna plucked her phone from her coat pocket, noting how red the back of her fingers were from the biting cold, and swiped to find Google Maps. The arrow spun this way and that and within seconds she huffed, her breath pluming out in front of her, and took a look at her options laid out in front of her. The traffic circle had five dials: the one she came from, the one to the right of the Post Office which bustled with the granny chatter, two either side of the medical practice and the one to her right.

'Eeny, meeny, miney … mo.' The cold had started to seep deep into her bones and her teeth were chattering loudly so she took her nearest option, walked to her right and turned down the first exit.

The shop fronts were painted pastel pinks, yellows and blues and hanging baskets sprouted from nearly every window, their bright flowers cascading down to their doorways. Although there seemed to be few customers, each shop seemed busy as Luna peeked in through the window. The hardware shop owner was stacking boxes of lightbulbs onto shelves and he tried to wave at Luna as she paused outside but only managed to jiggle his elbow before having to catch a box that was jostled. Luna quickly moved along to what turned out to be the second-hand bookshop. An elderly lady was pencilling prices into the front pages of a pile of books on the front desk whilst a younger girl was mostly obscured from sight as she was up a small wooden ladder nearer the back of the shop, sliding beautiful hardbacks into their rightful slots. Luna's feet drew her to the green painted door but one foot kicked over a chalkboard sign belonging to the shop next door. It clattered loudly and she felt lucky that there wasn't really anyone around to watch her awkwardly wrangle it back to standing. It was far heavier than it looked and every second that went by was another second that the voice in her head grew increasingly louder as it told her how ridiculous she looked and how embarrassing it was going to be if anyone saw her and what on earth was she going to say if someone came over. As Luna was about to lower it back down to the ground and leave it there for someone else to deal with, guilt being preferable over embarrassment at that moment in time, a loud bell jangled as the door to her left opened.

'Everything all right there, Miss?' Luna didn't dare look up at the man the voice belonged to. She could only bring her gaze up to the hem of the forest green apron hanging at his knees above his blue slippers.

'I'm sorry. I knocked it over and I can't seem to ... I'm sorry, it just won't ...' She stood but continued looking down only at the sad sign, its chalk writing now only displaying the word 'Coff', its Es smudged away by Luna's coat.

'No worries at all.' He bent down and deftly lifted the sign back to standing and pulled some chalk out of his apron pocket to adjust the writing. As he knelt into Luna's eye-line, her stomach dropped into her shoes. 'There we go!' His jolly face opened up into a smile as his bright brown eyes found Luna's briefly before she dropped them back to the pavement. 'Hang on a second. I *know you*,' said Beau.

'No. You don't.' Luna kept her head down and started to walk past the man, his sign and his shop.

'Yes, I do! You're the girl who won my pub quiz last year. The literary one!' She could hear his footsteps following along behind her so she picked up her pace. The moments of wanting to wrap her coat around her were long gone as now her skin felt fiery, beads of sweat making their way down the small of her back.

'That wasn't me,' she snapped. He caught up with her but as he rounded in front of her, Luna sharply turned herself back the way she came and for a moment, his footsteps stopped and she thought, she hoped, that he'd stopped pursuing her.

'It *was*. Your hair. I'd never forget that hair.'

'Not me! You've got the wrong person,' Luna called over her shoulder. She'd come to a halt just before the chalkboard sign outside his shop but continued to face away from him.

'No, no, it's *definitely* you! You're the one who entered the quiz on your own, caused a riot amongst my usuals and then—'

'Yes, I know what happened next.'

'So, it *is* you!' Even though she could hear the brightness in his voice, his laughter, her blood bubbled with every happy chuckle.

'I never meant to upset anyone!' Her throat had started to close up around her words.

'You didn't! I'm only teasing! I came looking for you the next day but you'd done a runner.'

'I didn't do a runner. That was when I was always leaving,' she lied.

'Not according to Mrs McArthur. She said you made a dash for it days before you were due to leave.'

'She's misremembering.'

'Are you always this difficult to talk to?' He laughed although it sounded like some, if not most, of the joy had left his voice.

'Are you always this persistent?' She turned to face him but still wasn't quite able to lift her gaze any higher than his apron hem.

'Blimey, I'm just trying to say hello! Get ... reacquainted.'

'We were never acquainted.'

'And I thought that was a shame.' A little flicker of something unfamiliar lit up in Luna's chest but she pushed it back down as far as it would go.

'Look –' he took a step towards her, ' – last time you were here, I put your prize money, that you won fair and square, may I add, aside in a jar and I made a deal with myself. I'd wait six months to see if you ever came back. If you did, I'd return the prize to its rightful owner. If you didn't, it would go back into the prize fund for the next clever clogs to win.'

Luna raised an eyebrow. 'It's been well over six months.'

'Yeah, well. Maybe I just had a feeling you'd be back.' He shrugged.

'A ... feeling?'

'Wishful thinking.' Beau smiled so warmly that it made Luna's skin prickle in a way she hadn't felt in so long that she put it down to the chill in the air.

'I told you last time, I didn't want it,' she mumbled.

'Well ... then at least let me get you a coffee? On

the house. Best coffee in Ondingside.' Luna sighed and forced herself to look at him, even if only for a short few seconds. His face was just as round and happy as she remembered, with all its warmth and soft edges.

'Is there any competition?'

'It'd still be the best even if there was, Miss ... ?'

'Miss Lark.'

'First name being ... ?' he said as he opened the door for her and the bell jangled again.

'I don't think we're on a first name basis,' she mumbled.

'Well ... I'm Beau.'

'I know.'

Beau's smile grew so wide Luna thought his cheeks would burst. 'So, you remembered me too, then?'

'Let me guess, you're a pour-as-much-sugar-and-syrup-in-until-it-doesn't-even-taste-like-coffee-any-more type of coffee drinker?' Beau's coffee shop was small, cosy, extremely well decorated but entirely empty. It only had four tables positioned in a square and yet not one of the eight chairs surrounding them was filled. Luna shook her head at Beau who was standing behind the counter, his hands poised, fingers twitching, itching to get his big green coffee machine grinding and whirring.

'Mocha?' he suggested. Luna shook her head again. 'Cappuccino? Latte?'

'Just a flat white, please.'

'Urgh! You didn't let me finish! That was my next guess!' Beau grinned as he flicked buttons and switches and the machine trembled into life. Luna could see the beans, visible through the clear plastic top, start to shift as some disappeared from underneath the mound to be ground into her drink. She fixated on the machine as she tried to squash that unfamiliar stir in her chest. Like her ribcage had trapped a mouse that was scrambling to get out.

'So, what brings you back to Ondingside?' Beau raised his voice over the machine.

'I guess ... I live here now.' She shrugged. Beau snapped his head up, almost sloshing milk over the side of the jug he was using for frothing, his eyes wide.

'Oh, God. *Why?*'

Luna supposed she would have to get used to people asking her, as a newcomer, why she was there. She felt foolish for not having a better prepared answer. *My family's dead and my childhood sweetheart abandoned me on the day of our wedding* was hardly the answer she wanted to give, nor did it give life to much positive conversation, *nor* was it who she wanted to be known as in this new life. 'Not that it isn't lovely to have you here!' Beau bumbled as he watched her try and muster an answer. 'I just mean ... there's nothing here. This place is a wasteland. It's where dreams and old people come to die.'

'*You're* here,' she said, her palms sweating in her pockets.

'Yes, but that's different. I grew up here. I don't know what I'm missing.'

'Surely you've been to the mainland before, though?'

'Not once.' Beau said, turning his attention back to expertly pouring the milk into the takeaway coffee cup.

'*Never?*'

'Nope. I've never crossed those train tracks.'

'Why?'

'Ahh.' He shook his head. 'Y'know. This and that. Life.' He shrugged and smiled but Luna saw that it was a sad kind of smile that made her heart ache for just a second. However, Beau was quick to blow away whatever cobwebs had clouded his mind for that brief moment and a real smile returned to his eyes as he placed her coffee in front of her on the counter. 'Ta da!' He flourished his hands around the top of the cup. Beau had shaped the foam of the milk into a beautiful leaf.

'Impressive,' she said. She reached for a sachet of brown sugar from the box next to the coffee machine.

'You don't smile much, do you?' Beau leant on the counter, bringing his face closer to her. She automatically recoiled from the intimacy and took a step back as she was pouring her sugar, which missed the cup as a result and spilt onto the counter top.

'I do!' Luna protested, sweeping the sugar into her hand.

'It takes a lot to make you smile then.' He laughed,

lifting up her coffee and wiping underneath it with his dishcloth.

'. . . That's not true,' she said, taking the coffee from his hand as he offered it to her.

'You just seem so . . .'

'So *what*?'

'Unhappy.' The word slapped her across the face and left her heart stinging. Luna didn't consider herself an unhappy person. What happened with her family was tragic, difficult and the memory of it did catch her breath from time to time. However, years had since passed and each year brought with it a little more anaesthesia to that pain. *Life goes on*, she always thought, and Luna planned to live her life in Ondingside writing her books and drinking coffee. *I might even get a budgie*, she thought.

'I'm not unhappy. I'm just . . . I'm just . . . well, I'm . . .'

'You're allowed to be unhappy, y'know?' Beau said with a tinge of pity in his voice that made Luna's non-coffee wielding fist clench.

'*I know*, but I'm *not*.'

'We've all got baggage,' he shrugged.

'It's not that—'

'No one expects you to be okay all of the time.'

'Right, but that's not—'

'Trust me, I've seen it before and I just think if you—'

'I'M FINE!' Luna put her coffee down on the counter a little too hard. It splashed up and splattered Beau's cheek.

71

'It's really convincing when you shout it,' Beau laughed, wiping his face with the bottom of his apron.

'I'm sorry,' Luna mumbled, using her sleeve to mop up the spill.

'No need to apologise. I'm just . . . looking out for you.'

Luna eyed Beau and was surprised when she couldn't detect any sarcasm or insincerity. His eyes were kind, if a little red from the sudden spritz of caffeine.

'You don't even know me,' she said, finally taking a sip of her coffee.

'True. I just recognise something familiar in you.' The corner of his lips turned upwards and Luna could feel it rubbing her up the wrong way.

'And what would that be?' She put down her coffee and folded her arms.

'Sadness,' he said simply, idly wiping down the counter again for something to do.

'I don't know who you think you are to judge me. How could you possibly know what you're talking about based on a single meeting?' She busied herself sipping her coffee.

'A second meeting,' he corrected her.

'I don't think the first should count seeing as I was severely inebriated and certainly not myself.'

'How would I know?' he shrugged. 'I "don't even know you".' A grin spread across his face. Luna felt her blood run hot and she could see that Beau noticed the change in the air around her. 'Look . . . ' Beau took a breath, eyeing her, and Luna could see the gears in his head in motion. 'Maybe I should get to know you better, then?'

Luna felt like she'd been punched in the gut. Was he asking her out? Was he actually suggesting they spend a prolonged amount of time together outside of his place of work so that he could ask her questions about things she maybe didn't want to be asked questions about? Then feel obliged to fire questions back in return about things she wasn't sure she wanted answers to?

'I'm not sure that's a very good idea,' she said before her thoughts on the matter were fully formed.

'Really?' Beau's cheeks started to flush.

'No.' She adjusted her coat again and took a step towards the door.

'Not really?'

'No, really.' Another step.

'Oh.'

Luna felt a pang of guilt as she watched embarrassment take hold of Beau and she wondered herself why she was so opposed to seeing him again. Luna felt tears prickle the back of her eyes as she wondered if the hopeless romantic that was once present in almost everything she did was entirely lost to the tragedies of her past.

'You're very ... sweet,' she continued before she cried in front of a complete stranger, 'and I'm happy being an occasional customer in what I have to admit is actually a very nice coffee shop with *really* good coffee, but I don't think it should be anything more than that.'

'Can I ask why?'

Luna felt a twinge of guilt. *Am I being too harsh?* she thought. *Or am I well within my rights to stand my ground?* Then she wondered why she was standing her ground at all, but she put a lid on the box that idea crawled out from.

'No,' she said.

'No?'

'No,' she confirmed and his smile quickly evaporated.

'So, I'm guessing I also can't ask why I can't ask why you don't think going on a date with me is a bad idea?' he laughed.

'I don't believe I need a reason! I just don't want to.' Luna reached the door and as she opened it, the noise of the bell made her jump. Beau held up his hands.

'All right. No worries. You're welcome in for coffee anytime.'

He's too nice. Why is he so nice? she wondered.

'Okay. Thank you. I'm going now.' A gust of cold air blew tendrils of Luna's hair across her face.

'Can I at least know your name?' Beau asked, hurriedly.

'Miss Lark.'

'I meant your first name ... '

'Then, no.'

Five

Luna decided it was best to go back the way she had come. She had had more conversations in one morning than she expected to have in a week and she felt drained even thinking about how many more the rest of the day might have in store. Drinking her coffee in her room and having a lie down was her plan. She would try venturing out again later on (or not ...).

As soon as her foot hit the pavement outside the coffee shop, the elderly lady she had seen through the window of the bookshop earlier walked out onto the street lugging a large, full, rusted watering can. Before Luna realised, the door closed behind her, ringing the bell. The woman, half raising the full watering can, did a double take and as she gasped, the weight of the heavy can pulled her arm back down to her side and she sloshed water over her fluffy slippers.

'You're the new girl!'

'Erm . . .' Luna faltered.

'Yes! You are! Mrs McArthur had said you looked like a city girl and boy, was she right! I could spot you a mile off! You stick out like a sore thumb!' The old woman threw her head back and cackled.

'Mrs McArthur. Of course.' Luna mumbled to herself. This woman seemed around the same age as Mrs McArthur, but her wrinkles weren't as deep set into her dark skin. Although where Mrs M was spritely and moved with ease, this woman had a stiffness to her and waddled as she walked towards Luna. Her Afro hair was twisted tightly into two lines that ran from her temples to the back of her head where it exploded into glorious disarray. Her lips were painted the same shade as a London bus to match her nails, a colour that she pulled off with dramatic ease. Luna envied her that.

'I'm Maggie! Mrs McArthur's oldest friend! And by oldest I mean we've been friends a long time. Not that I'm old because no one that's old could possibly pull off this eyeshadow!' Maggie closed her eyes and stretched out her face so that Luna could see her eyelids were heavily slathered in red eyeshadow. She cackled again. 'Come in! Come in! Wendy would be delighted to meet you!' Before Luna could respond, Maggie disappeared through the door, her watering can spilling water this way and that. Luna thought to herself, *I could just keep walking*. She had no desire to go into the bookshop if it meant having more forced conversation with people she didn't know. She would come back another day when no one was around or she would simply resort to buying her books online. However, Luna paused. She didn't want people prying into her life and her business but was that necessarily the same thing as shutting people out? She was private, but she wasn't mean. No. She would go in and explain that she could only stay a few minutes as she had prior engagements elsewhere. They didn't need to know that her prior engagements were with Julia Roberts and Richard Gere.

The shop was a burst of light and colour. The smell of soil and ageing books gave Luna the sudden urge to climb a tree or go for a picnic and she took several deep breaths, trying to cling onto the feeling of childish adventure.

'It's a lovely shop,' Luna said when the woman turned to face her and said nothing. She simply looked at Luna, up and down several times with the expression of a proud auntie.

'It's Wendy's.' Maggie slipped behind the counter and continued to pencil prices into the front of the pile of books on the side.

'Do you work here?'

'I used to! When Wendy's mum ran the place, but Wendy's been in charge ever since she passed away.'

'It's nice that you still help out.' Luna could hear herself and how fake she sounded but she figured Maggie had no point of reference so wouldn't know any different.

'I have to now that Wendy can't move around as much! Stacking shelves is hard when there's a great big bump in the way! I also used to be a midwife so I think I'm probably quite a handy one to have around.'

'Wendy's pregnant?'

'Is she?! You'd think with triplets if you didn't know any better! She's ginormous!' Maggie mimed the biggest belly she could whilst puffing out her cheeks. Luna wondered whether she would have exaggerated her impression so much had Wendy also been in the room but Maggie didn't seem like the sort to ever hold back. 'In fact, she's due today but no sign of Baby just yet. So, I help where I can.'

'Doesn't she have anyone?'

'She's got me!' Maggie grinned, holding up the book she had finished pricing as proof of how much help she was.

'Of course, but I meant ... well, the baby ...' Luna whispered.

'Ah! I see what you mean. No.' Maggie's smile fell away. '*He* did a runner. Didn't know she was pregnant but at the time, neither did she. He arrived last summer with a group of lads who wore biker jackets but had no bikes,' she rolled her eyes, 'and he left as quickly as he came without so much as a goodbye.'

'That's so sad.' Luna wondered if maybe she and Wendy might actually have more in common than she first thought. Luna wrote books and Wendy sold them and they both had felt the sting of people leaving too soon, albeit in different ways.

'Sad? Wendy and the little one will be better off without him. Someone like him doesn't deserve someone like her.'

'Does anyone know why he left?' Luna could feel the familiar prickle of inspiration lightly graze the back of her mind like a feather falling to the ground but the moment she started grasping for the idea, it dissolved on her tongue.

'Not for certain.' Maggie shook her head. 'If you ask me, I reckon he had a girl back at home on the mainland and he was playing away. Probably on a stag do or something. Just a fling for him, but our poor Wendy gets invested quickly. Guess she can't help but be invested now that a baby's on the way.' Maggie looked up at Luna who hadn't realised her concern was etched all over her face. 'She'll be fine!' Maggie laughed. 'She should be down in a second! I can't wait for you to meet her!'

Another familiar feeling crashed over Luna and her stomach flipped. Her skin tingled and her heart raced and she just knew meeting yet another someone new was too much for one day. Panic quickly set in.

'Actually, I really should be getting off.' Luna heard a thump in the rooms above their heads.

'Oh no, please wait for Wendy! She'll only be a moment.' Maggie pulled the curtain behind the counter aside and called up the stairs to the flat above the shop. 'Wendy! Someone's here to see you!'

'No, really, I need to get going now.' Luna hopped over

a couple of plant pots, ducked under a hanging basket and opened the door. Maggie rushed around the counter but took much longer to manoeuvre the assault course of pottery. Luna shuffled backwards out of the door. 'Thank you though! I'll come back! Tomorrow. Maybe. Tell Wendy hello! We'll meet another time. Thank you again. Bye!' Luna shut the door and walked at a speed she was certain neither Maggie and her short legs nor pregnant Wendy could match.

Six

Amusements

Luna let the door clatter behind her as she hurried down the street, hot coffee burning her hand as it erupted out the spout in the plastic lid. *Keep walking, don't look back. Keep walking, don't look back. Keep walking, keep walking, keep walking.* She'd been so certain that Ondingside was the place for her. She'd needed to get away from all the people who knew her story but she had underestimated the curiosity of strangers. She hadn't realised that getting away from people who knew her meant finding lots of people who *wanted* to know her. She'd run from everyone who had the full story and bumped headfirst into all the people who had all the questions. Luna had been certain of her logic but now she sensed a very large and very annoying flaw in her plan.

Luna followed her feet wherever they were taking her. She didn't look at street names, she barely even looked up from her shoes; she just ... travelled.

She took a left.

A right.

Another left.

She looked down the next left and saw a black cat cross the road.

'I definitely don't need that today,' she thought as superstition crept in. So, she took a second right towards the sea where she found Jacob's Amusements, the words in filthy, flickering lightbulbs along the front of a surprisingly long, open-fronted arcade. There was also a fish and chip shop and then five tall, narrow houses in various pastel colours. Luna ducked inside.

She posted a five pound note into a change machine and enjoyed the clinking noise as it spat out her many ten pence pieces. Three claw machines stood together near the front of the arcade, each one filled with indistinct stuffed animals, some bearing some vague resemblance to characters in current children's movies but only just. The temptation to spend more money and time than she had to spare on trying to win a toy she'd never use or even like all that much was almost overwhelming but she held steady.

'They're rigged, anyway. You just can't win,' she muttered as she peered in through the glass, trying to ignore the teddies that were reaching out to the metal claw that she was so sure she'd be able to win. Someone had once told her such machines were on a timer, designed to *let* you win every fifty goes or so and Luna clung onto that as gospel truth as she moved away from the three machines, removing herself from temptation. It was then that a machine in the back right hand corner of the room caught her eye. Unlike all the others that twinkled in the light with their silver cases, this one was made of dark wood and stood taller and narrower. Inside the glass was a large crystal ball, tarot cards and runes scattered around it on a sheet of purple crushed velvet. Above it on the back wall were the words FORTUNE FAVOURS THE BRAVE, surrounded by old bulbs. For an old machine the coin slot was still modern, made of black plastic with a bright yellow sticker that told Luna a single go would cost her a pound. Curiosity fired through her like a cannon-ball, ripping through her veins, and she quickly counted out ten pence pieces and pushed them through the slot as fast as her fingers would let her. The final coin wouldn't take and kept falling back through the return slot so she fumbled for a different coin. She pushed it through and when the lights on the inside of the machine burst into life she breathed an excited 'YES!'. The bulbs flashed sporadically, dancing around the sign, and it played a tune in a minor key that made the hair on Luna's arms stand on end but piqued her interest all the more. A projection of a galaxy swirled in the centre of the crystal ball but it looked like a very old trick, not carried out with up to date technology. More likely with smoke and mirrors. She wondered how often people came to these amusements, let alone how often this machine itself was used, but her thoughts were interrupted as the machine started to sing to the tune it played …

> 'Stare into the crystal ball and ask what
>   you require,
> Reach into your heart and tell me all that
>   you desire,
> If your future's dark as night or glowing
>   like the sun,
> It won't be hard for me to tell in three,
>   two, ONE!'

The bulbs turned off all at once and then their lights grew brighter and brighter and brighter until Luna could barely see the words on the back wall at all any more. The music swelled and with a final sustained minor chord the machine went dark. The bulbs went dead, the music was abruptly killed and all she was left with was her own disappointed reflection in the glass. She huffed and was about to walk away when a buzzing noise came from the machine. She stood back, taking the machine in, in its entirety. Nothing through the glass seemed to have awoken again but then a little slip of cream-coloured card appeared through a slot Luna hadn't noticed before. It seemed that the buzzing noise was a printer hidden within the machine that had produced something for her. She bent at the waist, plucked the card from its slot and inspected it. At first glance, it seemed to be blank, but as it caught one of the many lights from the surrounding arcade machines, the same words, *Fortune Favours The Brave*, glinted in swirling silver writing. Luna turned the card over where the writing was black and bold.

> **TO APPRECIATE**
> **THE BEAUTY OF A**
> **SNOWFLAKE, ONE MUST**
> **STAND OUT IN THE COLD.**

Luna stared at the writing and for a split second, she thought about letting it slip from her fingers and walking away, or trying to push *it* back into the slot it came from. Luna didn't like the cold, literally as well as figuratively. She felt like she'd been dealt enough ice to last several lifetimes and it was time she was due a little warmth and sunshine. *You can't have rainbows without rain!* was the first encounter she'd had with this sentiment. At her dentist's office, of all places, and she'd felt its insensitivity boring a hole in her as she waited for her name to be called. She didn't feel that losing her family and being left by her fiancé on her wedding day could be classed as a light shower or a cold winter's day. They were soul-destroying, life-altering moments that she felt she deserved the time to process. She didn't need cheery posters or stupid fortune-telling machines to essentially tell her to 'cheer up' despite her hardships. However, Luna couldn't help but feel like this fortune had been chosen for her for a reason, even if she did feel like it belittled the pain she'd endured in her lifetime. She brought out her purse from her pocket, tucked the fortune away behind her debit card and walked briskly away from Jacob's Amusements.

Seven

Vinegar

Today was the day. After thirteen years of companionship, years of umming and ahhing, too long wondering when the right time would be, he was going to take the plunge. He'd bought a nice diamond ring that was pricey but didn't break the bank and the rock was big enough to be impressive without being too showy. It was ideal. His relationship had been rocky for a while, to say the least, and he knew in his heart of hearts that it was his lack of commitment that sat at the core of their troubles.

'Thirteen years, darling,' she'd say. 'How long do we have to wait until we've proven that this works? That we work? Together?' And he knew it, of course. After the initial few years he knew she expected a proposal and the truth was he wasn't able to afford the ring, let alone

a wedding. Then his father sadly passed away and left his chip shop to him, as well as monetary inheritance, and financial difficulty no longer became the crux of his aversion to marriage. In all honesty, he didn't know what was. It was definitely fear, but not of her or of the life they might lead; probably of the unknown and complete lack of certainty. He'd bought the ring a year ago and had still been deliberating but enough was enough. Their relationship had fallen into 'make or break' – and it was time he 'make' her his wife.

He'd arranged a picnic on his lunch break along the seafront where they used to walk in their carefree twenties when they had time to play with. Now time was toying with him and those carefree days seemed distant and irretrievable. It was windy and it took him ten minutes to lay down the gingham cloth on the bench for them both to sit on. His bumbling and fumbling used to make her laugh, but today her face was stony and unchanging. She sighed as she sat down next to him. His cold fingers opened the basket and found the tightly clingfilm-wrapped cheese and pickle sandwiches he'd pre-made. He looked at the tattoo on his hand, the date they met in thick, black, bold numbers meandering across his knuckles.

'Kate, I've been doing some thinking,' he said as he opened his own little sandwich parcel. He reached down for the little black box in the picnic basket to his right, glancing at her empty ring finger on top of her unopened sandwiches, excited now at the prospect of

it being empty no longer. She stared straight ahead at the crashing waves, her brow beginning to crease in the way he loved when she was thinking about something intensely for too long.

'So have I, darling,' she whispered, her eyes watering.

'You have?' he said, his fingers just brushing the top of the box. She turned to him then and he froze.

'I'm done,' she said, tears streaming down her face.

'What?' he breathed.

'No more. No more waiting and wishing. No more hoping today would be the day. I've learned now that the day never comes and I will always be left longing for something that will never happen.'

'No ... but ...' He picked up the box, but couldn't bring himself to show it to her.

'I've made my decision. One of us had to.' She stood up, put her sandwiches on the gingham cloth where she'd sat, and walked away. He only watched her, his heart as numb as his hands. He slid the ring box into his pocket. He wasn't quick enough on the draw and had lost the most precious thing he had ever had in his life. She made sense of everything and without her, he felt like his world would surely crumble. It was now he knew that all along he shouldn't have been fearing commitment but fearing life without her. That was the real unknown. Sadly, these were all realisations that were found far too late. He sat on the bench alone, letting his body go numb in the icy sea air before he went back to work, empty and alone.

Saveloys, fried chicken and individually packaged pies sat in neat lines in the warm glass case on the silver counter and Luna's mouth started to water. The smell of chip fat, salt and batter was making her stomach gurgle at its loudest. No one stood behind the counter to greet her and she wondered what the protocol was to get someone's attention in this scenario. She'd seen those little bells on reception desks in hotels on television and movies but never really understood their necessity until now. Did she call out for someone or was it rude to shout? Did she just wait until someone came to check? Could she count on someone having heard the door open and close? Her stomach rumbled again.

'Hello?' Luna called out towards the kitchen behind the counter when her hunger outweighed her anxiety. She could see chip fryers and silver worktops but no one around to be working in them. She cleared her throat. 'Excuse me?' she said, though admittedly still not loud enough should someone be all the way in the back. However, there was the rustle of what Luna suspected was a newspaper being closed and the squeak of a chair against the floor. 'Are you open?' she called out, properly this time. A squat, middle-aged man with a good head of grey hair that was styled into a quiff at the front appeared and walked very slowly towards her, dragging his feet across the kitchen floor in a pair of blue slippers.

His white T-shirt was so stained with grease that very little of its original white colour showed through between the patches.

'What does it look like?' he said as he wiped his nose along the back of his tattooed hand with a great sniff.

'Sorry?' Luna asked, feeling the polite plastered-on smile, one that she automatically adorned for strangers, begin to flicker.

'The sign outside. What does it say?' He pointed to the door where the side of a sign facing them read CLOSED.

'It says Open?' She wondered why she'd said it as a question when she knew that was obviously right.

'Then we're open,' he said with an unkind smile that narrowed his eyes so much she could barely see what colour they were.

'. . . Okay.' She brought the rest of the change from her five pound note out of the bottom of her pocket and she could feel the man's hot breath as he sighed at the sight of all those coins. 'Could I just get a small portion of chips, please?' Her hands were starting to shake a little so counting the ten pence pieces was proving to be difficult, especially when her brain wasn't focused on the counting but on the way he was watching her fumble.

'Where've you come from, then?' he asked, with a bite to his words that made Luna step backwards.

'Sorry?' Her voice fluttered.

'Who *are* you?'

'I've . . . I've just moved here.'

'Why?' The man scoffed, phlegm catching in the back of his throat.

'Work?' she said. The quizzical inflection wasn't there to imply that she was unsure why she was on the island. She knew why she was here and was sure of her decisions. What she couldn't fathom was this man's abrupt curiosity for information that would seemingly affect zero per cent of his life, let alone his evening.

'Two pounds fifty,' he replied.

'Sorry?'

'Do you want the chips or not?'

'Yes.' Her stomach also rumbled its own answer.

'*Two pounds fifty.*' Luna started to count out the change and only a few of her muscles relaxed when he rolled his eyes and moved away to bundle up her chips.

'Could I get salt and vinegar on them ... please?' she asked as he started to wrap them closed. He rolled his eyes yet again as he violently shook the salt and then sloshed the vinegar, drowning her chips. He chucked the tightly wrapped parcel on the counter and she held her handful of coins out for him in the palm of her hand but he just looked down at the pile of silver as if she were handing him her freshly spat-out chewing gum.

'Sorry. I don't have anything bigger.' He rolled his eyes far harder than Luna felt necessary and opened his own hand for her to tip the coins into. He prodded a button on the till to his right and the drawer opened towards him with a clunk.

'Thank you,' she said as she hurried out of the door, clutching her hot parcel of wet chips against her chest, not waiting for a response as she knew there wasn't likely to be one.

Luna carried on walking the way she'd been headed before she'd met the chip shop man from hell and it was only when she reached the row of painted houses that she realised that actually, all she wanted to do was head home to the inn, cuddle up with a film in bed and eat her dinner undisturbed. Despite her phone telling her that it was only two thirty in the afternoon, Luna felt that she was already very much done with the day.

The door to the first house, its blue paint peeling in the sea air, opened and a man in a suit stepped out. He held the door open with his foot, a cup of tea in his hand and she was certain that he was looking directly at her. She slowed to a stop, unable to look away from the man, trying to figure out whether she was the victim of his gaze, but her eyes weren't good enough to tell.

'Hello?' he called out. 'Are you here for the house viewing?' He gestured to the sign secured to the railings with cable ties.

'No. Sorry.' She shook her head and the estate agent sighed.

'Nah, no need to be sorry. I knew no one would come.'

He sounded defeated but still smiled with all his very straight, very white teeth.

'No one at all?' Luna hugged her chips closer to her.

'Not a single soul,' he laughed.

'What's wrong with it?'

'Not it. *Them*. All five houses are for sale as a unit!' Luna looked at the neat row and whilst she knew she'd never be able to afford them, in a brief moment she saw her life living on the seafront flash before her eyes. Lemonade on a towel on the sand in the summer and cosy winter nights sat reading a book in the window overlooking the sea. She suppressed her longing for the life she'd created for herself in under ten seconds and focused. 'And there's nothing wrong with them at all! I mean, they're a bit old and need some TLC but they're structurally sound and a bargain if you ask me.'

'Then why has no one come to view them?'

'Everyone who lives here already has a home and no one new ever comes to the island.' He shrugged exactly like the emoji on her phone. She wondered if it was purposeful or if he'd been subliminally influenced.

'I'm someone new.' She shrugged back in the same fashion. He laughed so she guessed it had been a deliberate quirk.

'That is true – I've never seen you around before.'

'It's my first day here.' She was pleased that not everyone on the island was quite as coarse as the man in the chip shop.

'Well, it must be fate that we've met, because it's my last.'

'You're leaving?' Luna's hopes were dashed. Her first positive encounter all day and he wasn't even staying.

'There's a better job going on the mainland and I promised myself if no one showed up today I'd go for it. So . . . ' he shuffled his feet, 'are you here for the houses?'

'Oof,' she breathed.

'What?' He flashed his white teeth and she couldn't help but smile even if only a little.

'If I say yes, you stay and potentially remain in a job you clearly hate and if I say no, you take a huge risk on a job you might not get.'

'You're like my very own magic eight ball.' He shook an imaginary ball between his palms and then looked to her for an answer, eyebrows raised, mouth open and hopeful.

'Can I say maybe and remain impartial?'

'Aww c'mon, nobody likes it when the magic eight ball says "Ask Again Later"!' He chuckled as he reached into his pocket. He brought out a little blue card. 'Well, if you change your mind, call up and ask for Tony. That's me. If I'm not there, you'll know why.' Luna paused as she looked at the card he held between his fingers, and then took it.

'Thanks, Tony.'

As much as she quite liked Tony and his calm, easy manner (and his oddly symmetrical face) Luna turned swiftly on her heels and walked back past the chip shop. The idea of sinking into a bubble bath was getting stronger by the minute. She chanced a glance through the window of the chip shop as she passed back the way she came but the disgruntled man had disappeared back to his newspaper and so wasn't there to watch her walk back in the opposite direction, anyway. She dashed back past the twinkling amusements holding her warm bag of chips, trying to forget about the fortune-telling card that was burning a hole in her pocket. As she walked away from the man on the steps of the blue painted house, there was a faint click in the air as a door closed behind her.

Luna decided that she would walk back the way she came but she would walk as briskly as she could and that she would not stop for anyone or anything. She kept her head down as she passed Beau's coffee shop on the opposite side of the street but was sure she felt his eyes on her. The bookshop did its best to draw her to it and it was the only thing on the way back to the inn that very nearly made her cave in. She vowed she'd visit on a better day when she could enjoy all the old books and their stories to the fullest. As she approached the inn, Mrs McArthur opened the door, her make-up freshly done, wearing trousers and a blouse with a nice pair of low black heels.

'Miss Lark! Are you coming tonight?' Mrs McArthur wobbled over to her, clearly more accustomed to flat boots.

'Tonight?' Luna made her package of chips a little more obvious in an attempt to make it look like she already had plans, even if they were quite sad and lonely ones.

'Oh, you haven't forgotten already, have you? *The Wizard of Oz*! We're all going for dinner and then we're off somewhere over the rainbow!' Mrs McArthur's enthusiasm would have been infectious had Luna not felt so miserable.

'No, I hadn't forgotten – I'm just not sure it's for me. I'm not the biggest fan of musicals.'

'Not a fan of … my, my dear girl.' Mrs McArthur reacted as if Luna had said she didn't like puppies or ice cream. 'You sure you're not coming?'

'The Oompa-Loompas will have to do without me.'

Mrs McArthur tilted her head for a moment and then twittered a high-pitched laugh but when Luna was simply left staring at her, she abruptly stopped her giggling.

'Munchkins,' Mrs McArthur offered.

'… Hmm?'

'The people of Oz. They're called Munchkins. Oompa-Loompas are from *Charlie and the Chocolate Factory*,' she explained. She shook her head and laughed again, a little more haughtily, seemingly baffled how anyone couldn't know the very specific differences between the residents of Oz and Loompaland. It seemed that Luna was a very specific kind of racist that mixed up only the inhabitants of mythical realms.

'I see. Sorry. Probably more reason I don't come! Have fun, though!' Luna lifted her chips and wiggled them in the air to show off her simplistic dinner plans and scuttled into the inn before Mrs McArthur could protest.

Up in her room, she closed the door behind her and leant back against it, turning the latch to firmly lock herself in for the afternoon. She was grateful that Mrs McArthur had been on her way out as she'd arrived back for the night. She felt a little mean for having hoped she'd be too busy to pester her but her first morning in Ondingside had left a lot to be desired and she felt like she was allowed to want to be alone. *Just for a little while,* she thought, although she already knew it was sure to be longer. She had food, her laptop, her notebook and a bath. If she got hungry again later or needed anything from the outside world, she'd figure it out when it came to it but for now, she was content with what she had. She went to the bathroom and ran a bath, squeezing the last of the complimentary shampoo into the water in an attempt to create bubbles. As she shrugged off her coat, she realised just how bitterly cold her room had become. She had thought that leaving the window open would have given her room a fresh, crisp feel when instead it had made it almost uninhabitable. She pulled her coat back around her and rushed to pull the window closed and it was then that she realised how dark it had become. For three o'clock on a July afternoon, the world outside looked like Britain's deepest winter. The ceiling of cloud above the turbulent sea was almost black and Luna could see the wind whipping at the grass and the bushes that led down to the sand.

'Wow,' she said gasped as the gale whistled through every tiny crack in the inn's foundations. Luna wasn't sure how safe she felt in such an old building in this kind of weather but she figured it had survived upright this long at the very least. Luna jumped at a fervent knock at her door.

'Room Service,' said a voice but Luna already knew before she opened the door that it was Mrs McArthur. 'Hello, love. Terrible weather.' She shivered. 'Extra blanket for the night?' Mrs McArthur held out a neatly folded blue knitted blanket which Luna gratefully took.

'Yes, please. Thank you. Weren't you on your way out? Big night at the theatre?'

'I was, but I just wanted to make sure you were going to be all right. On your own.'

'Yes,' said Luna, her jaw clenching. 'I'm sure I'll manage.'

'Good. Good.' Mrs McArthur didn't leave and so Luna didn't close the door but neither said a word. Mrs McArthur smiled at Luna who wasn't able to manage a smile back. Instead she pursed her lips and raised her eyebrows, causing her to look a little sarcastically enthused. It wasn't her intention but neither was continuing a conversation and so she didn't do much to rectify the situation.

'Good day?' Mrs McArthur asked, certainly testing Luna's skills at saying only what needed to be said and nothing more.

'Not terrible,' she replied, which she felt was the best line she could find between not telling a lie but also not telling the truth.

'Meet anyone on your travels?' Mrs McArthur fiddled with the clasp on her bracelet.

'Has Beau been here, by any chance?' Luna asked. When Mrs McArthur had first questioned her connection to Beau, she'd felt a surge of anxiety and panic but now she just felt her patience and tolerance sinking far below average. Beau seemed to be becoming more of a nuisance than she expected, considering she didn't really expect Beau to be anything to her at all.

'No,' Mrs McArthur said with a nod of certainty.

'But you've heard from him?' Luna held the door with her foot and lobbed the blanket onto the bed, trying her hardest to make it clear that she wouldn't be inviting Mrs McArthur in for further conversation.

'Well ... he *may* have called.'

'Mrs McArthur ...'

'Yes, all right, he definitely did call but I didn't say anything! I didn't even confirm whether you were staying here or not but it's not hard to guess the exact whereabouts of people in this place. He only called because he's worried about you, dear.'

'I know, he made that abundantly clear.' Luna fought the urge to roll her eyes.

'What happened?' Mrs McArthur's sincerity made Luna think twice about being as abrupt as she would have liked. She was such a kind woman and despite her eagerness to know everything about everyone, Luna knew it didn't come from a place of gossip nor was she a busybody. It was simply that she'd never known any different. Living in such a small place with so few people, naturally everyone knew everything about everyone else. Mrs McArthur was simply a product of her surroundings and Luna just didn't feel able to berate her for that. After all, Luna had moved to their island and was invading *their* lives. Had it been the other way around Luna may have had a little more to say on the matter.

'I'm sure Beau has already filled you in,' Luna said.

'I've known Beau since he was a child. He does tell me everything, but I'm not asking him. I'm asking you.' Mrs McArthur reached out and touched Luna's arm and Luna let her, despite feeling a desperate need to recoil.

'Nothing *happened*, Mrs McArthur.' Luna managed a smile. 'He just pried a little too much and made far too many assumptions after not even nearly enough time.'

'Does that mean you'll be seeing him again?' Mrs McArthur clasped her hands together in front of her face, her eyes shining over the rim of her glasses.

'What do you mean?'

'You said he made too many assumptions after not nearly enough time ... will you be giving him more time?'

'Erm ... no, I don't think so.' Luna laughed, trying to lighten what had very suddenly become such serious mood.

'Why not? He's such a sweet boy!'

'I'm sure he is but ... I'm just not interested,' Luna said and Mrs McArthur took a step back from Luna to take her in.

'In Beau?' Mrs McArthur whispered in outrage.

'In *anyone*, Mrs McArthur.'

'Ever?'

'Not ever, just not now. I'm just not ready to be in a relationship at the moment.'

'So that's a maybe, then?'

'What? No, I just think that when the time is right—'

'Oh, that's marvellous news! I'm going to call him right this instant! Thrilled, my love. *Thrilled*!' Mrs McArthur was gone before Luna could correct her but weirdly enough, she didn't care. Luna watched the elderly yet spritely woman as she skittered along the corridor and down the stairs. She heard the door open and close behind her. Luna felt sick at the thought of the conversation that might be had between the two of them but instead of running after her and begging her not to say a word, Luna simply closed her door and locked it behind her once more. She was just thankful she wouldn't be around to hear what was said. Was it because she was learning to care less about what others thought? Did what people say behind her back when she wasn't there to listen not affect her as much as it used to? Or was it that little flicker of something familiar in Luna's chest that she had felt earlier in the day that was holding her back from rushing downstairs and knocking the phone out of poor Mrs McArthur's hands? Before she could think about it any further, the sound of running water invaded her thoughts and she ran into the bathroom to turn off the taps before she flooded the place.

From the bath, Luna texted Lottie with her somewhat dry hands.

> Safe and sound in Ondingside. The inn is still a shambles but still standing. First day was rough but tomorrow will be better. Please stop worrying! I'm absolutely fine.

She pressed send and slid her phone across the bathroom tiles so that she could soak in peace. Luna loved her best friend dearly but she had started to feel suffocated by her dedicated protection and incessant hourly check-ups since the almost-wedding. Luna knew it all came from a place of love but it was too much love too soon after the incident. She wanted to hide herself away to find some composure, some peace with what had happened and figure out a plan forwards. She found that the pinging of her phone every hour was a huge distraction not only from her own thoughts but also from her writing and when she turned her phone off, Lottie would only end up ringing her doorbell and inviting herself in for pizza, wine and a DMC (deep and meaningful conversation). Luna and Lottie had many similarities but they were polar opposites in how they dealt with a personal crisis.

Back in university, where the pair had met, Luna studying English Literature and Lottie Physics, Lottie often found herself in sticky romantic situations. Affairs that lasted mere hours, one-night stands, guys that were far too intense far too soon and guys that seemed to have interest in nothing but booze and sex with anyone and everyone: Lottie seemed to have encountered them all. On the many nights Luna came back to their dorm to find Lottie crying over a pizza and a bottle (or two) of wine, Lottie would grab her best friend by the hand, pull her into a hug and not let go until all of her tears were cried and all of her expletives had been expelled from her lungs. Lottie found solace and comfort in the presence of others whilst Luna only found embarrassment. Luna actually almost envied Lottie's ability to say exactly how she felt, when she felt it and deal with a problem in the moment so that it never sat and festered in her mind and soul for any longer than was necessary.

'When it comes to emotions,' Lottie used to say whilst mopping up her tears on her sleeves and trying to smudge her eyeliner back into place with her fingers, 'the same rules for burps apply ... better out than in!' This was why Lottie's initial reaction when Noel had, in her words, 'been a shit-head', was to pull Luna in for an embrace that lasted as long as it would take to make Luna feel better. Lottie wanted to hug her pain away and her encouragement to share only became more and more intense which caused an already retreating Luna to back away all the more. Luna loved Lottie with all her heart, she really did, but she felt she was old enough and ugly enough to be trusted to deal with her own issues by herself. It was already a year since Noel and as much as she was over him and his idiocy, she knew deep down she probably wasn't as fine as she would have Lottie (and now Beau ...) believe and she just needed time by herself to figure out a way forwards. Luna was telling herself that Ondingside was her very own permanent self-care retreat where she could lick her wounds, heal and become stronger than she ever had been before. Constant supervision and prying eyes were not ideal conditions for Luna to do any of that, Now, come to think of it, Luna wished she had added a few emojis to her message to be a little more convincing. Although, Luna knew Lottie would take the hint and would send maybe only two more texts before the night was out. She certainly wouldn't try to call again but Luna really did intend to call her back. Just not today. Today was hers and hers alone to enjoy her bath, eat her chips and watch a movie. Everything else, could simply wait for her and life would resume tomorrow.

And Luna did exactly that. Her day was boring by most people's standards but it had been exactly what she had needed: time spent doing not a lot. She even wrote a few more notes in her notebook which she let herself feel proud of despite the fact they were nothing to do with her novel. *Writing is writing*, she told herself.

Day one could have been better but it could have been worse. However, I'm deciding that the glass is half full despite being thirsty for much more than Ondingside has currently offered. Have I made a huge and miserable mistake? Or is this the adjustment period I should have been expecting? I'm hoping it's the latter but I'm terribly worried that it's the former, especially now that someone is showing far too much of an interest in me. I just need to stay strong and do what's right for me. Time to be a little bit selfish.

She put down her pen but felt unsatisfied so then picked it back up and added,

Beau can do one.

and felt a little bit better.

When nighttime finally came and the world outside the window became dark, the wind whipped louder, the clouds grew thicker and Luna actually felt a shiver of panic shudder through her bones. There was no thunder and no lightning, just bitter cold seeping into every available space of the inn and a darkness like no other she'd seen before. Luna knew that the light pollution in somewhere like Ondingside was far, far less than London and so she expected the skies to be blacker but not like this. There were no stars and the moon was barely visible through the thick sheet of cloud. This kind of darkness blanketed everything with the intention of suffocating the light from the world and came with a sinister edge that Luna couldn't put her finger on. Whether it was the howl of the wind or the bite of the icy air or the fact that all of this was occurring on what should be a balmy July evening, this still didn't seem like the kind of night for a cosy sing-song around the fire. This seemed like the type of night where people went to bed not knowing what kind of weather damage they would wake up to the next morning. Fallen trees, crushed cars, broken windows ... Luna didn't feel a huge sense of safety in the rickety old inn but even so, sleep was pushing down her eyelids with its forceful hands and so, with heavy limbs, Luna went to the window and with one last wave towards the moon, she pulled her curtains closed.

Luna opened her eyes and saw nothing but white. A tear streaked down her cheek as a snowflake caught her eye and she blinked to make it melt. She was unable to see anything more than the sheet of snow tumbling down in front of her. She lifted a hand in front of her face and saw a vague shadowy outline but nothing more. Luna called out but her voice only echoed into a great expanse of emptiness. She took a step forward and her bare foot crunched the snow beneath. The skin of her soles tingled. As if she'd been asleep with her legs curled underneath her and like her mind, they were only just waking up. Wrapping her arms around her naked body, she trudged onwards. The flakes whipped at her face and she fought against her long hair dragging in the wind behind her shoulders. An ache in her chest throbbed and with each definite pang it filled her body with a heaviness that made pushing onwards into the blizzard hard and tiresome. The frost violently whipped at her cheeks but she only felt the light kiss of ice on her lips. She called out again and her voice carried through the blizzard but no one came. Luna forged on alone.

Eight

Day One . . . Again

July 17th 2019

In the night, a dog sniffed along the bottom of the garden fence, the smell of last night's kill fading in his nostrils. The dirt from his dig covered the garden and although the catch had been marvellous, the dog's owner hadn't seemed as happy as he had hoped. In fact he'd shouted and hadn't thrown his ball with such gusto on their daily walk. The dog felt a tickle on his nose. Then on his back, and then all over. He looked up to see the sky speckled with white. It was only a light sprinkling at first, but then the flakes started to fall thick and fast. The dog jumped high into the air trying to catch the snowflakes, as if they were rabbits, but the kill certainly wasn't as satisfying or triumphant when they melted quickly on his tongue. The dog landed on the ground with a thump, his head suddenly foggy. The wagging of his tail slowed and he sneezed as a snowflake landed in his nostril. The dog looked around at the garden. He saw the overturned soil sprinkling the grass and smelt the faint scent of dead rabbit. The Jack Russell remembered the trample of his own feet as he bounded towards the rabbit's bright eyes. He remembered the squeal as he bit down against the flesh of its neck and the triumph as he left it in the centre of the grass and squeezed back under the fence. Yes, tonight's *hunt had been a good one. The dog stuck his snout under a small gap underneath the fence and pushed until his head popped through and he peered into next door's garden. He still couldn't see any sign of where he'd left the rabbit. He was sure he'd felt its neck snap in his jaw but maybe it had only been injured and managed to move to safety in case the dog came back. The dog walked back to the back step of his own house, tail between his legs, and just before he retreated back into the warmth of the kitchen through the flap in the back door, he took one last glance as the snow covered the evidence of his hunt and wondered where he'd gone so wrong.*

Getting out of bed had never been Luna's strong suit. Her alarm jolted her out of unconsciousness and she fumbled around in the half-light until the pads of her fingers illuminated the screen of her phone. Then she just kept prodding until she found the orange button of her alarm and the sound ceased. She lifted the phone onto its side and, through foggy eyes, Luna looked at the time. Ten o'clock. She made a howling sound as she yawned then she positioned all four pillows behind her and lay upright against them. She opened Twitter, Instagram and Facebook and expertly swiped between each app, waiting for them to load ... but none of them did. She closed and opened them all for a second time and waited far longer than expected and she was still met with 'No internet connection', 'Nothing to see here' and a spinning wheel. All the bars in the right-hand corner of the screen were a miserable faded grey instead of their usual bold black and the absence of the 4G made Luna groan. Lottie hadn't texted before the signal had gone so Luna quickly wrote another text to send that would hopefully deliver whenever 4G sprang back into life.

> Signal here is terrible. If you don't hear from me, I'm not dead, just dead bored without Instagram.

Putting down her phone, she swung her legs out of bed and that's when the ice took a good and proper bite out of her skin.

111

'Oof!' she said, pulling her bare legs back into the warmth. Then in her still groggy state she realised she could see her breath in front of her face. Cupping her hands in front of her mouth, she breathed hard into them to try and stop them from numbing. Luna couldn't bear to get out from under the blankets but her curiosity was too strong not to go to the window. She worried that when she opened her curtains she'd see that whatever weather was bringing forth this freeze would prevent her from going outside on her first day in Ondingside. Even so, she just had to know. She bundled the duvet and another blanket – that, although she didn't remember seeing it on her bed the night before, she was very grateful for now – around her shoulders and, holding them tightly around her, waddled to the window. The hair on her skin raised and the skin itself pimpled as she walked closer to the curtains. She wriggled one unlucky arm free and quickly yanked the curtain back. The light from the outside world blinded her tired eyes for a moment and she scrunched them shut but even closed, all she saw was white. Luna carefully opened her eyes once more but the light was just too bright. She blinked a few times but they just didn't seem to adjust. She pulled the other curtain back as well and as she leant closer to the window she noticed the faint line of something all along the outside windowsill, pressed up against the glass.

'It can't be . . .' She looked up and realised that what she thought was simply light from the sun was actually a blanket of bright, white snow covering every inch of grass, soil and sand.

'Holy hell!' A laugh escaped her and then she laughed again at how surprised she was at the sound of her own voice. The air was still and the snow seemed to have gently hushed the world into silence. Even the sea seemed to ebb reluctantly but where the water met the snow-covered sand, it had frozen. Luna pressed her hand flat against the cold glass and the frost on the other side blossomed around her fingers. A little sliver of ice dropped away as the heat from her palm started to seep into the outside world. She stood back, pulling her hand away from the window, not wanting to disturb such a perfect picture. She plonked backwards onto her bed and, in her warm cocoon, she just watched. Birds swooped in the air and Luna wondered if they were heading south, confused why home had suddenly become so cold, so early. Whilst the snow was fluffy and fresh, the sky was still filled with grey clouds that, if Luna didn't know any better, still had bellies-full of snow fit to burst at any moment. The Earth seemed confused with itself and yet content to be so and Luna couldn't help but smile.

Downstairs, the inn was in chaos.

'The heating won't turn on and our chef can't get to us,' Mrs McArthur shrieked down the phone. 'The roads are covered in snow and ice and there's no one to cook! I refuse to tell my guests that they can only eat if they trot into the kitchen to make it themselves.

I just won't have it and I—hello? Hello? The absolute bas—oh, hello . . . '

'Hello.' Luna waved without conviction and so it simply looked like she'd tried to catch a fly mid-air.

'Sorry about that. I'm not too keen on being hung up on, especially in such a crisis. Have you looked out of the window?' Mrs McArthur's hair was in wild disarray and Luna counted the rubbered ends of three pencils sticking out from behind her head, keeping her hair in place.

'Yes. Snow.'

'*Lots* of the blasted stuff! I bet you didn't expect that when you travelled down yesterday!'

'Does it always snow in July here?'

'Never. This is certainly a first. I checked the news. Nowhere else seems to have been hit by it. A freak snow-storm, they're saying.' Mrs McArthur came out from behind the desk and ran to the front door to open it a crack and peek out at the Christmas-card scene outside. Almost as if she were checking that all that snow was still there and that one of the local boys wasn't pulling some kind of daft prank.

'Wow,' Luna said, her breath dancing in the air.

'Wow, indeed. You're not going out there, are you?'

'Well, it is my first day here. I was hoping to see what was around.'

'Hmm. Just . . . wrap up warm, won't you?' Mrs McArthur embraced herself and rubbed her shoulders as she went back behind her desk where she'd lit the fireplace; Luna couldn't recall when she last saw an actual working, indoor, wood-burning fire. As for wrapping up warm, Luna certainly hadn't packed for snow and her baby blue coat, with its three-quarter-length sleeves and its inability to actually do up at the front, certainly wasn't designed for a chilly spring, let alone a winter freeze. Even with a long-sleeved jumper on underneath, it wasn't ideal but Luna nodded at the kind lady's words of concern – despite the cold gust freezing the tip of her nose and ears immediately as she opened the door and ventured out into Ondingside for the first time.

Snow had always been Luna's favourite kind of weather. She didn't much like the cold if she wasn't dressed for the occasion but nothing could make her smile quite like the satisfying, wholesome crunch of snow underfoot or the feeling of snowflakes getting caught in her eyelashes. Luna was convinced that snow wasn't nature or simply the science of water evaporating, freezing and falling, but that it was actually a kind of magic. Magic that she was allowed the luxury of witnessing each winter, if she was lucky. She was, and always had been, enchanted by its ability to calm and quieten even London's hustle and bustle. Ondingside didn't need as much calming and quieting but even so, the beauty of turning something from a luscious green to pure white in one single night, especially in the middle of summer, was mesmerising.

Luna walked to the hill around the back of the inn that

overlooked the sea. Unsurprisingly, the white beach was empty. Ondingside was small and sparsely populated on the best of days and so Luna wondered how many souls she would actually encounter when the more tempting option was to stay indoors where there were blankets, hot water bottles and hot chocolates. The thought of hot beverages made Luna very aware that her stomach was as empty as the beach and instead of walking on the snow-covered sand, Luna continued along the way she was headed.

'Morning,' said an elderly gentleman as he threw a tennis ball for his dog.

'Morning,' Luna replied although she wasn't sure she said it loud enough to be heard.

'Looking for town?' The man called after her as she passed him. She turned back and nodded. 'Well, you're headed the right way! Just keep going past all those houses until you hit the roundabout. Although,' he chuckled, 'we don't got much!' The man's face had been nipped by the air and the end of his long nose was bright pink but he smiled all the same as his Jack Russell, a little hodgepodge of black, brown and white, bounded over, kicking snow over his owner's brown boots.

'I don't need much,' Luna smiled. 'Just coffee and a good book.' She dipped her head and took a couple of steps backwards.

'Well then, you're in luck!' he said, closing the distance she'd started to create. 'Our lovely Beau opened a coffee shop just a few months ago! Doesn't get many customers. Bit too ... what's the word? Hipster?' The man chuckled. 'Us old fogeys don't quite understand all that. Nothing beats a cup of tea for me! I'm sure Beau'll be pretty glad to see someone nearer his own age.'

An icy breath caught in the back of Luna's throat. 'Sorry, excuse me, did you say Beau?' The name triggered a memory that made her feel as sick as she had felt a year ago.

'I surely did.' The man retrieved the tennis ball from his dog's mouth and threw it as far as his arms would let him.

'As in ... the same Beau that used to work at the Green Arrow?' Luna just had to make sure before she unknowingly walked into the spider's web.

'That's him! Know him, do you?'

'... Old acquaintances.' She tried to smile but her stomach was turning.

'Well then, make sure you pop in! All right, all right, Welles!' The Jack Russell had dropped the ball at the man's feet and had started to bark. 'Hope you manage to find your old friend!'

The man tipped his flat cap to her and as she turned she muttered, 'I'm not sure *I* do.'

Luna reached the roundabout, then veered to the right and took the first exit. Her feet seemed to guide her without much thought but she was happy to slowly wander, watching her boots sink into the inches of powdered snow. She spotted the books in the window of the used bookstore and smiled at her own brilliant sense of direction. Just beyond the bookshop, however, there was a chalkboard sign on the pavement that read CONGRATULATIONS! YOU MADE IT OUT OF BED! A cup of coffee had been drawn underneath it. The sign was sweet, if a little lopsided. Luna smiled in spite of herself and edged towards the shop. She wasn't thrilled about the prospect of seeing Beau but she was certainly in need of caffeine. Just as she was weighing up the pros and cons, a bell rang as the door to Beau's shop swiftly opened.

'It's warm in here if that makes coming in any more tempting.' Luna hadn't seen Beau's face in almost a year and yet she couldn't explain why it felt far more familiar than she had expected. Her memory had always been pretty accurate but it struck her as odd that she knew him instantly, without that usual few seconds of buffering that it usually took to recognise someone you hadn't seen in a long time. Especially when she had only met him once before and over a year ago. Beau held the door for her as she entered the shop and for a moment, Luna thought he might have forgotten.

'Hang on, a second . . . ' Or maybe not. 'I know you.'

'Do you? I've been told I just . . . have one of those faces.' Luna turned away from him to peruse the menu behind the counter written in chalk on the black wall.

'No, I definitely know you.' Beau followed her behind the counter and took a moment to scrutinise her face whilst she pretended to ignore him.

'I've still got your prize money!' He grinned as the penny dropped. Luna thought for a moment about denying it, she even thought about running out of the shop altogether. Instead, she stood her ground, even if she wasn't looking him in the eyes.

'You've got a good memory,' she said, cringing.

'So, it *is* you. Returned at last.' He spread his arms wide and gave a little whispered cheer. 'How's the island treating you on this visit?' Luna thought about explaining how it wasn't just a visit and it was for good this time but then she remembered her rule. *You're Miss Lark. Not Luna. Miss Lark,* she thought. *No one gets on a first-name basis and no one needs to know who you are or why you're here.*

'Well, thank you.'

'I work here now. Well … I own this place. But I don't work at the Green Arrow any more. Traded pints for coffee.'

'It's nice.' She smiled.

'Less people throw up in here too,' he joked but she winced. 'Too soon?'

'Maybe just a little,' she admitted. 'I'm not sure I'll ever laugh at that memory.'

'Ahh, you've gotta laugh. Otherwise you'll cry.'

'I'll drink to that.'

Beau's face suddenly flushed and all expressions dissolved. 'You actually want a coffee?' he half whispered.

'You ... *are* a coffee shop, right?'

'Well, what can I get you?' He clapped his hands together loudly. 'Latte? Flat white?'

'Flat white sounds ideal.'

'Coming up!' He bashed and banged behind the machine which whirred and huffed in response.

'So what brings you to the island again? Business or pleasure?' he asked when the noise had quietened down.

'Business.' *That's technically true,* she said to herself, thinking about the book she had to write.

'Here for long?' He kept glancing up at her with his big brown eyes and she couldn't help but be a little taken aback. They looked almost velvety and swam with a warmth and kindness she'd not seen in a while – yet something in her still wanted to pull back despite her yearning for someone kind.

'A while.' She nodded.

'Not leaving as quickly as last time, I hope?'

'No,' she said. He banged the silver milk jug on the table, Luna sensing the cogs in his head turning.

'I came looking for you, y'know,' he said, concentrating on the milk as it flowed down into the coffee and up to the surface.

'I heard.' She smiled whilst he wasn't looking.

'Mrs M.' He sighed.

'Who else?'

'She means no harm. I think she fancies herself as a bit of a matchmaker,' he said and then his tongue rolled out the side of his mouth as his wrist moved in fluid motions, expertly drawing on the top of her coffee with the jug.

'I see.'

'Ta-da!' he said as he delicately placed the small flat white in front of Luna. A frothy milk snowflake floated on the top of her coffee.

'Wow.' She nodded. 'Impressive!'

'My portfolio of latte art is small but luckily, this is one I can do well and it seemed fitting for today of all days.' He gestured to the snow-powdered street outside.

'Does it usually snow this much in July here?'

'First time I've ever seen it and I've lived here all my life.'

'You've never left the island?'

'Never needed to!' he said in a sing-song way. Luna felt that awkward moment of lull in the conversation looming and wasn't sure what to say in order to keep the dialogue going. She was amazed at herself for wanting to chat for a little while longer at least but she had nothing interesting left to ask him and nothing that she wanted to divulge about herself.

'Well, it was good to see you again, Beau.'

'Yes, you too . . . oh my God. I've forgotten your name.' His face flushed.

'You haven't!' she quickly reassured him. 'I just never told you. I'm Miss Lark.' She knew it hadn't gone unnoticed that she hadn't provided a first name but he nodded.

'Mysterious, Miss Lark. A pleasure, as always.'

'This time was probably more of a pleasure than the last time, though, let's be honest.'

He chuckled then and the fun of making him laugh fizzed through her; she enjoyed the feeling of her face stretching into a real smile.

'You're, erm ... you're not going to *The Wizard of Oz* tonight by any chance, are you?' Beau asked.

'*The Wizard of Oz?*' Her hands were starting to sweat against the heat of the coffee.

'The school play. It's kind of a big deal here. It's such a small place so the whole island ends up going to watch, seeing as all the kids are someone's son, daughter, grandson, granddaughter, niece, nephew so on and so forth ...'

'A musical?' she said, scrunching her nose.

'Not a fan?' He raised an eyebrow and she shook her head. 'You don't like musicals?'

'Not my thing.' She shrugged.

'Well ... see you soon?' he said and Luna liked how it was a question.

'Maybe. Tomorrow?' She didn't like how she was answering in questions, however, so she settled on, 'Tomorrow,' and nodded as she walked out into the cold street, feeling a little warmer than before.

The coffee was so creamy, so sweet and so exactly what Luna needed, she felt like running back into Beau's shop and giving him a hug. As first days go, she thought, this was shaping up to be quite a good one. The sun managed to burst out of its dense, grey cage for a moment and the world all around her started to glisten. The sparkling snow, the sound of it compacting under her boots and the steam of her coffee warming the tip of her nose as she clutched it in both hands at her chin, squeezed Luna's soul in all the right places. Before she quite knew it, a smile had crept over her face and she found herself beaming as she blissfully ignored the street signs and let her feet guide the way.

She took a left.

A right.

Another left.

Luna looked to her left again as a black cat crossed the road ahead of her. They locked eyes for a moment and Luna thought about trying to befriend it, but it slunk under a car so Luna turned right, which brought her to a row of amusements. The bulbs in the sign were old and rusty, some flickering whilst others just weren't working at all. Luna stood outside, looking up at the sign and all the whirling lights shining out at her from inside. Something deep in her memory stirred, like something was trapped in a box but wasn't strong enough to get out. A book she'd read? A movie she'd seen? In which someone went somewhere similar? *Big*, maybe? *I love that movie,* she thought as she went inside. Luna pulled out her purse and counted out a pound in ten pence pieces. She wasn't sure when she'd accumulated so much change, considering she often paid for everything on card these days, but she was thrilled she'd get to have a go on the claw machines. As she wandered over to three glasses cases filled with various stuffed toys, some from recent kids' movies and some very generic stuffed teddies, a machine in the very back corner of the room started flashing its lights. She could see a crystal ball in the centre of the machine's wooden frame and her intrigue piqued.

'Fortune favours the brave . . .' she read. Luna peered into each of the claw machines as she passed and decided that none of the toys seemed to be accessible enough to grab. *Claw machines are usually rigged, anyway,* she thought.

Luna slipped all ten coins into the machine in the corner and watched as it whirled into action.

> *'Stare into the crystal ball and ask what*
> *you require,*
> *Reach into your heart and tell me all that*
> *you desire,*
> *If he loves or loves you not, if she will*
> *stay or leave,*
> *It won't be hard for me to tell in one,*
> *two, THREE!'*

Luna quickly made a wish like she used to as a child before blowing out the candles on her birthday cake. The lights flickered and fizzled until they all switched off.

'That can't be it, surely?' Luna searched around the machine before hearing a buzzing noise. The machine spat out a little card that Luna excitedly snatched out of the slot.

> **WHEN WRITING THE STORY OF YOUR LIFE, DON'T LET ANYONE ELSE HOLD THE PEN.**

The guilt from all the work she had yet to even make a start on for her next novel hammered into her brain like a very large nail. Sadly, said nail missed pinning down all the good ideas that were floating around in her mind. She checked the clock on her phone.

'Nine a.m.?' She'd woken up well after nine o'clock in the morning so she knew that couldn't be correct. She had a fiddle with the settings on her phone but none of it seemed to make any difference. She opened up her usual social media apps but still, not a single one would load. 'Urgh.' Luna wasn't sure how she felt about being *this* cut off. The purpose of moving to Ondingside was to give her the physical space she needed but being entirely detached from everyone she knew (and everyone she followed) seemed a little *too* extreme, even for Luna. With thoughts of her book that she'd vowed to begin today, and the feeling of isolation starting to make her feel a sort of chill that even the snow couldn't match, she decided to go in search of people.

Nine

A Not-So Blank Slate

He had woken up to an empty bed, not knowing where his girlfriend had disappeared to. Luckily, she'd only wandered to her sister's house, not far from their home, although she was unsure how she'd got there. She agreed to meet him for the 'spontaneous' picnic he'd been planning for months. She'd been so sad and so distant for so long and he knew it was his doing. He knew he wasn't communicating in the way she needed him to, in the way he should have been doing all along and he was letting his fears of their future get in the way of actually living it.

They wandered down the beach together, in spite of the cold and the snow, and found a quiet bench to park themselves for sandwiches. He braced himself for the speech he'd prepared. He reached down into the picnic basket to his right and his fingertips brushed the small ring box, tucked next to a flask full of sweet tea.

'Kate, I've been doing some thinking.'

'So, have I ... ' *She trailed off, her eyes fixed on the snowy horizon. His heart skipped a beat and something in his chest forced the words out of his throat, not wanting the moment to pass.*

'No, please let me finish.' *He cupped the box in his hands like he would a live butterfly.* 'You've been by my side for thirteen years. Through everything. You've taken all the bad with all the good without complaint and I've been too stupid and too stubborn to give you the one and only thing you've ever asked for.' *He opened the box then to reveal the ring and the little light that shone through the cloud made rainbows dance in his palms. She looked at him and only him, a tear trickling down her face.* 'All you've ever wanted is the promise that I'll be yours forever. I thought it was enough to just say it – and it is, I suppose, in a way, but if I say it and I mean it, I should be able to prove it, too.'

'Oh ... ' *she sobbed.*

'I'm yours, Kate. I always have been. Will you have me?' *He took the ring from the box but she laid her hand over it and pushed it down, her gaze still firmly on him.*

'You daft bugger,' *she said and in just a single moment, he saw the face of the girl he'd fallen in love with all those*

years ago. Then she kissed him and for a brief moment,
he turned into the boy he had once been, too.

'Hello!' beamed the man behind the counter. 'What can I get for you today? We do saveloys and pies, even fried chicken! Or is it the classic fish and chips you're looking for today?' Luna remained stood at the door, not knowing why her stomach had flipped and her palms were sweating nor why she had this nagging feeling that she'd somehow seen this man before, even though she was certain they'd never met.

'Just some chips, actually.' Luna slowly approached the counter.

'No worries, no worries.' He grinned with all his teeth. 'Small or large?'

'Small is fine.' Her stomach rumbled in protest but something else in her gut told her not to stay in this man's shop for any longer than necessary.

'Lovely, lovely.' His face contorted into a smile, his eyes widening over his strangely thin and twisted lips. 'Not at school today, then?'

'School? No. I'm ... I'm twenty-six.' She would have laughed had the hair on her skin not been sticking up on end. It wasn't déjà vu. It was just instinct, a hunch that this man wasn't what he seemed.

'Twenty-six, eh? Shouldn't you be in work, then?' He

jostled the chips in their frying basket and Luna wished they'd fry faster.

'I'm a writer,' she said and was startled when he laughed in response.

'Ahhh, so you can write from anywhere?' He looked up at her, his eyebrows lifting and Luna nodded. 'How marvellous! Anything I would have read?'

'No, I don't think so.'

'Oh, go on! Try me. I read all sorts back there and if I've not read it, I bet my … *fiancée* … has.' His smile beamed brighter.

'No, really. You won't have heard of me.'

'Well. Maybe one day you'll break into the market!' He smiled and Luna took a deep breath. He hummed as he wrapped her chips and didn't ask any more questions, probably sensing she wasn't in the mood. She handed over her change and as soon as the warm parcel of chips was in her hands, she was halfway down the road. The door hadn't even closed behind her before she wondered if maybe she had been a little rude.

Ten

Round the Houses

He peered out of the curtains. The sign was definitely up and visible.

VICKERS AND HEWES, OPEN HOUSE! WELCOME!

Although he knew no one would show. Even he didn't want to live in Ondingside so what were the chances that there were five separate individuals looking for properties right on the freezing seafront of an island most of the population of planet Earth didn't even know existed? Especially when these particular houses were painted in such twee, childish colours. Hope was in short supply but he was clinging on to the last thread.

Property was his passion and there was no denying that he had a real knack for matching up the personality of a person with their perfect property. As a child he'd watched Homes Under The Hammer, 60 Minute Makeover *and* Location, Location, Location *with the same avidness that most children his age had watched* Spongebob SquarePants. *Nothing gave him a thrill like handing over a set of keys and dubbing someone a Home Owner.*

'Twenty minutes. I'll give it twenty minutes more and then …' he dusted off his hands, ' … I'm done.' He stood from his cross-legged position on the empty floor and peered through the living-room curtains out onto the seafront. A woman was approaching, clutching a bag of chips to her chest, but she slowed and he just knew she wasn't meant to be there. She wasn't late for the open house nor, he bet, did she even know these houses existed before she turned left out of the chip shop but even so, she continued walking towards him. He ran out of the room, his foot catching a loose bit of carpet, and stumbled into the hallway. He opened the door but the wind blew it out of his hand and he jumped back as it clattered against the wall. He looked towards the woman who was now standing still in the snow, watching him. He half raised his hand to wave but felt it would be unprofessional so instead he straightened his tie. Just as he was sure the woman would turn around, she continued to walk towards the house.

Luna saw the door to the first of the five houses burst open with a bang. A man skittered out onto the front steps and, his brogues certainly not meant for the ice, slipped down the first step but managed to catch himself on the railing. She clocked the sign and the prospect of finding somewhere to live on her first day on the island drew her closer.

'Are you here for the open house?' the young man called out to her. He was tall, good-looking and broad. Luna felt he was far too handsome to be an estate agent and he seemed much more suited to a personal trainer or Hollywood actor. If his steely blue eyes and well-coiffed dark hair weren't enough to make Luna weak at the knees, his broad Scottish accent soon had her swooning.

'No, I'm not.'

'Oh.' His shoulders dropped.

'But I am actually looking for somewhere to live. So maybe . . . I am?' Luna clutched her chips closer as the sea wind threw a few icy flakes into her face.

'Really? That's brilliant!' He clapped his hands together but Luna couldn't tell if it was because he was happy or cold as he then started to blow warm air into his clasped hands.

'It is?' she asked.

'What I mean is, I didn't think anyone was going to turn up today. Not because the houses aren't lovely, that is! They are! Great houses! It's just that everyone who lives in Ondingside already has somewhere to live and no one ever moves here.'

'Well, you're in luck! I've just moved here. I'm staying with Mrs McArthur?'

'Ah, yes! Nobody's Inn! A fine choice!' Luna shouldn't have been surprised he knew Mrs McArthur and the address at which she currently resided but she'd have to get used to just how small Ondingside really was if she was committing to the permanent move. Looking at these seafront houses was a big step towards making that commitment.

'Do you want to come in?' the man asked, quickly catching the door before it blew shut.

'Can I take a card?'

'Of course.' He beckoned her up the steps to him as he held the door open with his foot and fumbled in his inside jacket pocket for one of his glossy business cards. 'Are you certain you don't want to take a look?' Luna looked up the steps to the open door and the warm light that was glowing from inside. If she looked around, would she have to commit? Would she have to make promises she couldn't keep over a house she probably couldn't afford? Was it rude to look even if you knew you weren't going to purchase? There were too many questions with a lack of answers.

'Maybe another day. I'll have a think and ... and come back? Maybe?' The man began to nod but his brow creased for a brief moment and he paused for longer than necessary.

'Sorry ... I just ...' He bit his bottom lip. 'I had a really

weird moment of déjà vu just then. Do you ever get that?'
He smiled.

'Not really . . . no,' she admitted.

'I just have this really funny feeling that I've seen your face somewhere before.' Luna studied his face, every missing wrinkle, his naturally straight teeth and his perfect hairline. If she'd met someone as handsome as him before, she knew she would have surely remembered it.

'I don't think so.'

'Well, I actually leave the island tomorrow so if you call, tell them Tony sent you.'

'Ah. Your last day is my first day!'

'Really? It's your first day here?' He looked over Luna's face again.

'First day! So we definitely can't have met before,' she said, praying that he hadn't been at that pub quiz a year earlier and he was just mistaken. He shook his head and Luna felt a little rush of relief. He held out his hand and Luna shook it, hoping this wasn't the sealing of a deal because the likelihood of her actually returning was small.

As she moved away, she turned back and watched the man disappear back into the first house. They were admittedly beautiful. Luna could even almost see herself living there. In fact, she'd love to live there, right by the sea. She'd be thrilled about being so close to the amusements but less happy about that particular chippy being her local. However, she certainly wouldn't let one singular judgemental man ruin what could potentially be the beginning of a happy, quiet life. It could be amazing. Maybe. Just maybe.

Eleven

Naked

The coffee shop was empty not only of customers but also of Beau as she glanced through the window on her way past. She lingered with the excuse of checking her hair in the reflection and then actually did pause for a moment to inspect her appearance. There was a slight softness to her face that felt new and pleasing. A brightness to her eyes that she was glad to see after a long time of vacancy. She concluded that the fresh sea air seemed to be doing her some good.

The bookshop, with its green paint and colourful interior, seemed so deliciously enticing that Luna didn't think much about any potential forthcoming interactions and stepped inside to peruse. No one was there and the silence felt calming and tranquil. The warmth of the shop was enough to keep her inside. Every radiator must have been turned on to its fullest. Luna was surprised the plants weren't wilting but she was grateful nevertheless and loosened the grip on her coat and her hot package of chips. The books smelt old but Luna could see they were spotless. Not a speck of dust and the pages hadn't yellowed nearly as much as she would have expected for how long ago many of them had been published.

'Hello?'

Luna jumped at the voice and the book she was holding slipped from her hand but she managed to fumble and catch it before it hit the ground. A head had appeared around the curtain behind the counter. The woman's make-up-less face was surrounded by a halo of deep vermilion curls and her big coffee eyes looked out at Luna through large round spectacles with frames so thin, Luna almost couldn't see them. The woman remained behind the curtain.

'Hi. Hello. Sorry. Was just looking around.' Luna slid the book back into place.

'That's okay! I didn't hear you come in. I'm going to be honest. I'm naked behind here.'

'Right …' Luna said, averting her gaze even though she certainly wasn't able to see anything the woman didn't want her to see.

'I'm Wendy. I'm very, *very* pregnant. Ridiculously so and I'd been sat in this sweltering shop for so long that I knew if I didn't take a cold shower, my uterus was going to turn into an oven and hard-boil my baby.'

'Why is it so hot in here?'

'It's freezing outside! I overcompensated.' Wendy shrugged and almost lost grip on the curtain. 'Whoops! Didn't think I'd have any customers today so I thought I was safe and now this is extremely embarrassing for a myriad of reasons.'

'It's fine! Honestly!' Luna said to her feet.

'Well, I'm going to waddle my way back upstairs and I'll be down in a minute! Keep browsing!' Wendy and her curls slipped back behind the curtain.

'It's okay, I was only here for a minute anyway ...' Luna said but trailed off as she heard Wendy begin to sing the theme song to *Saved By The Bell* as she climbed the stairs and realised she either couldn't hear her or wasn't listening any more.

Luna did a lap of the shop but Wendy didn't return. She snuck to the curtain and was certain she could still hear the sound of the shower running. Luna wasn't sure she would be able to look Wendy in the eye, anyway. There was a pencil on the desk and a stack of sticky notes next to the phone so Luna wrote, 'Had to dash off! Will come back soon!' and stuck it to the centre of the desk before departing. As she walked away from the shop and thought about the ridiculous nature of entering a book-shop and encountering the naked owner, Luna enjoyed the pleasing stretch of a grin in her cheeks.

Twelve

Atlas

Luna had decided to save her chips until she got back to her room, unwilling to devour the source that was keeping her fingers toasty. Mrs McArthur had tried her hardest to tempt her with steak and ale pie in the bar downstairs and for a moment, Luna did wonder if maybe she should. However, the hungry ache in her stomach and the subsiding warmth of her chips forced her to politely decline, much to Mrs McArthur's disappointment.

Once in her room, she donned her pyjamas, knowing that the chances of her leaving for any reason other than a fire were highly improbable. She watched an episode of something happy and easy as she ate every last crispy bit at the bottom of the bag and then sat at her desk. She opened her notebook to the next blank page and dated the top right-hand corner.

It's funny how the lack of something can feel so heavy. I haven't felt the cool breeze of inspiration or the fire of creativity in so long and their absence weighs down on my shoulders. As if I were Atlas carrying the Earth. With each day that passes in which I don't make some sort of start, its weight increases and my back is closer to breaking. It's strange to think that the addition of something would make me feel lighter. I eagerly await the day they return and I can cease my run of being my editor's biggest disappointment.

Luna paused her pen for a moment, willing the return of some kind of creative spark. She listened intently for even the mere whisper of an idea, but there was nothing. She moved her pen to the next page. *Write about what you know,* she thought and began to detail her day. She wrote about her reasons for moving to Ondingside and her fears for what the future would hold if she stayed and where she would go if she left. It may not have been the beginnings of her next novel and it may not have lessened the great big cloud of a deadline that loomed over her head, but it did let her breathe a little easier. It felt good to let some of her fears leak out onto the pages of her notebook so that she could look at them clearly. As if she'd ensnared them so they couldn't follow her from day to day, fogging up her mind and dampening any positivity that did enter into her life. Luna closed the notebook.

She spent the rest of the evening reading one of the many novels she'd brought with her in the hopes that something sparked an idea. Instead she sat wondering why she bothered writing at all when authors like these existed, to whom she could never match up. Maybe books weren't worth writing if they weren't going to go on to be great works of literature that school kids groaned at the idea of studying. Luna actually *wanted* kids to hate her because they were forced to read and peel apart every sentence. Then again, did someone have to always be the best at something in order for it to have worth? Was life that black and white? Could she merely be just okay at something, even good at a push, and be content with just telling stories that made people feel things, despite not winning awards left, right and centre or knowing her name as an author wouldn't be remembered and revered for the rest of time? Luna ruminated on those questions all evening until sleep swept her up in his arms and kissed her goodnight.

Luna opened her eyes and yet saw nothing but white. She blinked as snowflakes barraged her eyes and clasped her arms around herself tightly as the cold began to sink into her bones. Her naked skin felt the sting of the whipping snow like tiny razors slicing past. She lifted a hand in front of her face and could just see her long, red raw fingers stretching out but she surely couldn't feel them. Luna called out, her voice hoarse and quiet, drowned out by the roaring of the blizzard. She stumbled forwards, her toes numb and useless, the soles of her feet sore and tingling. She trudged onwards, her hair loosening as the wind dragged it out behind her. An ache in her chest began to throb, like a hole was opening up inside her. There was a rumble beneath her feet and just as she looked down the ice split, the jagged crack perfect between her feet. The split became longer and wider, the ice beginning to part. She leapt to the right, almost wobbling into what had become a giant chasm from which a wailing rose up into the white sky. Just one singular voice echoed from the black chasm and through the void but it was a voice Luna could not mistake ... as it was her own. She threw her hands over her ears but the sound could not be blocked. The voice was desperate, grief-stricken, pitiful and painful for Luna to listen to. It was the voice she dare not let anyone hear. The words she dare not speak. It said 'Help me', 'I'm lost', 'I'm alone' and 'I'm scared'. It wailed and it moaned whilst Luna clutched her ears and then her chest and back and forth and back and forth until she was dizzy and aching and she slipped in the snow to the ground. She crawled to the edge of the chasm, her fingers gripping the edge of the ice and yet she closed her eyes, unable to stare into the void below her.

'Not yet,' she whispered. 'Not yet, not yet, not yet.' The voice hushed for a moment. The snow slowed in the air, still falling but quiet and calm, and her voice called out from the void and said, 'Then when?'

Thirteen

Day One . . . Again

July 18th 2019

In the night, a dog sniffed along the bottom of the garden fence, snow building up against his muzzle. He was sure there was a rabbit next door but there was no scent to trace. He went to dig under the fence only to find that the soil underneath the snow was already loose and came away with ease underneath his paws. Another dog had dug here before him! He sniffed in rapid circles. If there was another dog on his territory he'd be sure to find it but alas, there was no scent to follow. The dog looked up at the black night sky just as it became littered with specks of white that floated down and licked at his nose and ears. He barked upwards, into the abyss, but no one answered back. The dog whimpered and walked up the steps to the back door of his owner's house. He curled his tail around him and closed his eyes as the snow came down once more.

Reality can seep into your dreams. When you can hear your mum calling you down for breakfast, the ogre in your head starts to sound remarkably like her as it chases you up the mountain. Faces you pass in the street become the cast of your night's sleep and our daily anxieties cause us to turn up to school or work completely stark naked in our unconscious minds. However, Luna had never experienced her dreams seeping into reality before. She'd dreamt of a blizzard so fierce that she could barely see her own hand in front of her face and here she was in Ondingside, trudging through ankle-deep snow.

'Town' didn't seem too hard to find although 'town' in Ondingside wasn't filled with your usual Primark, Costa, Waterstones and Pret A Manger. It was all quaint, independent shops that gave you the necessities and little else. Luna prayed there would be a coffee shop and that the second-hand bookshop held a few gems. She seemed to naturally gravitate towards town without any difficulty. Just as she yawned she approached a sign that said GOOD COFFEE with an arrow pointing to the door. Underneath there was another arrow pointing in the opposite direction and next to it read ... DRAGONS MAYBE? WOULDN'T RISK IT. COME ON IN! Luna skipped the last few steps to the door and revelled in the ring of the bell as she entered the shop.

'Hi there!' said a cheery voice and as Luna bounded over to the counter, eager to order her flat white as soon as possible, she saw the owner's face and recognised him instantly.

'You ...'

'*You* ...' he replied with a grin. 'You still need to collect your winnings!'

'You've got a good memory,' she said, tucking a loose strand of hair behind her ear.

'You made quite the impression.' Beau smiled again and Luna wondered why he did that so often. Then she wondered why she didn't and who out of the two of them was abnormal.

'Sorry about that.' She dug dirt out from the corner of one of her fingernails.

'Don't be. That's one of my favourite stories from my time working at the Green Arrow.'

'You actually *tell* people about that?' She massaged out the creases in her forehead and looked at Beau from between her fingers.

'There's very few people left to tell considering most of the people who live on the island were actually there to witness it.' Luna groaned and Beau laughed. 'Hey, it's not the weirdest thing to have happened in that pub, I promise.'

'Really? Someone throwing up in your pint of beer isn't at the top of the list?'

'Nope.' He shook his head and a strand of his slicked-back black hair wriggled loose and fell over his face. Luna felt her lips tighten and it took her a moment to realise that they were trying to smile.

'Well, now I'm just annoyed.'

'Why?' Beau's eyes sparkled as he watched her try to suppress her moment of giddiness.

'I maxed out all levels of humiliation that night! At the very least I wanted my moment of drunken madness, which has never been repeated, may I add, to be at the top of *some* kind of list. Otherwise it's solely the single most embarrassing night of my life.'

'Okay, I lied. It's definitely the weirdest thing.'

'Promise?'

'I promise.' He crossed his heart with a finger. 'Who could possibly top that?'

'Well, I should hope so.' Luna felt a flush of heat rush through her body. *Are you actually ... enjoying yourself?* she thought. *In the company of another human?* Luna had completely forgotten what it was like to have a conversation with someone that lasted longer than a few minutes, let alone to have a conversation that she actually wanted to continue.

150

'Besides, if that's the most embarrassing thing you've ever done, you're doing pretty well.'

'Sounds like that's a story …' *A story I actually want to hear … !* She couldn't quite believe herself.

'So, what can I get you? Let me guess … latte?' Luna shook her head.

'You don't seem like the sweet and syrupy type of coffee girl …'

'Correct. I still like to be able to taste that it's coffee.'

'Me too.' He winked and her stomach flipped. Beau pursed his lips and narrowed his eyes. 'I'm gonna go with … flat white?'

'Bingo.' She pointed both her forefingers at him with her thumbs in the air. It was such a bizarre thing to do, not just for Luna, but for anyone in a social situation. However, now that she'd fully committed and Beau had been witness to it, she wiggled her thumbs as if her hands were now guns and made a 'pew' noise. Then she prayed for a sinkhole to appear beneath her and swallow her right down to the burning hot centre of the Earth where all of her humiliation could go to die but instead, the corners of Beau's eyes wrinkled as he chuckled at her and she thought she might vomit from relief. Had anyone been so utterly ridiculous in her presence, she probably would have found a way to vacate their proximity in t-minus ten seconds.

'One flat white coming up! So, what brings you back to Ondingside?' Beau started to press buttons and levers with expert deftness and Luna actually leaned a little over the counter to watch. She shrugged. 'I live here now.'

Beau's head snapped up from his work. 'What?'

'Yeah, yeah, I know. My landlady has already given me the "but there's nothing here for you" lecture.'

'But ... there's nothing here for you,' he parroted.

'And that's exactly why I'm here.'

'What are you running from?' Beau's words hit her and for a moment she was numb.

'Excuse me?' she asked, shaking herself out of the moment.

'The only reason why anyone from my generation has ever come here is because they're running from something. Bad relationships, ghosts of the past, tragic events ...'

'Try all of the above,' she mumbled, her palms starting to sweat in her pockets.

'That bad, huh?'

'I just wanted a change of scenery. Plus the quieter the better.'

'Not much of a people person?' Luna scrunched up her nose and shook her head. 'Well, this might not be the best place then.' Beau plucked a little box of toothpicks from his green apron pocket, pulled one from the bunch and, behind the large coffee machine, set all of his focus on something seemingly intricate out of Luna's view. 'It's such a small island, everyone knows everyone. We're busybodies, us lot. When you can keep track of every single person's business, nothing is secret.'

'I don't have any secrets.'

'That's what people with the most secrets say.' He placed her coffee in front of her. In the foam of the latte, he'd crafted a beautiful snowflake.

'Impressive,' she said and she actually meant it. Luna had tried latte art at home but nothing she'd attempted had ever been successful unless what she'd been attempting was a sorry excuse for Mickey Mouse's silhouette. 'I don't want to ruin it.'

'Trust me, the coffee is better than the snowflake. You'll want to ruin it.'

'Humble!' she scoffed.

'No, no. Just entirely confident in my own skills as a barista. I'm terrible at everything else. Let me have this.'

'Fair enough,' she said, forced to admire his honesty and envy his confidence. Luna flicked through the portfolio of her very few skills in her head and pondered in which she had the most faith. She knew it was her writing but she wondered how many books she would have written had she had the confidence Beau showed in his coffee. Luna pulled out her purse from her pocket.

'Ah, ah, ah!' Beau held out his hand. 'On the house.'

'Really?' Luna couldn't help but glance at the empty tables in his shop.

'Really,' he reassured her.

'Thank you, Beau.'

'You're more than welcome ... um,' Beau's cheeks flushed. 'I'm so sorry but ... I've just realised that I don't know your name.'

'That would be because I've never told you.' There was a pregnant pause. Luna toyed with giving him a fake name so as not to seem rude but felt that would be far weirder than not giving him any name at all. Omitting the truth was the lesser of two evils when the other option was outright lying. Beau's face was so cheruby and child-like that she felt awful not giving him what he so clearly wanted in that moment but Luna had set herself rules for her new life. Breaking those rules on the first day because a stranger had given her a free coffee was not the precedent she wanted to set.

'Well ... I'd best be off,' she said with a smile and a bob of the head as she backed towards the door.

'Oh.' Beau hurriedly came out from behind the counter.

'First day in my new home town. Got lots to be getting on with.'

'Of course.' He smiled, but his glee seemed to have dissipated.

'I'll be back, though,' she added.

'You will?'

'Apparently, you're the only place that does coffee, full stop. Let alone the place that does the best coffee.'

'I win by default.' He waved his hands in celebration.

'Exactly.' She opened the door.

'You're really not going to tell me your name?' he called after her. Luna smiled over her shoulder.

'Maybe tomorrow.'

'On The Street Where You Live' suddenly popped into Luna's head and although never blessed with the ability to carry a tune, even if given a bucket, Luna found herself humming it all the way down the road.

She took a left.

A right.

Another left.

She looked to her left and a black cat sat in the middle of the road staring at her with its giant green eyes. Luna made a kissing noise to try and entice it towards her. It tilted its head but when it saw she had nothing but empty hands it licked its lips and slunk under a car. The sound of clunky fairground music to her right caught her attention anyway and she found that it was coming from a place called Jacob's Amusements. Three kids were crowded around one of the three claw machines, slotting in coin after coin trying to rescue a multicoloured stuffed owl that was now lying upside down, its pink feet sticking up in the air.

'They're all rigged, Andrew!' one boy said, as the other pushed more coins into the slot and the machine's music cranked up again. 'You'll never win.'

'Just one more go, I swear,' said Andrew as he deftly manoeuvred the joystick.

'You said that about ten goes ago,' said the dark-haired girl to his right, with a roll of her eyes. As the machine dropped the owl for the umpteenth time in amongst the other toys and it sounded a miserable wah, wah, wah, waaaahhh, Andrew threw up his hands.

'All right, I give up,' he huffed.

'I told you, they're all fixed!' said the other boy, throwing an arm around his shoulders.

Claw machines had never been her strong suit, she was always better at the penny pushing machines, and Luna knew that the young boy was probably right, the machines were rigged to only grab onto the toys every fifty or so goes. However, the idea that she might be the lucky one that the machine chose to reward was far too enticing for Luna to resist. If it was indeed a timed machine, that boy was sure to have used up quite a few of those goes so maybe she would get lucky. Who was to say! She pushed three pound coins into the change machine.

'I could have sworn ...' she muttered, as she waited for her coins. She opened every slot in her purse as she was certain there had been a five pound note in there. She shrugged and collected the coins in the palm of her hand. With a burst of excitement she approached the children.

'Excuse me ... can I try?'

'We're playing right now, *lady*.'

'*Andrew!*' The taller and older boy gave the imperti-nent one a shove.

'Well, how about if I use my change *and* I promise to give you the winnings?' His eyes lit up. 'How old are you, Andrew?'

'He's ten.' The dark-haired girl appeared from the back of the arcade holding a little white card in her palm and a lightbulb in Luna's brain briefly flickered. 'George is thirteen and I'm Amber. I'm sixteen,' she said with a swish of her hair.

'Well, Amber, seeing as you lot clearly have the run of the place and you're quite obviously in charge, what do you think of my proposed deal?' Little Andrew turned to Amber with his hands clasped together.

'Please, please, please, please, please!' he said eagerly.

'All right, short stuff, say it don't spray it,' Amber said, wiping her arm. 'Go for it.' She nodded to Luna and the three of them parted, letting Luna at the machine.

Inside, the toys were all awfully bright, cheap things with large glittering eyes. The claw was dangling neatly in the back left hand corner. Luna pushed five ten pence pieces into the coin slot which, according to the little yellow fading sticker on the black coin slot, would allow her three attempts to win.

'Any suggestions?'

'The rainbow owl!' Andrew said, squeezing himself between the machines and pressing his nose up against the glass to get a better view. The rainbow owl didn't really take Luna's fancy but ultimately, she was just in it for the thrill of the win so what she won was up to Andrew. 'Nah, I think you're better off aiming nearer the back,' George said, peering over Luna's shoulder on tiptoe.

'It's your call,' Luna said to the boy leaving fingerprints on the glass. He looked into the machine once more, his brows meeting above the bridge of this nose. The owl with its multicoloured feathers was lying upside down, wedged between a yellow lion and a pink panda, with only its feet to grab onto. Finally, Andrew nodded in agreement with his brother, George.

'The bear at the back looks pretty cool ...' Andrew said, so Luna pressed start and began to manoeuvre the claw with the joystick towards the back of the machine. On the first attempt, she caught the ear of the little grey bear. It seemed to be slightly more raised than the other toys and looked like a relatively easy target. The claw pinched its ear for a moment but the pincers slipped past each other and the bear didn't budge. The machine played its 'wah, wah, wah, waaaahhhh' tune and the kids groaned in unison.

'Try the penguin,' said George.

'Penguin?' she asked and Andrew nodded again. It was lying face up and was almost entirely spherical and so she thought if she aimed the claw perfectly above its round, white belly, the claw might not be able to avoid scooping it up. The penguin gazed upwards, the three

158

metal pincers reflected in its glassy eyes as they clamped around it, lifted it an inch into the air but then the penguin rolled out of one of the sizeable gaps between the pincers. The machine played its tune of failure again as the claw swung back to its corner and the kids sighed.

'It's useless.' Andrew climbed out from between the machines and folded his arms across his chest.

'One more go. How about you take this one, Andrew?'

'Really?!' He looked at Luna and then his sister, who nodded, and this time Luna stepped out of the way, letting Andrew take control of the machine.

'I reckon that bear at the back is still up for grabs.'

'Yeah, me too!' said George.

'Me three,' said Amber.

'Let's do this!' Andrew hit the start button. The bear was sitting forward, leaving a little gap between the back wall and his furry behind and Luna wondered if Andrew would be able to get the claw that far back in the machine. Andrew wiggled the little black joystick to the right and then to the back as far as it would go. It clunked to a halt precisely above the bear. Andrew waited for the silver claw to stop swinging so violently and when it was still enough for his liking, he pressed the red button on the end of the joystick. The claw lowered down, slowly, until it reached the grey bear, his black eyes shining at Luna as she looked hopefully back at him through the glass. The claw tucked neatly between the back wall of the machine and the bear's back. The machine played suspenseful music in funfair tones and even though all that would be lost if this attempt were to fail were five ten pence pieces, Luna's heart still raced like she were a child with all her hopes riding on the back of that little grey bear. The claw clamped around the bear's grey fuzz and started to lift. He rose an inch. Then another. Then up and up and up until he was at Luna's head height. She thought how cruel it would be to get Andrew's hopes up this high only for the machine to let him plummet back into the pit of cuddly toy despair. She was already counting out coins with her fingers in her palm, ready to spend at least the three pounds she'd changed in the machine to try and win him. But there was no need. He was still sitting comfortably in the grips of the claw that was shuddering its way over to the hole in the front left-hand corner, right in front of Luna.

'Come on . . . come on . . . ' she coaxed, hoping the gods of funfair fate were listening.

'That's it!' George said, loudly.

'Yes, yes, yes!' Andrew chanted, clenching his fists tighter and tighter. With every jolt, her heart skipped, praying that the bear would survive the journey. Then the claw opened and he fell through the hole that led to the little hatch by her feet. *Diddly-dum-de-dum!*, the machine chimed in triumph.

'YES!!!' they cried together. Luna dropped to her knees and pushed open the flap where her new-found friend was lying face down on a grubby patch of carpet inside the machine where a few sucked lollies had been abandoned for won toys, now collecting dust and hair. 'Well, hello, Mr Bear,' she said, patting him on the head, then gave him to Andrew, who turned him over in his hands, inspecting him for any signs of damage. He was a teddy bear that had cost her fifty pence, but the look on Andrew's face was priceless. At a time when she felt like she'd had very few personal wins, even the smallest triumph felt gargantuan and she swallowed a lump in her throat. At this moment in time, she would take whatever she could get. Andrew gave the bear a hug but then pulled it away and looked at it for a moment before holding it out to Luna.

'I think you should have him, Miss.'

'But you won him! Fair and square!'

'He's got loads of toys,' Amber whispered to Luna over her little brother's head.

'Looooaaaaaddddsss,' said George.

'Why do you want me to have him, Andrew?' she asked, not yet taking the bear, knowing how fickle children could be. Andrew shrugged.

'Dunno. I just feel like he was meant for you.' He pushed the bear into Luna's hands and skipped off shouting, 'I WANT CHIPS!'

'Thanks, Miss! Andrew, wait up!' George said as he ran past her.

'Thank you,' Amber said with a smile as she calmly walked after her brothers, leaving Luna with a new friend and a full heart.

> '*If your future's filled with love,*
> *Or anger or with hate*
> *One coin is all I ask of you,*
> *To let me tell your fate.*'

The lights on the machine in the far corner started dancing and a sultry female voice sang to Luna to entice her over, as if the mysterious wooden box knew she was there.

'One coin, my arse . . . ' she said, reading the sign that told her this particular machine would cost her ten of her ten pence pieces. Curiosity had taken hold of her, though, and she knew she wouldn't be able to resist, so she willingly gave over her money. The lights started flashing brighter and it started to sing again.

> '*Stare into the crystal ball and ask what*
> *you require,*
> *Reach into your heart and tell me all that*
> *you desire,*
> *Forget whatever came before for now it's*
> *dead and gone,*
> *Your fate will be revealed in just three,*
> *two, ONE!*'

The bulbs in the machine seemed to be in full working order as they blinked on and off so brightly, Luna had to squint. Luna wondered what this machine actually did as all it seemed to do was blind her but eventually, it ceased its flashing and spat out a small card from a slot near her knees.

She read the card twice over before letting herself believe that was actually what it said. It felt so oddly, specifically, perfectly suited to her life right now that it gave her the odd feeling that she was being followed or, at the very least, watched. Luna kept reading the card over and over as she left the amusements and followed the smell of food.

'Afternoon!' The man behind the counter greeted Luna with a smile so broad, Luna was sure she'd be able to count all of his teeth.

'Afternoon,' she responded, tucking the little white card from the fortune machine into a credit card slot in her purse.

'And what can I get for you today?' He turned behind him and gave the basket in the chip fryer a quick toss, the oil hissing in reply. 'I've got some fresh chips here that will be perfect to eat in … ooooh, about … thirty seconds. That's not including cooling time, mind you!' He shook his head and chuckled.

'A small portion of chips would be perfect, thank you.' Luna smiled but she noticed that it didn't entirely feel natural. She couldn't help but feel herself pulling back from this seemingly lovely man. Instinct was a funny thing and Luna felt inclined to trust her gut. The last time she had ignored it she'd ended up humiliated in front of all of her living relatives. Even though she wasn't entirely sure why, Luna let her guard rise.

'Small portion of chips, coming up! Aren't you a little too old for toys?' He pointed a chubby finger at the bear in her hands.

'Oh ... um ...' Before she could answer, he continued.

'So where've you come from, then?' he asked, taking a moment to give her face a once-over before removing the basket from the fryer and draining Luna's dinner. 'I've never seen your face before and I know everyone around here.'

'I'm ...' Luna caught herself before giving away her name too freely. 'I'm living here now. Just moved yesterday.'

'From?' he asked and the muscles in her jaw clenched.

'From London!' she said, a little too shrill.

'Oh, a city girl! Only been there once,' he said. 'Too busy. I like the peace and quiet and simplicity of island life, me. Nothing fancy about it. Just is what it is.'

'Me too,' she said, softening.

'Really?' He paused as he poured the chips from the basket onto the paper.

'Yes, why?'

'Not running from anything?' The man smiled to himself and Luna felt a heat start to rise from the pit of her stomach.

'Why would I be running from anything?' Although, he, admittedly, was the second person to say this to her today, she didn't feel entirely sure this time it came from the same place of simple curiosity or with the same sense of care. However, she then also wondered what made her so sure Beau had, in fact, cared . . .

'Salt and vinegar?' the chip shop man asked with a smile and a raised eyebrow. Was he actually enjoying watching her squirm under pressure? Was he enjoying putting her on the spot? She nodded as she watched his eyes a little closer. 'We get young 'uns like you washing up on the shores every now and again. Trying to get away from something. Or *someone*?' He shook a hefty amount of salt over her dinner.

'What about you?' her mouth said before her brain caught up and convinced her otherwise. 'Anyone special in your life?' Once her mind raced in front of her speech, it actually also agreed that firing questions back might give him a taste of his own medicine and take the heat off her.

'Funny you should ask me that, actually,' he grinned. 'I proposed this morning.' He looked up at Luna and didn't look away until she acknowledged his statement.

'Awww,' she obliged with an unconvincing smile.

'Funny thing is though, she was already wearing the ring! Says she woke up with it on, but that's just an excuse!' he said, placing Luna's wrapped and bagged chips on the counter. 'She was probably snooping and jumped the gun but I'm glad she did. It looks perfect on her.'

'How odd . . .' Luna said, leaning a hand on the counter.

'What, that she said yes?' His face fell momentarily.

'No! No, that she found the ring and just . . . assumed.'

'She assumed correctly, so all turned out just as planned.'

'That's lucky.'

'No, my dear. *I'm* lucky.' He smiled as he handed over her order. Luna was bowled over by his words and his sentiment and a pang of envy tightened in her chest. He seemed to be taking lines right out of romantic novels and she wished Noel had shown the same kind of affection towards her. However, the idea of Noel at all made her grimace and a strange kind of pride made her smile. If cringing over past exes wasn't growth, she didn't know what was.

'That's actually very sweet,' Luna said. 'I'm sure she's very lucky too.'

'Let's hope so. On the house.' He winked and shooed her out of the door with a playful waft of his greasy hands. 'Welcome to Ondingside!'

Luna wasn't entirely sure what had made her do it or where this sudden burst of courage had come from but she knew this was an opportunity not to be missed. Clutching the little grey teddy bear and her portion of chips, she approached the row of houses with the open house sign outside.

'Are you here for the open house?' was the first thing the man said to her after he'd swung the door open with such surprising fervour that he almost knocked himself off balance. Luna herself admittedly felt a little weak at the knees. This man didn't look like your average estate agent. In his blue suit, he looked more likely to play James Bond or to be attending some kind of swanky film premiere. Not standing in a tiny house on the shore of a shabby seaside town.

'I ... I guess so, yes. Yes, I am. I wasn't supposed to be. I was just passing by but ... well ... I'm actually looking for somewhere to live right now and this seems actually quite ... perfect?'

'*Brilliant*!' He grinned with all his straight, white teeth. 'Well, come in! Come in! Look around! I won't hover over your shoulder like most estate agents do. No pressure. I'll be in the living room when you're done.'

Luna went through the small hallway past the first door which Luna guessed was the living room as that's where the dashing estate agent had disappeared into. The door right at the end of the hallway corridor led to the lavender-painted kitchen which spanned the entire width of the house. Although the house wasn't huge, whoever had designed it had made the most of the space and made sure the rooms felt as big as they could be. She peeked through the little square window in the wooden back door and saw that the house came with a garden. It wasn't a large patch of land but it had hedges down either side that came about two feet above the fences. She'd be completely sheltered from any neighbours' view and it looked like a corridor in a maze from a children's book. Upstairs, there were two bedrooms, one master and one smaller but still decently sized, and a bathroom with a bath that Luna noted would certainly be big enough to soak in for hours but not so small that her feet stuck out the end. She took one more whizz around the rooms, not letting herself feel excited just yet at how perfect this house would be for her. It wasn't too dissimilar from the house she grew up in and certainly had the potential to be just as cosy.

'What do you think?' the estate agent asked as she entered the living room (which, she noted, had once been two rooms but a wall had been knocked down to make it one large spacious room with a dining area that looked over the garden).

'It's lovely,' she said. '*Really* lovely.'

'Great! Did you want to see any of the others?' He moved to the door.

'Erm … others?' Luna followed him out into the hallway where he was already opening the front door out into the cold.

'Yes, sorry, didn't I mention? This whole row is up for sale. All five houses.' He smiled with all his teeth and Luna swallowed, hard.

'*All five?*'

'Yes, it was an entire family. Started off as a mother and father with two children. When the kids grew up, they then bought the houses on the other end of the row and when the middle two became free, the grandparents bought the remaining two houses!'

'Where are they all now?'

'The grandparents passed away not too long ago and they left the rest of the family a small fortune. They're all still in Ondingside but in a much nicer row of houses.' He chuckled. 'Look, obviously, no one's expected to buy all five. That's quite a scary prospect ... but I will tell you that they're currently priced at fifty thousand each.'

'Excuse me?' Luna blinked rapidly several times.

'I'm guessing you're used to London house prices.' He laughed again at Luna's stunned expression. 'Little different on an island of this size.' Luna had sold her parents' house before moving to Ondingside for £750,000. Even after paying off the £300,000 that was left of her parents' mortgage, she still had enough to afford all five houses with money left over to completely refurbish and redecorate. Again, she swallowed her excitement and said, 'Yes, that's ... definitely different than what I'm used to.'

'Well, you have my card. Go away and have a think. It's not like you've got much competition at the moment.'

He winked and this time Luna definitely couldn't keep the smile off her face.

'Actually, I don't.'

'Don't what?'

'Have your card.'

'Oh, I could have sworn I gave you one.' He took a card out of his pocket and handed it over. 'Our slogan is "Small Island, Big Dreams" but personally I think it should just be "Cheaper Than The Mainland".' Luna laughed and stopped abruptly with a snort when she realised she'd not heard that sound in a while.

'You're good at this.'

'At what?' He opened the front door for her.

'. . . Estate agenting,' Luna giggled.

'Do you mean selling houses?'

'Yes, that is what I mean,' she nodded, pulling her coat close around her neck and cuddling her chips and the teddy bear close to her chest. 'That. You're good at that.'

'Technically, I haven't sold you a house yet so how good can I be, really?'

'Better than you think.'

The estate agent held out an arm to her which she gratefully took and together they descended the icy steps together.

'Can you tell that to the company I'm applying to? I could do with all the help I could get.'

'You're leaving?' Luna wasn't sure why she assumed he was leaving the island altogether. *How many estate agencies could Ondingside possibly have?* she justified. He paused for a moment.

'Yeah. I am,' he said, nodding. A smile slowly spread across his face. 'Yeah, I am.'

'Good for you. Good for you.' She laughed and he laughed with her.

'Sorry. I think I only just really made up my mind. I've been humming and hawing for a while but only because ... well, it's a bit scary, isn't it? I was going to leave tomorrow morning but I feel like if I don't get on a train tonight I'll probably never get off this island.'

'You should go for it. Seems like the universe is trying to balance itself out. Like the population of Ondingside can't be more or less than what it already is.'

'How so?'

'I arrived here last night. We're being traded.'

'Well, I wish you a happy life here on the island. Hopefully in one of these lovely houses.' He handed her a card. 'I probably ... no, I definitely won't be there if you decide to call but make sure to tell them it was me who sent you. Might help me persuade the other agency to give me a job!'

'I will. And good luck ...' she quickly read the card, 'Tony.' Luna held out her hand and Tony shook it with such fervour he almost lifted her off the ground.

Luna turned to look at her potential new home before she headed back towards the amusements, away from the seafront. There was so much potential. Five houses turned into one super house where she could write her books in isolation away from the world's prying eyes. It would be idyllic. Exactly what she wanted and needed and Luna knew that wanting and needing didn't often collide. The estate agent locked the door and turned to wave at her at the top of the stairs before he slipped on the ice of the top step and skidded all the way down to the bottom. He looked up and caught her stifling a laugh and threw up his hands with a roll of his eyes. He waved goodbye again and Luna waved goodbye to him and hello to the beginning of her new life in Ondingside.

Fourteen

Second-Hand Books

The woman carefully hammered the needle through the spine of the book.

Thud.

You don't need him, she thought. She moved the needle down to the next mark she'd made in pencil.

Thud.

You don't love him.

Thud

You can do this on your own.

Thud, thud, thud.

She raised her head from her work and took a moment to breathe. She put a hand on her giant beach ball of a belly and hummed a quiet tune, squeezing her eyes shut tight. She shook her head and looked back to her work.

This had always been *her* shop, *her* passion and *her* life. For a brief moment she'd been swept off her feet. Or rather, swept someone else off their feet who definitely wasn't ready for the hurricane that she was. He whirled out of her life as quickly as she'd whirled into his. Of course it was only a few weeks after he'd left her in bed, snuck out of her room and fled the island that she realised how much her boobs hurt and figured out why she was feeling so sick in the mornings. She hadn't even known his name. So it was just her and bump, together against the world.

Thud.

You can do this.

Thud.

You're not alone.

Thud, thud, thud.

She wiped away a tear before it fell and soaked into the endpapers of the book. Her baby kicked out as if it were saying 'Snap out of it, Mum!'. The woman laughed and gave the spot the baby had kicked a gentle prod.

'Okay, baby. Okay,' she whispered.

Luna traced her steps back the way she had come, having opened her chips on the way. She was almost wearing the bag like a horse's feedbag as she revelled in the steam that poured out of the bag and onto her face if she positioned it just right underneath her chin. It was close to burning but Luna was addicted to the vinegary scent. Just as she reached the street Beau's coffee shop was on, Luna finished the last of her lunch and slowed her steps. She wanted to visit the second-hand bookshop next door to Beau's shop but didn't want him to think she was wandering past just so she could catch a glimpse of him. *Although seeing him again wouldn't be so bad,* she thought. *But that's not why I'm here again and I definitely don't want him to think that's why I'm here again.*

Isn't that why you're here again? said the voice in her head.

Maybe a little, she admitted to herself, *but that's certainly not the sole reason I'm here. I'm an author. I want to browse some books.*

There was nothing for it. She'd just have to walk past without looking in the window. She couldn't possibly look in the window. *I can't possibly look in the window.* If she looked in the window he'd think she was there for him. *Or would he?* Her steps were quick and assured but no matter how many times she chanted 'Look down, look down, look down' in her head, her eyes disobeyed. Luna glanced up and to the left and there he was, wiping down his coffee machine for want of anything better to do. His shop was still empty but his temperament still seemed upbeat despite that. *His face is still beautiful . . . did I actually just think that?* She looked back down at her shoes just as she was sure he would notice the shadow of a potential customer looming in the doorway and she darted into the green doorway of the bookshop.

At first glance, Luna wasn't sure if she'd entered the right shop. Hanging from every corner of the ceiling were baskets overflowing with cascading flowers, mostly orange, pink and purple in colour. Some Luna recognised, like the petunias and geraniums, but the rest were unknown to her. Behind the counter were shelves with a few books dotted here and there but mostly they were filled with pots upon pots of cacti. Big ones, small ones, some as big as Luna's head. There *were* books, of course, shelves and shelves of them, but you had to weave past vases and plant pots piled full of flora to get to them nearer the back of the store.

'Hello?' Luna said as she tripped over a pile of pots. It started to topple but she caught the pots before they crashed to the ground. A curtain next to the counter swished open and there stood a woman dressed in green floor-length robes who couldn't have been much older than Luna herself. Luna felt a little foolish that she had expected an elderly woman to own a shop that was full of plants and books. She berated herself for thinking that reading and gardening were an older person's hobby when she herself loved flowers and books; then she forgave herself a little when she remembered that the average age of Ondingside's population was probably about seventy and so the chances of someone younger owning any of the shops on the island were slim at best.

The woman's eyes were magnified slightly by her mottled amber-framed glasses so the autumnal reddish-brown of her eyes stood out against the forest green of her clothes. A dark green scarf encompassed her head, causing her short, curly, deep red hair to stick directly outwards at the back. Two earrings dangled by her cheeks and upon closer inspection, Luna saw that they were dream catchers, purple feathers swinging underneath them. Luna thought she looked like Mother Nature herself. When she opened her mouth, a twee and delicate Scottish accent came forth.

'Who are you?' the woman asked.

'Just came in to browse,' Luna smiled, wiping some soil from underneath her foot onto her other leg.

'But no one comes in to browse.' The woman breathed as she steadied herself against the counter. 'How old are you?' Luna was a little taken aback by the abrasive question but again, when you've been surrounded by the cast of *Cocoon* for your entire life, meeting someone of your own generation must be quite an unexpected change.

'I'm twenty-six,' Luna replied.

'*I'm* twenty-six. Why are you here?' The woman rushed behind the counter and awkwardly raised herself onto a stool. Luna hadn't noticed before but as she arched her back to hoist herself upwards, her baby bump very quickly made itself known as it pushed up through the fabric like a beach ball floating to the surface of a paddling pool.

'I just moved here,' Luna said, fiddling with a clump of soil under her shoe so as to give the woman a little privacy to get comfortable without being watched and scrutinised by a total stranger.

'You just moved. *To* Ondingside?' Her big eyes blinked.

'Yes,' Luna said, wondering how many more times she'd be asked that question and feel judged for moving to a place that the other person already inhabited.

'Why? That's crazy.' The woman laughed a laugh so high-pitched Luna was sure some of the plant pots rattled on their shelves. 'Everyone our age has moved *away* or is, at least, trying to.' The woman leant against the counter and into the conversation.

'*You* haven't.' The woman's abrupt questions somehow seemed to raise Luna's own confidence. She had set the bar and Luna took that as her permission to match it.

'Touché.' The woman smiled now and her face softened.

'We all have our reasons, I guess.' Luna shrugged.

'And what are yours?'

Luna wondered which version of events she should explain. That she was running from the ghosts of her past and needed a little space, like she'd told Beau? Or would that be two people too many who knew a little too much? She'd decided that no one need know who she was or who she would be and that it was her business and hers alone. Beau was currently her sole exception.

'Actually, I'm an author,' she said, finally. 'I wanted to move somewhere slower. Quieter. Somewhere with fewer distractions so I could write a little faster than I have done in the past.' Luna gave a final nod.

'It's definitely quieter, that's for sure, but I couldn't think of a place with less inspiration for a novelist.'

'Today's only my first day here so I'm willing to give it a chance. So far I'm impressed with the weather. I like the snow,' she smiled.

'Oh, so you're like ... *properly* new,' the woman said, shifting her bum on the stool.

'Brand spanking!'

'So an author, huh? That's exciting! Published?'

'Yes.'

'Ooooh! Anything I would have read?'

'Oh, I doubt it,' Luna said, batting the air.

'Go on, try me. I own a bookshop. I've read loads.'

'Well ...' Luna loved writing and was proud of every single word she had ever written which meant she wasn't able to explain the amount of nausea that overcame her when someone asked her one of the following questions:

Where do your ideas come from?

Have you written anything I would have read?

Can you tell me a little bit about the novel you are currently writing?

Each one brought with it a sense of embarrassment that caused all of her insides to simultaneously shrivel in on themselves as she fought through her brain to find some kind of an explanation that she wouldn't deem 'wanky'.

Her blood ran hot as she quickly said, 'The novel that went down the best is probably the one I wrote called *Cloud Walking*.'

'Oh, that's— wait . . . wait, wait, wait. Now, you hang on just a hot second . . .' The woman's smile had been fixed for a moment and she'd started to reply to Luna far too quickly with a practised answer she had prepared for when every second person inevitably told her they were an author, that they wanted to write or that they'd been published but had only sold six copies and that was to their parents, nan and three distant cousins. But then the rosiness in the woman's cheeks dissolved, her magnified pupils dilated and her breath caught. 'No . . . no, no, NO!' She hopped off the stool as fast as she could, which was surprisingly quick considering her bump was fairly large, and she disappeared through the curtain for certainly less than ten seconds and then reappeared with another swish and a skid of her socks – this time, Luna's side of the counter and with a book in her hands. Although it wasn't just any book. Luna would have recognised that pale blue cover anywhere.

'This book. This is *your* book. *You* wrote *Cloud Walking* and *A Little Ray of Hope* and *Nothing Short of Magic* and *The Pleasure Is All Mine* and *The Day The Darkness Left*. That's all you. *You* . . . are Elle J. Lark.' The woman left very few pauses and Luna wondered how long it had been since she'd blinked.

Luna's pseudonym was Elle J. Lark. Lark was obviously

her real last name and the J came from her real middle name which was Jane but, even before coming to Ondingside, Luna had become a little touchy about her first name. It was the name her parents had given to her and for that reason she loved it, but if she was asked one more time whether that was *really* her real name or if her parents were hippies or if she howled when the moon was full, she would move to a small island and become a recluse ... oh, wait. Calling herself Elle was her little way of making a joke as 'L' was her first initial so technically, it wasn't a lie. Well, it was the small, white kind that didn't count because it didn't hurt anyone. Plus, she honestly didn't think enough people would care enough about her, let alone her writing, to warrant worrying all that much about having to answer any questions regarding her pseudonym.

'Wow. Yes. That's me.' Luna laughed as she took the book the woman was handing her and flipped to a page near the back where a picture of her fresh-faced, twenty-year-old self was trying an expression somewhere between coy and clever that had just ended up looking constipated. 'Yes. I'm me.' She held up the photo next to her own face for an awkward moment.

'Well ...' the woman sighed, 'fuck me sideways and call me Nancy.' A grin spread across her make-up-less face. A laugh escaped from Luna that she didn't expect and therefore could not stop. 'You're actually her? You actually wrote those books? You're not having me on?' She pointed a black-painted nail and narrowed her eyes.

181

'Can't you tell from the horrendous photo? No one would own up to that photo willingly unless it was really them.' Luna held up the photo again and tried to replicate the expression that indicated tummy troubles.

'I just . . . I can't believe it.' Luna noticed she was finally blinking. 'You're my favourite author.'

'I find that incredibly hard to believe.' Luna put the book down.

'No, I mean it!' The woman gently took Luna by the elbows so she couldn't avoid looking directly into her goggling eyes. 'I'm only just reading *Cloud Walking* but I've read *everything* else you've ever written. Even all the early stuff that you entered into writing competitions as a teenager that you posted on your blog. I read your blog!' she added. 'When you used to post, that is.'

'Yeah I don't really do that any more. It all got a bit . . .'

'Personal?'

'Yeah,' Luna breathed. 'The more you give people the more they expect. I found that hard after a while. The boundaries started to blur.'

'I'm not surprised! Most people wouldn't even tell a stranger on the bus their first name but then expect celebrities to tell us who they're sleeping with, when they're getting married, when they're pregnant and what ridiculous name they're going to give the baby!'

'Yes! Exactly! Although I'm not even a celebrity. A few thousand people read my blog each week and even then I felt the pressure. I can't imagine what *actual* celebs go

182

through.' Luna shook her head but she could feel the muscles in her cheeks starting to stretch outwards. It had been a while since she'd enjoyed a conversation this much, which was surprising considering this was someone Luna didn't know and recently she'd found talking to strangers so difficult.

'There's wanting to write and then there's wanting to be a celebrity,' the woman agreed. 'Sometimes the two go hand in hand but sometimes they don't and when they don't, us fans just gotta be a bit more understanding. I'm guessing that's why you've never done any signings?' She looked over the top of her glasses, momentarily shrinking her eyes. Luna nodded. 'I'd always suspected that was the case. Every time one of your books comes out I always hope that there'll be an announcement of a signing somewhere. Scotland maybe, somewhere close enough that I could come and get my collection signed. Y'know ... tell you how brilliant I think your brain is. I never in a million years dreamed you'd move to Ondingside, let alone walk into *my* shop! My God, what a world, eh? *You're in my shop*!' She leant an elbow against the counter and flattened her other palm against her bump, frowning a little as the baby shifted inside her. Luna wondered if the baby was feeling the woman's excitement and was trying to join in. Luna stroked a stray strand of hair behind her ear and looked everywhere but at the woman.

'I could ... I could sign them now ... if ... if you wanted me to?'

The woman took her hand away from her bump and encircled her fingers around Luna's wrist.

'Are you being serious? I mean … *actually* serious.' Luna couldn't help but let out a giggle. Her books weren't sought-after enough for bookshops to chase her up to do signings and so the only level of fame she had reached were the thousand or so people who read and commented on her blog. She had a few lovely reviews on Goodreads and Amazon but she was never recognised, she never received any fan mail and she certainly had never had anyone fangirl over her, even mildly. A proud glow spread through her.

'Yeah. I mean … I don't think I've ever signed a book that wasn't for one of my uncles or cousins so I can't promise it'll look anything like my name but … yeah. I'd be happy to.'

'Oh. My. God. Wait. There.' The woman disappeared through the curtain again and this time Luna could hear the thud of her steps as she clambered up the stairs, carefully so as not to jostle her baby too much.

Luna moved further into the shop whilst she waited and finally waded far enough through the foliage to find all the books within. She still had to move a few cacti out of the way to pull out the titles she wanted a closer look at but it was undoubtedly a well-stocked store. The owner certainly had an eye for beautifully bound books. Most had leather covers in brown, black or blue, and the majority were bordered in shiny gold foil, some even intricately patterned. There were classics upon classics like *Wuthering Heights, Silas Marner,* and the complete works of Shakespeare and Dickens but then there were some other titles that seemed like they'd only ever be bought as gag gifts in today's day and age, such as *Men, Women and Pianos* and *A Beginner's Guide to Grass.* If Luna was being honest, there were very few books that piqued her interest and even fewer that she'd actually consider paying good money for. No book in the shop was younger than fifty years old but although she was already quite certain she would leave empty-handed, Luna would make sure to ask the woman if she had any recommendations at least. She had been kind to her, after all, and Luna could appreciate how hard it must be running a small, independent business, especially when living on such a tiny island with an extra mouth to feed on the way.

'Here we are!' The woman reappeared, pushing her way through the curtain backwards as her hands were underneath a pile of books that she was holding steady with her chin. 'Now, are you *sure* you don't mind?'

'Not at all.'

The woman quickly snatched a pen out of a pot on her desk and handed it to Luna. Luna found the page near the front with enough space for her to personalise and sign and poised the pen above the page. 'I'm so sorry. I've just realised I haven't yet asked your name.'

'Wendy. Wood.' She held out her hand and the moment

Luna took it, Wendy shook hers so vigorously, Luna thought she might drop the pen in her other hand.

'Lovely to meet you,' Luna said. She hadn't signed many books in her lifetime and although she had a pseudonym she knew she never felt comfortable signing something that wasn't actually true so all she ever signed was her last name which she had down to a fine art. The L was large and completed in one languid movement and the 'ark' didn't look much like an 'a' an 'r' or a 'k' but the squiggle Luna left looked professional and calligraphic enough to be enviable. She personalised and signed each book in turn whilst Wendy watched on, thanking her after she closed each cover.

'This is incredible. I don't know how to thank you enough.'

'Honestly, it's nothing—'

'WAIT!' Wendy disappeared through the curtain for a third time but reappeared almost instantly holding another book. 'All of the books in here are old and most of them are boring but the ones that aren't boring people have already read. Y'know: Dickens, Shakespeare, George Eliot, Austen, you get the idea. SO ...' She held out the book to Luna. It looked like an ordinary book at first glance, not unlike all the others on the shelves, but upon closer inspection Luna noticed some subtle differences. The blue fabric cover had been cleaned and patterned fabric had been added to the spine and trimmed in dark blue ribbon. When Luna opened the book she saw that new endpapers had been glued in and the pages of the book had been carefully cut out and replaced with blank and patterned pages, all carefully hand stitched into the old cover. 'I saw someone online doing it and thought I'd give it a go, considering I have an abundance of resources.'

'This is beautiful. Wendy, you could sell these.'

'Noooo,' Wendy said with a smile but then she said, 'Really?' with a furrowed brow. 'You're the first person to see the finished article and I'd love to sell them but ... is it good enough?'

'It's brilliant. I'd buy one!'

'You can have that one! As a thank-you for signing all my books. Well ... actually for writing all your books in the first place.'

'That's my job!' Luna laughed.

'I know, I know, but your job makes a lot of people happy. Your job allows Muggles like me to escape my incredibly dull and meaningless existence for a little while and pretend I'm Misty the Cloud Walker or Hope Hawthorn who's "never wrong ..."'

'... and "right on time."' Luna finished.

'Your job allows people who don't always get treated right feel less alone, and can even convince them that they do deserve better.' Wendy's hand snaked up to her stomach and she took a deep breath, her eyes closing and without a word, Luna reached out and took Wendy's other hand. 'Oof. Sorry about that. That went a little deeper than I had intended but I guess that's what happens when you've not to spoken to someone your own age in quite a while and the first person you come across is also your favourite author!' Wendy shrugged and laughed but the laugh caught in her throat and Luna could see how glassy her eyes looked through her frames.

'Well, thank you. For the journal. I'll make sure to write the notes for my next book in it.' Luna took a step towards the door.

'You're working on something new?'

'Trying to,' Luna said, thinking of her empty notebook. 'Finding this one a little . . . challenging.'

'Well, if you ever need a quiet place to work, no one *ever* comes into this shop.' Wendy said with a roll of her eyes. 'I could set up a table back there next to the window?'

Luna looked into the back of the shop and noticed how pretty the light was as it shone through the leaves and petals of the hanging baskets in the window and scattered pale colours onto the wooden floors and the spines of already beautiful books. Luna felt like this could be the kind, less murderous version of Mushnik and Son from *Little Shop of Horrors*.

'Do y'know what? I'd actually love that. I couldn't think of a better place to write than surrounded by some of the world's greatest authors.'

'And some of the world's worst. Seriously . . . some of those novels back there are stinkers. They can teach you how *not* to write a book.'

'Could I start tomorrow?' Luna asked before her brain had a chance to talk her out of it.

'Absolutely!' Wendy clapped her hands together. 'I'll get the coffee in from next door!'

'Actually . . . I'll do that.' Luna smiled even though she tried hard not to.

'Are you sure?'

'Yes. Definitely. It's the least I could do to say thank you for letting me work in your shop.' It wasn't a lie. It just wasn't the entirety of the truth and Luna was happy to settle for that.

As she left the shop, Luna thought about turning right and going back into Beau's shop. She could claim she wanted another coffee and this was pretty much the only place to obtain a good one. She *did* want another coffee, but was that too keen? Did she care if she looked too keen? She wasn't the 'play hard to get' type but she also knew she couldn't be keen without seeming *overly* keen. Luna had no in-between and she knew it. She was either the ice queen or Lavender Brown. She had no . . . Jessica Rabbit mode. Luna sighed and turned left, wishing she hadn't eaten all of her chips.

First days were miserable, according to Luna's personal experience. On her first day of primary school, a boy named Jake Taylor yanked up the hem of her skirt so that

189

everyone got a flash of her lime green Teletubby knickers. Kids called her Dipsy right up until high school. One boy even asked if he could show her his Tinky Winky, which she declined with a firm fist to the face. On her first day of high school, she couldn't open her locker and was forced to carry around seventeen text books in her rucksack, causing her to be hunchbacked for a week afterwards from the sheer weight. She thought the terror of first days and the fickle, somewhat cruel nature of children wouldn't carry over into her adult life, especially not in places of work – but it seems that some people just never grow up. After university, Luna first went into editing, starting with a small online magazine. The office was small but her boss was a woman who liked things in a peculiar and yet particular way. Any small deviation from her particular way was punishable by firing. Luna was just thankful that she had a job writing for the magazine in which she could keep her head down but it was the PAs, who were ever present in the boss's office, bringing her post, tea or telephone messages, that seemed to take the brunt of her rage. She went through personal assistants like Luna went through bourbon biscuits. The average life expectancy of a PA was approximately ten days and after a while, Luna stopped bothering to learn their names. They would turn up bright-eyed and bushy-tailed and leave downtrodden and bewildered, sometimes sopping wet from a launched mug of whatever the boss's drink of choice happened to be that day: usually cold tea but on an occasional Friday, a parma violet gin. That wasn't just a difficult first day for Luna, but a difficult eighteen months.

So Luna wasn't quite able to believe her luck that her first day in Ondingside had brought with it snow, a potential friend and, gulp, somewhat of a crush. *Am I actually crushing though?* she thought. *Or am I just excited that he was friendly and he made good coffee?* But her stomach somersaulted at the idea of picking up her flat white and a caramel latte for Wendy tomorrow morning. That little flutter was answer enough. The snow seemed to have stuck fast to the ground – however, it was a little slushy on the sand under Luna's boots as she trudged back towards the inn. The sky was still just a thick sheet of grey without a single break where the sunlight could creep in. Even as she looked out over the sea, the ceiling continued for miles. A wind pushed against her back and forcibly moved her along the beach and into the door of the inn.

Fifteen

Dinner

'Miss Lark!' Mrs McArthur spread her arms wide as Luna arrived back at the inn, shaking off the icy breath of Jack Frost as she fought against him to close the door behind her. 'Good day?' She looked a little more glamorous than usual but Luna realised she was wearing almost an identical outfit to when Luna arrived except her jumper was a burgundy that matched her lipstick.

'Surprisingly good, actually,' Luna said, her cheeks thawing. 'Heating back on?'

'Yes, yes, all's fine now. We even have some help in the kitchen whilst Ralph can't get to us. He's only on the other side of the island but he's got a little girl and between school being cancelled and their nanny not being able to get to them . . .' she waved her hands about in the air,

'... ugh, I just gave him the day off on the proviso that he sorts it all out and is back with us tomorrow. In the meantime, the Green Arrow have very kindly shared some of their staff with us in this great time of need and—'

'The Green Arrow?' Luna's heart thumped.

'Yes.' Mrs McArthur pulled her glasses down her nose so that her eyes pierced Luna. 'Why?' She asked, pronouncing it 'huuuuwhy'.

'N-no reason. Does that ... does that mean Beau's here?' Luna asked, looking only at her feet as she thoroughly wiped them on the doormat.

'Oh, my love, you don't need to worry about bumping into him! He doesn't work there any more. Owns a coffee shop in town now. Not that he'll be there for long, mind. Don't think business is quite as booming as he had hoped.'

'Of course.' Luna shook her head and laughed at herself. *Get a grip, you idiot.*

'So, no. Beau isn't here and dinner is definitely back on the cards for tonight! Double win for you!' She raised her arms in celebration and Luna got a waft of her floral perfume. 'We do a lovely steak and ale pie with chips for eight pounds fifty ...' she tempted.

'D'ya know what, Mrs McArthur? That sounds perfect. I'll be down a little later for it but count me in.'

'I'll reserve you a table!' Mrs McArthur clapped her hands together just as the door clunked behind them. The air gushed inwards and sucked all the heat from the reception area and the sight of Beau's rosy cheeks as he walked into the room sucked all the breath from Luna's lungs.

'What on God's green Earth are you doing here, you buffoon!' Mrs McArthur squeaked.

'Blimey, Mrs M! Hello to you too!' he said, wiping his feet. 'Oh ... hi,' he said as his eyes fell on Luna and his face split into a smile that filled the room with warmth once more. 'I just came to see if you could use an extra hand.'

'Shouldn't you be grinding beans instead of my gears?'

'I usually close at six anyway.' He shrugged.

'It's three forty-five!' Luna winced at Mrs M's shrill tones.

'Yes, well, it's not like anyone will be too disappointed.' He ruffled his hair with his hand but the momentary sigh he tried to hide did not go unnoticed by Luna.

'Look, I've just told the lovely Miss Lark here that you were not on the premises and I would like to keep it that way.' Just as Beau unzipped his coat, Mrs McArthur opened the door with one hand and placed the other on the centre of his chest, pushing him back out into the snow.

'Mrs McArthur!' Luna rushed over and put a hand on her shoulder. 'It's fine. Really. I actually bumped into Beau this afternoon.' She swallowed. *He knows I've been talking about him,* she inwardly groaned whilst trying to keep her face neutral.

'Yes – *Miss Lark,*' he said slowly, 'came in for a coffee. See. People do actually like my coffee, Mrs M.' He narrowed his eyes at Mrs McArthur. 'When they do come in ...' he added. Mrs M rolled her eyes at him but there was the hint of a smile on her lips.

'I'm sure the coffee is wonderful, Beau. It's probably the conversation that drives them away,' she said, a smile playing on the corner of her lips.

'Ahh, Mrs M. You always know just what to say to warm my heart. Behind the bar?' He gestured towards part of the inn Luna had yet to visit.

'All right.' Mrs M rolled her eyes again. 'Go on. You know where everything is.'

'Maybe, I'll see you in a bit?' Beau touched Luna's shoulder for a moment and then that moment was over but Luna could still feel where his fingers had been.

'Save me a cider,' she tried to joke but she couldn't seem to make her eyes meet his. Still, she knew he was smiling. *He's always smiling.*

Once he was out of sight, Luna raced up to her room and threw off her coat, put the journal Wendy had given her in a drawer in the desk and rummaged through her case for something smart and yet casual. Something bold yet understated. This was way more Lottie's area of expertise and Luna wished she was there telling her which top went best with which pair of jeans and which shoes were the perfect height and colour for whichever outfit she chose. Luna picked up her phone and started to write out a text but quickly hit select all and backspaced. Lottie would have a field day if she knew there was someone she was trying to impress and Luna wasn't sure she had the capacity to deal with both Beau and Lottie at the moment. Lottie came with questions, most of which Luna was sure she wouldn't have the answers to. Besides, Luna noticed that the right-hand corner of her screen still displayed no 4G symbol, nor were any of the bars of signal white. Just a plain and miserable grey, not unlike the clouds outside that were no doubt the culprit for all the interference. She threw down her phone and went back to rummaging and trying to match random items from her poor excuse of a wardrobe. Luna was quite firmly comfort over fashion. She liked her Doc Martens and when she wore out the soles or the zip broke, she'd simply replace them – often with the same pair, maybe in a different colour. Occasions like this, when Luna actually needed to look smart and somewhat 'dolled up', were rare but when they did occur, Luna often made a vow to actually listen to Lottie's advice when they were out shopping and to 'actually buy something worth borrowing'. Those moments, however, much to Lottie's dismay, were always fleeting.

Eventually, after much switching and swapping and mixing and matching, Luna settled on a simple black button-down shirt with three-quarter-length sleeves that tied in neat little bows at her elbows, paired with her grey jeans and a pair of black boots. The boots were indeed made by Doc Martens, but they had a thick heel that gave Luna height without making her teeter on her tiptoes or giving her cramp in the centre of her foot that could only be remedied by taking said boots off and massaging it out. Getting your manky feet out whilst trying to impress someone would be somewhat counterproductive so Luna was pleased with her choice. She knew they were a pair of boots even Lottie wouldn't have been able to resist. She only touched up her make-up, resisting the urge to take it all off and start from scratch and before she changed her mind, she gave her hair a quick zhuzh in the bathroom mirror, picked up her phone, purse and keys and headed downstairs.

The restaurant and bar area was exactly what Luna had expected. Quiet and deserted, much like the rest of the island. She had hoped to be pleasantly surprised and find it bustling like the Green Arrow had been last year but that was certainly more of a pub for the locals whereas Nobody's Inn was for tourists and guests, of which Ondingside had few. In fact Luna wondered if maybe she was the only one. Every table was vacant but one in the far corner near the window had a little chalkboard centrepiece that told Luna that it was reserved just especially for 'Miss Lark' and she made a mental note to thank Mrs M later. As she walked past the bar she glanced over the many beer taps, emblazoned with logos and names of beer she'd never heard of before, hoping to catch a glimpse of Beau, but he didn't seem to be around. *Maybe he went home,* she thought as she picked up a menu from the small rack on the table that held condiments and cutlery. *Maybe he was actually just here to help. Maybe he wasn't here for you at all and once he'd felt he'd done enough to help out Mrs M, he just simply . . . left.* She browsed the menu, even though she already had her heart set on the pie and chips Mrs M had promised, but even so, her mind wasn't able to focus on the words dancing in front of her as it was running away with thoughts on where Beau might be right now, why he would have gone home and whether he was as interested in her as she somehow, strangely seemed to be in him. The feelings of a new infatuation were so delicious but they lost their sweetness when the sudden fear set in that maybe the infatuation was a one-way street. Just as Luna was about to swallow that very bitter pill, she felt someone, presumably a waiter, approach her table.

'Hello, madam. My name's Beau and I will be your personal waiter this evening.' Luna's head snapped up and sure enough, there were his eyes, shining through a tidal wave of his black hair. 'Is there anything I can get you? Food, drink, company?'

'Is it greedy if I say all of the above?'

'I'd say that's perfectly reasonable.' Beau took her order to the bar, pie and chips and a bottle of cider, and returned to her table but this time, he slid into the booth opposite her and her stomach flipped. *You're just hungry,* she thought, knowing full well it was actually the effects of Beau's grin.

'It's such a coincidence that you just *happened* to show up and offer your services where I just *happen* to be staying,' she toyed as she took a sip from the bottle Beau had placed in front of her.

'Are you suggesting I'm *stalking* you?' Beau mock-gasped.

'Not stalking. Just ... following closely.'

'Aren't they essentially the same thing?'

'Depends how you want to come off!'

'Following closely it is!' He smiled and took a swig of his own pint. 'You're not going to ruin this one too, are you?'

'Oh, stop it,' she groaned. 'This will be my one and only drink of the night. Promise.' And she meant it. 'Actually,' she said, starting to peel at one of the stickers on the bottle, 'I'll be coming in to properly purchase two coffees tomorrow.'

'Two?' Beau asked and Luna wondered if he was thinking the second coffee was for a date.

'One for me and one for Wendy. In the bookshop. Next door to you,' she clarified.

'*Wendy*? As in Wendy Wood, Wendy?' He laughed.

'As in Wendy, Wendy.' She held her hands out in front of her own stomach, fingers splayed across a large, imaginary, pregnant belly. 'Yeah ... why?'

'She's as mad as a box of frogs!'

'She is not!'

'Oh, come off it. She dresses like she teaches at Hogwarts and she spends all day talking to plants!' he howled.

'I quite liked her style! Besides,' Luna said, shaking away her own smirk, 'she's lovely and she's offered me a space in her shop to work.'

'You don't have conversations with cactuses as well, do you?'

'It's cacti and *no*, I don't. I'm a writer,' she said with conviction.

'Oh, I bet Wendy *loved* that.'

'She did, indeed.'

'Anything I would have read?' She studied his face and when she was sure any trace of mockery had disappeared she carefully considered her answer.

'Do you even read?' she asked.

He paused for a moment. 'I *can* read.'

'That's absolutely not what I asked.' She grinned at him.

'I've read a few books in my time!' He leant over the table and batted her arm with the back of his fingers and Luna's skin tingled at the touch.

'Mr Men and *The Hungry Caterpillar* don't count.'

'Well, then I've read one book in my time.' She caught herself smiling at him, her eyes starting to glaze over and she blamed the cider, knowing full well that it was not the cider. 'No, I used to read a lot but not so much any more. Definitely not as many as someone who writes them for a living, though.' Luna nodded her agreement. 'Then let me try again.' He leant forwards on his forearms. 'Have you written anything *Wendy* would have read?'

Luna thought to tell him how Wendy had almost lost her mind when she'd found out that the novels she had written just happened to be the ones she loved the most but she wasn't sure she felt like putting herself in the spotlight. Not this early on. Besides, her last boyfriend had transitioned with her from wannabe writer to published author and so she wasn't sure how to approach the subject of her career with someone entirely new. She knew there was a difference between pride in your work and arrogance but she didn't want to risk tripping over the line between them and falling flat on her face. Especially not in front of Beau.

'Don't think so.' She shrugged. 'I'll have to ask.'

'Can I read anything you've written?'

'I doubt Wendy's store stocks my books, somehow. All of her books are ...'

'Older than Jesus?' he asked just as Luna took a sip of her cider and she tried her hardest not to look like she was choking. Beau took a napkin from the table rack and handed it to her. *Smooth.* 'Sorry, I'll try not to be funny any more. So, that's a no then?' He laughed.

'My books are published so if you can find one, you can read it.' She wiped her mouth, careful not to smudge her lipstick.

'I'll need a little more than "Miss Lark" to put into a search engine, then.'

'Maybe that's the challenge.' She smiled.

'You're really not going to tell me your name?' The wrinkles in his forehead deepened.

'What's this obsession with names?'

'I don't think it's an *obsession*!' he scoffed. 'I've just never met someone with such an odd reservation. I could easily ask you what's your aversion to telling people your name?'

'Touché.'

'No, I'm actually asking.' He looked at her, his eyes wide and pleading, but no matter how soft and kissable his face looked (*did I really just think his face is kissable?* she thought), the nervous rumble in her chest outweighed how much she might want to hear him say her name.

'Telling someone your name is like inviting them into your life,' she explained. 'It removes a very large boundary. When people are on a first-name basis, they're no longer acquaintances. It's one step closer to friendship.'

'So you're telling me you don't have any friends?'

'I have friends. Well, one in particular. Lottie. She's been my best friend since uni.' Luna looked at her phone, the signal still missing from the upper right-hand corner.

'That's it? There's no one else?'

'Not really.'

'Not even Facebook Friends?'

'Does there have to be?'

'I suppose not but ... aren't you lonely?' Luna thought about it for a moment and realised that loneliness had

203

never been an issue for her. She had Lottie and Lottie was amazing and they were there for each other but other than that, she had always been happy in her own company. Even before she had lost her family, she'd been an independent child and she had never yearned to share her life with a multitude of people. Even on social media her tweets were few and far between, her Instagram pictures were always of places and objects, rarely of her own face, and whilst Luna was an avid browser of Facebook and she enjoyed watching the lives and families of the people she knew grow and unfurl, she couldn't even remember the last time she actually posted something about herself. The most recent picture on her profile was a photo someone else had taken, posted and tagged her in from when she was about seventeen. Perhaps she ought to post something more current as she wasn't sure she liked the idea of everyone she knew remembering her as a dorky, gangly teenager that hadn't quite yet mastered the art of colour co-ordination. She was an anxious person who didn't desire a large amount of human interaction nor did she require much attention on a day-to-day basis. That being said, Luna wasn't incapable of making friends. She'd met Wendy, whom she liked and had plans to see quite a lot in the foreseeable future. Luna just liked her life the way it was and had no desire to let an abundance of strangers into her private business.

'I'm not lonely. At all. I have everyone I need,' she said, not sure she was even entirely convincing herself. 'I just don't need the approval of strangers to continue with my life.' That was true at least.

'Strangers are just friends you haven't met yet,' he said as if reading it off a motivational poster.

'Is that what they teach you at stalker school?' She took a swig.

'Yeah, it's our motto.'

'Catchy,' she said, smacking her lips.

'I'm serious though,' he said as he doodled through the condensation on his pint glass with his index finger. 'It's one thing to need the approval of strangers to function through everyday life. That doesn't sound healthy. But it's another thing entirely to never open yourself to the possibility of friendship.' He swivelled the glass around to her to reveal he'd written the word 'please' that shone through in the bright amber colour of his beer.

'Y'see, now I can't tell if you really believe any of this or if you're just saying anything you possibly can in order to make me tell you my name.' She narrowed her eyes and pursed her lips.

'What if it's a little bit of both?' he asked, and she shook her head. 'You're *really* not going to tell me?'

'That would make us friends.'

'And what's wrong with being friends with me?' He wiped away the word he'd written on his glass with his hand and then ran his dewy fingers through his hair.

'I don't know you at all!'

'That's the point of being friends! Getting to know

someone!' He laughed but Luna could see that it didn't reach his eyes and that he was starting to tire of the chase. She wasn't intentionally trying to be difficult, nor was she playing 'hard to get'. She was just simply making sure she was sticking by the rules she'd set herself.

'I thought the point of getting to know someone was to become friends? You need to get to know someone before you can decide whether they're worthy of your friendship, surely?'

'Go on, then.' He readjusted himself in his seat and put his hands flat on the table.

'What?' she laughed.

'Get to know me. Put me to the test. Let's find out if I'm worthy of being your bessie mate.'

'... All right.' *I might enjoy this*, she thought. 'Favourite colour?'

'BZZZZ!' He pressed an imaginary buzzer on the table and made a gameshow noise so loud that it startled Luna and she giggled. 'Orange,' he chuckled.

'Ooooh, that's quite "out there". Not my personal fave, but I like a bold choice.'

'Ten points to Hufflepuff!' He raised a triumphant fist in the air.

'Favourite movie?'

'BZZZZ!' This time he hit the table and a passing waiter looked over his shoulder with a scowl. 'Sorry!' Beau mouthed and Luna covered her mouth, stifling laughter. '*Chamber of Secrets*.'

'I meant in general!'

'See if you can guess.' Beau cleared his throat. '"Feed me, Seymour! Feed me all night loooonngg"!' He sang as loud as he buzzed. Luna scrunched up her nose.

'*Little Shop of Horrors*? Really?'

'*What*?!' he gasped. 'It's a *great* movie!'

'It's a *musical*,' she said with an exaggerated roll of her eyes.

'And what's wrong with musicals?'

'People randomly burst into song and dance! Isn't that a tad ... unrealistic?'

'Unrealistic? Er, you write books. Are you telling me there's nothing in your books that is even just the teeniest bit unrealistic?'

'That's different!' she said, feeling her cheeks start to burn.

'So you can suspend disbelief for some things and not others?'

'Not for musicals, no,' she said and Beau pouted. 'I'm sorry but ... people do experience stuff like "love at first sight" and couples do get married very quickly. It might be young, stupid and ill-advised and they may end up getting divorced but the point is it happens. But large groups of people literally *never* burst into song in real life and know all the lyrics *and* choreography right off the bat without having had prior extensive rehearsal.' Beau stared at her blankly and for a moment, she didn't know if she had actually really offended him.

'You've thought about this way too much,' he said finally, the hint of a smile returning to his lips.

'I'm a writer. I'm meant to think about things too much.'

'"Love at first sight", eh? So, you write romantic fiction, then?'

'Hey, I'm supposed to be interrogating you!' She leant across the table and batted his arm, mimicking his earlier action, and Luna liked how smooth and warm his skin felt under her cold fingers. She wished she could have made it last longer but thought that would cross the line into creepy. Especially as they were currently having a conversation about how she was trying to keep him at bay.

'All right, all right!' Beau held up his hands. 'She's bossy, too!' He winked and Luna felt her heart rise a few inches. 'Continue ...'

'Sweet or savoury?' she asked.

'Cheese,' he said without hesitation.

'That's not an answer.'

'Yes it is. Cheese is savoury.'

'What?'

'When it comes to dessert, I always go for the cheese board. The savoury option.'

'That was a weird way of answering. You're weird,' she grinned.

'Does that earn me any points for Hufflepuff or will there be a deduction for strangeness?'

'You don't earn or lose any points. It's just an observation. You're just … weird.' He paused for a moment and then nodded with his bottom lip protruding.

'I can live with that.'

'Favourite season?' she continued.

'Season three.'

'Huh?' She raised an eyebrow.

'Season three. Of *Friends*. Y'know … "So no one told you life was gonna be this waaaayy",' he sang and then clapped four times.

'I meant season of the year. As in summer, winter …'

'Oh.'

'But season three is a good one! It's the one with Phoebe's doll house.'

'I would have said spring …'

'*Spring*? Why spring?'

'So judgemental, Miss Lark!'

'Sorry. I just don't know anyone who would pick *spring*.'

'That's because you have zero friends.'

'Not zero. Lottie. I have Lottie.'

'You don't have a Lottie. You have little friends.' There was a moment of silence in which Luna simply blinked at Beau and then slowly her lips stretched across her face and a howl of laughter erupted from her lungs. Her eyes began to stream, her breath was stuck somewhere between her lungs and her throat and an ecstasy she hadn't felt since she couldn't remember when flooded through her body. Laughing so hard your stomach hurt

209

and your throat was hoarse was something Luna hadn't done a lot of in recent years and she'd completely forgotten how beautiful it felt. To be so filled with childish joy that it bubbles up and up and up until it shoots out of your mouth in a guffaw, like a shaken-up coke bottle. It was safe to say that her bottle lid had been unscrewed and she wasn't sure if the giggling would ever end.

'Oh, Beau. That was brilliant.'

'Word play. The author likes word play. You're too predictable, Miss Lark!' He sipped his beer with difficulty due to his lips still wanting to smile.

'So, tell me again. Why do you like spring?' she said, still laughing.

'It feels all fresh and new. Plus there's Easter and I like chocolate.'

'I thought you said you were a savoury person?'

'I still like chocolate! I'm not a monster! But when they invent eggs made out of Brie I'll be first in line to buy one of them!' Luna watched him and the way he didn't just smile nor did he just *look* happy but he embodied happiness. His face *was* a smile even when it wasn't smiling. It didn't seem to know anything other than positivity. It was as if happiness and good thoughts shone out of him and once you'd seen it, it made no sense to look away. If Luna had been made of ice, she was sure she would melt in his warmth.

'So how have I done? Are we friends yet?' Oof. He was kind, funny, clever (although not as well read as she would have liked but no one was perfect ...) not to mention he was beautiful and made exceptional coffee. Luna's heart was bouncing around, doing backflips off the walls of her chest, howling to get out and jump into Beau's hands. However, not too long ago, Luna had put her heart in a cage in a desperate attempt to protect it and had thrown away the key. It had proved that it just couldn't be trusted and gave itself up too fast and too fully. It was time her head was in the driver's seat. Her brain made rules that she could stick to and kept her from getting hurt. She could feel her heart going crazy, trying to push her towards him but she filled her lungs to steady it. *Sorry heart,* she thought, *I just can't risk it.*

'You're sweet ... ' she started.

'I get it,' he said.

'I really do think you're lovely!'

He drained the last of his beer and shuffled sideways out of the booth. 'Honestly, it's cool. I tried my luck and I failed. I get it. I really do. But this is my cue to ... back off.' He placed his beer glass on the tray of a passing waiter.

'Beau ... '

'Miss Lark.' He smiled and held out his hand which she took in an instant. He sandwiched her fingers between his and kissed the back of her hand where she was sure a fire must have started for how much her skin burned and tingled under his lips. 'Although brief, it's been a pleasure.' His fingers lingered in hers for a moment but as soon as their hands disconnected and he slipped away and through a door behind the bar, Luna's heart slumped to the bottom of its cage.

Urgh, she groaned to herself. *That ... was horrible.* She chanced a glance at the bar but Beau had well and truly disappeared.

Luna only ate half of her pie and pushed the chips around the plate, doodling with them in the gravy. She stayed for as long as she felt acceptable, paid her bill and slunk upstairs, grateful that Mrs M was somewhere else in the building as she trudged past reception. She let herself fall backwards onto her bed and closed her eyes whilst a knot in her stomach wrangled and wrenched tighter. *Why didn't you just ... see where it went?* she thought. *He wasn't proposing, he just wanted to be friends.*

'I know. I know,' she said out loud to her achingly empty room. She sat up abruptly and went to her bathroom mirror where she was actually a little taken aback by how well she'd done her make-up and even more surprised by how pleased she was by her own reflection. It was certainly the first time in a long time that she didn't avoid her own gaze. 'But hear me, *Miss Lark,* and hear me good and proper.' She grasped either side of the sink with her spindly fingers. 'Rules are rules. You put them in place for a reason and you can't just go breaking them for the first handsome face you meet on this stupidly tiny island. No matter how ridiculous his smile is.' His face faded into her mind. The way his expression visibly changed when he knew he was about to say something clever or funny that was sure to make her laugh. The way he practically bowed to say goodbye as he kissed her hand like a character straight out of an Austen novel. And that smile. Oh God, that smile. That big, toothy, could-take-a-bite-out-of-a-sadness, everything-will-always-be-okay kind of smile that Luna had only ever seen in movies. She didn't think anyone who wasn't an actor had one of those kinds of faces and she certainly didn't think she'd ever meet them if there was. But there was Beau and she had met him and she had just turned him down. She shook her head. 'But you've turned him down for someone more important right now and that's you.' She stared into her own blue eyes and forced herself not to look away. 'No one's gonna sort your shit out for you, Luna. So knuckle down. Get your book written. Get your life sorted. Then you can think about relationships or friendships or whatever. But that's not what you *need* right now. You moved here, to this tiny speck on a world map, specifically for zero distractions. It's been one day and you've already found the biggest distraction this little island probably has to offer. Well, enough. No more.'

Luna got into her pyjamas, took off all of her make-up with her nice new cleanser that she'd bought before going away and a muslin cloth that, no matter how many times she washed it, still remained a grimy grey from her mascara and eyeliner and she sat at the desk in front of the window. She opened her laptop, already knowing her mind definitely wasn't in the right place for writing but she hoped with a little bit of force and perseverance she'd be able to get it in gear and find 'the zone' to start her novel. A novel that currently had no plot, no plan and currently to Luna, no point. Ideas seemed elusive and ungraspable. Like those cute, small dinosaurs in *Jurassic Park* that flee before the giant T-rex, trying not to get eaten. Luna was the T-rex and all her ideas were trying not to become dinner. She opened the file she'd created a few weeks ago entitled 'New Book' and a blank page appeared on the screen.

'Okay,' she huffed. The good news was that the signal was still down. No 4G meant no social media to distract her. The last picture to have been uploaded on her Instagram feed before the signal went down was a selfie by Lottie from one of her raucous nights out. She scrunched up her face at the camera, a dark club behind her, a drink in her hand in the corner of the shot. She looked happy and like she was having as much fun as when Luna had last seen her. Although she knew it wouldn't send, Luna left a comment to say *I'm having just as much fun without you too!* and an emoji of a little bright yellow bald head rolling its eyes to convey her desperate sarcasm. Seeing as she knew it wouldn't properly send, she added *In fact, I even went on a date tonight, so there!* As soon as the comment was written and sent but not delivered, Luna closed the app. She was the world's worst procrastinator and even when the app

214

wasn't technically live and working, she knew she would still manage to use it to waste time. Usually, when it was working, she would reward herself every hundred words or so with a fifteen-minute scrolling session on Instagram or a nosedive down one of YouTube's many rabbit holes. Without it, she had no option but to simply crack on.

Fifteen minutes later, Luna was still staring at a painfully blank screen and she had checked her locked phone screen at least twenty times, knowing full well there would be nothing new to see. She closed her laptop. The temptation to pack it in until tomorrow was within reach and was calling to her with a sultry voice and blinking its puppy dog eyes. Tomorrow she would have an office, of sorts. Tomorrow she would be in close proximity to a fan of her work who would hold her accountable if she wasn't doing something, anything that contributed towards her next book. Tomorrow would be a better environment for starting a novel. Tomorrow, tomorrow, tomorrow ... however, Luna knew herself too well. The last two months had been full of tomorrows and it had always been too easy to take temptation's hand and let it lead her down the path of watching Netflix whilst sat in a bath or seeing how many cups of tea it was possible to make and drink within one evening. Tomorrows came and went and the document on her laptop remained plain white, lacking the glorious scattered black markings of all the words she'd conjured up and arranged into pretty sentences. Sentences that made people say 'aww' or 'oh my goodness!' and even shed a tear or laugh out loud in public spaces. 'Tomorrow' didn't mean anything to Luna. It was right now or never. She'd written novels before and she knew she could do it again – and she needed to do it soon and quickly or her editor was going to internally combust – she just needed to know what it was she was actually writing about.

'I'm not giving up,' she told herself. 'I'm merely taking a different approach.' Luna slid her laptop away and pulled her black leather notebook across to her and opened it to the next blank page. She had a habit of dating the top right-hand corner, like she was still in school, as her nostalgic, sentimental side loved looking back through old notebooks and knowing exactly where she was when having her mostly terrible yet sometimes brilliant ideas.

A woman goes into a coffee shop, she wrote. *The barista has an award-winning smile that has surely never won awards otherwise he'd probably be standing in front of an expensive camera wearing an expensive suit for an expensive brand. Instead he asks what her name is to write it on the side of a paper cup. Instead of giving him her real name, like an idiot she gives him a pseudonym because she's convinced herself she doesn't need anyone other than herself, that work is more important, that relationships only hurt you and that dying alone is the best option she has because it's better than getting hurt over and over and over and over and over ...*

Luna slumped forwards onto the page of words that she only half meant and gave herself a moment to have a little cry. She felt a large, unusual sob heave upwards from somewhere in her soul that hadn't exposed itself for quite some time. It was a little ball of grief and self-pity that came out like a tangled set of headphones and for a moment, Luna felt the urge to dig her fingers in and start untangling, strand by sorrowful strand. For a second, she actually thought about dealing with it instead of stuffing it back into her rucksack of blissfully ignored emotions that was close to bursting at the seams but ultimately, Luna did just that. Fear of what she might find in the centre of that mess of feelings and personal issues was much too much for a night on her own on an island she'd only just moved to. That was something that really could wait until tomorrow.

'You're okay,' she breathed. 'I'm okay.' Luna sat up and closed her notebook. 'Okay. If I say tomorrow, I really mean tomorrow. I'll be in Wendy's shop and if I don't get any work done in front of her it'll be super embarrassing and disappointing and just ... awful. So tomorrow. But *actually* tomorrow.'

Luna opened her laptop again but this time she opened up her iTunes and clicked on a romcom that she'd bought and downloaded months ago. *For inspiration,* she thought as the beginning credits rolled, inevitably listing Hugh Grant as the male lead, as he seemed to be in all the good romcoms, not that Luna (or anyone really ...)

was complaining. The soothing soundtrack played in the background and before she closed the curtains for the evening, she looked up at the sky and could only see a light patch of dark cloud where the moon was desperately trying to look at her. Luna waved anyway.

'Tomorrow,' she said, not knowing that tomorrow really never would come.

She crawled to the edge of the chasm, her frozen, raw fingers gripping the edge of the ice and yet she closed her eyes, unable to stare into the void below her.

'Luuuuunnnaaaa!' Her own voice screamed a deafening roar and then the whole world around her fell silent. The wind went still and the roaring from the chasm hushed. A silhouette appeared through the curtain of snow. It stood tall, with its shoulders back and head held high. Its footsteps fell with confidence in a direction it was sure of. Luna could only wish for such certainty. The silhouette came closer but never into focus and Luna wished she had a chance to meet that person before consciousness pulled her away.

Sixteen

London

July 19th 2019

'I'm not following you again on one of your ridiculous chases, Jaxon. The last time nearly got me killed.' Bella Brown lifted an empty suitcase from their cramped bedroom cupboard and opened it out onto their bed. She pulled her dirty blonde hair out of her almond-shaped brown eyes and began pulling clothes from their hangers and haphazardly slinging them into the open case. She quickly became sweaty and pulled at her T-shirt over and over again, trying to waft some cool air down her cleavage.

'You only fell out of a boat, Bella. It was hardly Armageddon.' Jaxon appeared in the doorway, still wearing his leather jacket despite London's heatwave starting to reach its peak. He had paired it with a stained T-shirt and knee-length denim shorts. Bella looked at him as he leant against the doorframe, rolling a cigarette with his fingers, seeing now what her mother always saw and she felt a headache start to pinch behind her eyes.

'I was under the water for what felt like an hour because *someone* hadn't even realised I'd gone overboard!' She took off the watch he'd bought her for her birthday and threw it at him. Jaxon just managed to catch it before it smashed against the wall next to his head.

'I knew! It just took a while to see where you'd gone! We were in the middle of a storm, Bells! It was dark, y'know!' He laughed.

'I hit my head on the side of the boat, Jaxon. I had concussion and had to have stitches.' She pulled entire drawers out of their slots in the dresser and tipped the contents into the case. 'I'm lucky it wasn't worse than it was!' She touched the scar on her head.

'All right, all right, maybe it *was* quite bad,' he admitted.

'Then stop smiling,' she said through clenched teeth.

'I'm sorry!' He laughed again. 'I just think you're making a mountain out of a molehill.' He shrugged, licking the edge of the rolling paper.

'Me ending up in hospital because my idiot, thrill-seeking boyfriend thinks it's a brilliant idea to try and get struck by lightning *is* a mountain. And one I'm just not willing to climb any more,' she sighed, hurriedly trying to neaten up the contents of her case.

'Oh, come on, Bella! You used to *love* this kind of stuff!' Jaxon stamped his foot and she looked at him for a moment. She didn't know whether to laugh at just how *done* she was or cry at how long she'd spent with someone who would actually stamp their foot like a toddler during what was meant to be an adult disagreement.

'I've *never* loved this stuff, Jax! I came along for the ride because I loved *you*! But I'm done. I can't keep doing this and more importantly I can't keep *funding* this.' She closed the case but it didn't quite shut so she clambered onto the bed and laid across the top of it on her stomach, desperately trying to make the sides meet. 'I want to get *married* one day, Jax. I want to have kids and a house and build a family.' She shifted further across the case, its plastic clasps straining against her hands. 'I don't have the money for that *and* your crazy habit.'

'I don't do drugs, Bells!' He laughed as he began to light the cigarette. Her head snapped up at the sound of the lighter fizzing into action.

'If you light that in here then I *will* kick off.' Her eyes were wide and glaring.

'You mean this isn't you kicking off right now?' He pulled the lighter away from the end of the cigarette but still kept it ablaze.

'Oh, honey, this isn't even scratching the surface,' she spat. He huffed and put the lighter back into his shorts pocket but kept the cigarette between his lips. He slicked his hair back and wondered if he looked as much like James Dean as he thought he did.

'Your storm-chasing is an addiction, Jax, surely you realise that?' She looked at him as she pulled her knees up onto the case and rocked from side to side, trying to force the case shut. 'And I can't keep paying to come along on these outlandish trips with you and your goons, only to end up in hospital, broke *and* broken.' Jax watched Bella struggle but made no move to help. Whether that was because he didn't want her to leave or didn't want to help was still unclear to both of them.

'Marriage and kids sounds . . . great. One day,' he said, tugging at the hair on the back of his head. 'But I want to go on adventures first, babe. That's what this is about. I'm getting it all out of my system now so that one day, in the future, I'll probably settle down.'

'But, y'see, that's the thing. Probably isn't enough for me. *Marriage and kids* is meant to be an adventure. It's supposed to be one of the greatest adventures two people will ever have and you Just. Don't. Get. That,' she said very clearly. 'I don't think you ever will. And I'm not gonna stick around waiting to see if you do.' The case finally clicked into place and she quickly whipped the clasps closed and heaved the case off the bed.

'Where the hell are you even gonna go?' he asked as she waddled past him with her case and dumped it in the hallway.

'My sister has said I can stay with her.' Bella grabbed her coat and laid it over the top of the case, still sweating too profusely to even think about putting it on.

'How long have you been planning to leave?' He sat on the top of her case and she batted him off it as she raised its handle

'I dunno. A month or two. Too long, Jax.' She went back into the bedroom for a moment and returned with her blue rucksack.

'Well, thanks for letting me know,' he scoffed. Bella turned to him then and put a gentle hand on his arm.

'Jax, you and I both know that you've always had one foot in this relationship whilst the other was waiting to run. Probably after some hurricane or tornado or whatever. What's this next one then, eh? Thunder? Lightning? Whirlpool in the middle of the ocean that sucks you straight to the centre of hell?' She smiled and for the first time, Jax felt his chest tighten.

'Blizzard, by the looks of things.' He took the cigarette from his lips and fiddled with it in his hand.

'A blizzard?' she laughed. 'Are you sure? It's July.'

'Yeah, some kind of freak, extreme weather change. In Ondingside. Y'know that place just off the coast of Scotland? All the trains have stopped running there and no one's been able to contact anyone on the island for days. It's like the island has just ... gone dark.'

'Is everyone okay?' Her brow creased and Jax wanted to kiss her to make her worry go away.

'No distress signals. No accidents have been reported. It's just like ... no one's there.'

'Has no one tried to get to the island?'

'A couple of boats have tried but they've had to turn back as the water gets too rough the closer you get to the shore. There's only one train track out to the island but it's totally iced up. Everyone says it's too dangerous so until there's some kind of distress signal, they'll just wait until the island thaws out.'

'So how are you planning to get there, then?' she asked, but Jax knew she already knew what his plans were.

'Train tracks.' He smiled with all of his teeth that surprisingly had only yellowed slightly considering how much he smoked.

'Don't be ridiculous. What are you planning to do, *walk it*?' She laughed but he nodded.

'Yeah.'

'You're out of your mind.'

'I thought that's what you loved about me.' He brushed a strand of hair out of her face and for just a moment, he thought if he leant in, she would let him kiss her. The moment was brief. She looked down at her shoes and pulled away as she backed towards the door.

'It was. It's also why I'm leaving.' She tightened the straps of her rucksack, checked the time on her phone and opened the door, wheeling her case out first. Bella looked back and saw something in his face that reminded her of the youthful, carefree boy she fell in love with two years ago. When things were fun without the added element of danger that had scared her into leaving for good. 'Just ... be careful, okay?'

'You're not gonna try and stop me?'

'Would it work if I did?'

Jaxon really did think about it for a few seconds. He thought about what life would be like if he took off his jacket and said he'd forget about the whole thing. How he would feel about being a husband and a dad ... but his chest tightened further and the walls started to close in and he knew nothing would make him feel more trapped than a ring on his finger and a baby to feed.

'No,' he said with certainty.

'Exactly. Bye, Jax. Don't get yourself killed.' She closed the door behind her, leaving him in the hallway.

'I'll try,' he said as he took the lighter from his pocket and finally lit his cigarette and went to pack a bag of his own.

Seventeen

Ondingside

July 20th 2019

Wendy sat up in bed, the covers pulled down below her bump, her nightshirt pulled up above it. Wendy knew the idea behind meditation and mindfulness was simply to let thoughts come and go as they pleased, like cars on a road whizzing past. She took deep breaths and watched her belly move as the baby inside her stretched its limbs. However, eventually a monster truck always decided to park in front of her and often she wasn't able to stop it running her over.

'You're alone,' the thought whispered. 'You're unloved and unlovable and you can't provide the life your child deserves.' Tears splattered onto the skin of her bump and

trailed their way down to her protruding belly button. Wendy slid her fingers under the rim of her glasses and pushed against the corners of her eyes. She'd cried too much in the recent days and while she could put it down to the hormones racing around her body, Wendy knew it was more than that. It was fear, worry and insecurity that became harder and harder to fend off the closer she came to bringing a new life into the world. Wendy shook her head and reached for her book and for a moment, she remembered meeting its author earlier that day and what a moment that had been. How nice she'd been and how Wendy had made her laugh. Wendy made plans to rearrange some of the plants in the morning to make it a more conducive working environment. The idea that a novel may be written in her bookshop not only excited her to no end but also might be good for business. And not only might it be good for business, it also might be good for her. Friends of her own age were few and far between on the island. Since falling pregnant she'd had conversations with other mothers but everything they said dripped with pity and sometimes judgement and Wendy felt happier when it was just her and Maggie and her books and her plants. But now there was Elle J. Lark. Wendy opened the book to the signature and a tear slid down her cheek once more but this time, it was a happy one.

Luna awoke to a great banging at her door. At first she was certain it was just inside her dream. It was the sound of the ice splitting apart beneath her feet, opening up to reveal a great, dark cavern from which her own voice howled in agony. However, as her conscious mind moved forwards in her head, she realised that it was actually the sound of fists against the wood of her door.

'One sec!' she croaked as she stumbled out of bed too fast and almost crashed into the desk in the darkness. 'One second!'

'It's me, darling! Mrs M! Please open the door! Quickly!' she whisper-shouted up against the crease of the door. Luna didn't have many pieces of furniture in her room nor had she unpacked much of her case but still, she managed to walk into everything until eventually she reached the door and opened it without taking the latch off first. The chain reached its limit and pulled back against Luna's hand, and the door, slipping from her grasp, slammed shut in Mrs McArthur's face.

'Sorry!' Luna corrected her mistake and opened the door once more. 'Sorry, sorry! What's wrong?' Mrs McArthur was practically walking in circles, like a frantic bird pacing in a cage.

'First aid. There's a man downstairs. Do you know it? He needs help. I don't know first aid. Do you?'

'I don't, Mrs M. Did you say there's a man downstairs? Is everything okay?' Luna took hold of the elderly woman's shoulders and rubbed her thumbs in calming circles.

'He came here in the night. All by himself! I found him asleep on the floor in the hallway.' A sob began to rise in her throat and so Luna rubbed her thumbs in faster circles.

'Mrs M, you're not making any sense,' she said in the most soothing voice she had.

'He walked the train tracks, Miss Lark!'

'What? Why? Couldn't he have just got a train?'

'Well, according to him, no.'

'Mrs M, I'm sorry, I just don't understand.'

'Neither do I! He's talking gibberish! I think he's got hypothermia.'

'You're saying he walked the train tracks? The tracks that go over the sea? From John o'Groats?'

'Oh, just go and talk to him yourself.' Mrs M gently broke out from Luna's grasp. 'I need to find someone who knows first aid or a doctor or anyone who can give him a once-over. Make sure he's all right.' Mrs M skittered off down the corridor and began to bang on the next door. Luna closed her door, turned on the lights and hurriedly got ready.

Mrs M was right. The man certainly had slept in the hallway: she could tell by the giant puddle he'd left. It looked as if someone had tipped over a full bucket. *It must have been raining pretty heavily last night*, Luna thought. She pulled on her rucksack straps, securing the bulk of her backpack tightly against her back, and had to hop, skip and jump over the lake in the hallway to follow the noise of clinking glasses in the bar area where she first saw the man Mrs M had been twittering about.

'Hello? Hi. I'm assuming you're the person Mrs M is seeking first aid for?' There was no answer. She knew he'd heard her, even though he had his leather-clad back to her and the hood of his hoodie underneath his jacket was pulled tightly over his head. He'd turned his chin over his shoulder just enough to show he'd registered her presence, even if he wasn't going to fully acknowledge it. He was behind the bar, pouring himself what looked like a glass of whiskey with no ice.

'Are you supposed to be behind there?'

'*Mrs M* said I could help myself.'

'She probably meant to food and water. Maybe even a cup of tea. Not whiskey.' She watched him swig again and grimace. 'She's trying to find a doctor for you.'

'Is that what she's doing?' he said, downing the glass and proceeding to pour himself another.

'Is everything all right? Are you okay, I mean?'

'I'm fine. The daft old bat is worrying over nothing.' He turned to her then, his face pale and washed out under the large lights hanging over the bar, accentuating the dark rings under his eyes. *No wonder Mrs M is so worried*, she thought. *He looks like a grungy grim reaper.* However, there was a sadness that flickered over his gaunt face as he stared into his quickly emptying glass but it was gone in an instant. Replaced by a roll of his eyes and a small smile filled with a smugness that made Luna's skin crawl.

'Wow.' She folded her arms across her chest.

'Excuse me?' he said flatly.

'She's just trying to help you. And you stayed here last night for free and knowing Mrs M, she'll let you have that. Show a little respect.'

'All right. I'm sorry.' He shrugged, slugging back his drink. *You're not sorry,* she thought. *I don't think you've ever been sorry for anything in your entire life.*

'What's *supposedly* wrong with you anyway?' Luna pulled her arms around her tighter, a draught whistling through the bar.

'Nothing.' He shrugged, leaning against the shelves of bottles that rattled a little under his carelessness.

'Mrs M said you … you walked here? On the train tracks.'

'That's right.'

'Why didn't you just get a train – y'know, like normal people do?' She sniggered.

'The trains out here have been down for days, babe,' he said, cleaning dirt out from under his nails with his teeth.

'Don't call me babe. I came on a train here yesterday.' She tutted. 'You could have been killed walking the tracks like that. What are you, some kind of thrill seeker?'

'I am, but that's beside the point. What date do you think it was yesterday?' His face contorted into a Grinch-like expression, full of sinister glee.

'The fifteenth, why?' She sighed. This man's whole attitude and demeanour was entirely boring to Luna. She didn't like it when people didn't just say what they meant. Games weren't her bag, at all.

'Yeah, it's the twentieth today, babe.' He turned away from her again. 'Like a kid in a candy store' was definitely an appropriate phrase for the way his fingers wiggled in front of the rows and rows of bottles of liquor, wondering which one would he would let dance on his tongue next.

'I hope you're gonna pay for all that booze you're knocking back this early.'

'Sure thing, babe,' he said raising a bottle above his head before continuing to pour.

'Stop calling me babe and no, it's not the twentieth. I arrived here yesterday. I'll go and get my ticket to prove it if you like.'

He laughed and Luna felt heat rush through her veins. 'It wouldn't be any good.' He turned to her again, his smile wider now, his teeth bared. 'You may have come here on a train on the fifteenth but yesterday was not the fifteenth. See?' The man held up his phone with his red, grubby fingers and showed her the date hovering above a well-lit selfie of himself. His phone screen confirmed that it was indeed the twentieth of July.

'Your phone must be broken.' She shrugged, pulling her own phone from her coat pocket. Her screen said that today was the sixteenth.

'Well, it's broken *now*. It wasn't before I walked the ice tracks of doom, though.' He opened and closed several different apps, none of them opening any further than the home page where nothing seemed to load. 'No signal, no 4G, no nothing. I thought it might be because this place is in the arse end of nowhere but I think it's the blizzard that's on the way. It's messing with everyone's technology.' He sniffed, put his phone away and then wiped his nose on his sleeve.

'Ice? Blizzard? What are you on about? It's the middle of July.'

'Says the girl who's shivering. Look outside if you don't believe me.' He gestured to the window with his newly filled glass of amber liquid and he watched with contentment as Luna rushed to one of the big windows in the bar and pulled up the blind. She squinted in the brightness of the white light that filled the room and blinked until she could see the vast amount of snow that covered everything in sight. It was piled almost a foot high on the tables out front and the driveway had completely disappeared.

'You have *got* to be kidding,' she exhaled.

'It's been snowing here for like ... four days.' He sipped at his drink.

'No, it hasn't.' She shook her head and turned back to him, her eyes still adjusting to the brightness. 'I arrived here yesterday and it was cold, fine, but it wasn't snowing.'

'I've been tracking the blizzard that's headed for this island for ages.'

'You can't have. You're not listening, I only arrived yesterday.'

'That's great, but you won't have come by train because, like I said, the trains haven't been running for the last four days. So unless you walked the tracks like I did, there's no way you got here yesterday.'

'Did you fall and hit your head?' Luna could feel her head start to pound. She wasn't awake enough for this.

'And it's been snowing here for ages and it's going to keep getting worse until the blizzard finally hits tomorrow at midnight.'

'What are you, Cinderella?'

'No.' He grinned. 'I'm Jaxon.' Jaxon raised his glass to her.

'Jaxon?'

'With an X.' He winked.

'And you're a ... a ...'

'Storm-chaser.'

'Right.'

'Which is how I know there's a blizzard on its way and you either need to leave the island or batten down the hatches because it's gonna be a big one.'

'Leave the island? You mean via the tracks?'

'No other way out unless you want to swim it.'

'Well. I hope you're good with disappointment because yesterday was the fifteenth, today is the sixteenth and there is no blizzard on the way.' Luna turned on her heels and almost skidded on the puddle Jaxon had left in the hallway.

'All right, babe! See you later!' Luna could hear the smug smile in his voice.

'You're really gonna need to stop calling me that,' she hissed and ventured out into the snow.

A kind man near the beach gave Luna directions into town before she'd even built up the courage to ask. His dog bounded over to her, covering their shoes in snow. She made a fuss of the happy canine and the man tipped his flat cap as she left. It was a cheery start to her first day in Ondingside but Jaxon's words kept rolling over and over again in her mind, casting a cloud over her head.

The trains out here have been down for days, babe.

I've been tracking the blizzard that's headed for this island for ages.

There's no way you got here yesterday.

She was certain none of it was true. How could it be? He was surely either delusional or a prankster who got his kicks from fooling seemingly gullible people into believing the most outlandish scenarios he could possibly dream up. Luna shook her head and breathed in the cold, crisp sea air. She'd brought her backpack out with her laptop and notebook tucked neatly inside in the hopes of finding somewhere cosy and safe to get some work done for the afternoon. A productive first day was exactly what she needed and so she exhaled all the negativity that Jaxon had cast over her morning. Right now, all she wanted to think about was enjoying her first day in her new home but before the enjoyment could commence, Luna needed to be caffeinated.

As her mind had raced and retraced her ridiculous conversation with Jaxon, her feet had absentmindedly led the way and she was unsure how they'd led her, so brilliantly, right to the doorstep of a coffee shop. Quite a nice-looking one too. Much more modern than she'd expected for such a shabby seaside island. A chalkboard sign outside read:

BEHIND EVERY SUCCESSFUL PERSON IS A SUBSTANTIAL AMOUNT OF COFFEE.

As she pushed on the door, a bell rang out to signal her entrance and, for some unknown reason, her empty stomach somersaulted.

'Hello?' Luna called out and almost immediately she heard the squeak of a chair against the floor and the thunder of footsteps.

'Hi! Hello! I'm here! Hello! Hi!' Luna could hear the man shouting through the door behind the counter before he burst through it and almost tripped as he took his place behind the counter. 'Sorry! I was just going through the CCTV footage.'

'Everything all right?' Luna said, suppressing a smile.

'Yeah, all fine. Well ... things have been going missing and being moved. Just making sure no one's nicking anything whilst I'm in bed!' He laughed but then he went quiet and looked at her, properly, and his eyes narrowed. 'I *know* you.' Almost simultaneously, Luna had realised who he was, too, but she had been hoping she'd get away with it, if she could keep the dawning of recognition from her face.

'You won my pub quiz last year!' Beau laughed. She winced.

'Yes, it's me. I was hoping you wouldn't remember.'

'Remember? How could I forget?!' He smiled, his plump lips spread ear to ear.

'I suppose I did make a lasting impression, didn't I?' Luna clutched her reddening cheeks, trying to cool them down with her frozen fingers.

'I still have your winnings saved! They're at the Green Arrow in an envelope waiting for you. Unless the bar staff found it hidden behind the clock on the mantlepiece behind the bar. In which case, will you take an IOU?' He pulled his hands up by the side of his face in a little held shrug that Luna couldn't help but think was quite adorable. She thought, if he asked, she could blame her flushing cheeks on the sudden change from the cold outside to the warm shop. *I'm just thawing out,* she thought.

'How did you know I'd come back?' she smiled, wondering if maybe she was thawing out in more ways than one. He shrugged.

'I didn't. It was just wishful thinking.' Oof. Luna almost swooned at that one. What was wrong with her? She felt so unlike herself today. Usually, social interactions with strangers for longer than a few seconds made her start to feel a little trapped and panicked, like she was being held against her will and she needed to find a way to escape. She would start to think up exit strategies and ways she could verbally excuse herself from further conversation. Worse than that, often Luna would even avoid going into quiet coffee shops such as this one because the risk of one-on-one conversation was higher than if the shop were heaving with customers for potential chatter. She hadn't thought too far into why she felt this way but it didn't take a genius to figure out that Luna had always been abandoned by those she loved more often than most and in more ways than one. Her family were taken from her and then the man she loved *chose* to leave of his own accord. Any normal human would react in the same way as Luna: hold people at arm's length because if they didn't get close, when they eventually left it wouldn't hurt as much. And yet, here she was. Happily bundling into an entirely empty shop, where small talk was highly likely to be unavoidable, without hesitation or overthinking and although she had already met Beau once before, he was still practically a stranger ... so why did she feel so comfortable talking to him? Why did she actually *want* him to ask her questions about her life? And more importantly, why did she want to share the answers?

'Well, I gave the winnings to you,' Luna said, trying to clear away the rosy fog that had suddenly clouded her mind.

'I didn't feel it was fair, you won them.' He smiled, lopsidedly, and Luna cleared her throat.

'Well ... thank you. Maybe I'll come and collect them at some point?' *Are you hinting that you want to see him again?* she thought. *Oh my God, Miss Lark ... are you* flirting? Luna couldn't seem to get her head around the idea.

'I don't work there any more. Opened up this place a few months ago.' He gestured around at the empty chairs and tables and rolled his eyes.

'Well, I'm glad you did. There doesn't seem to be much else round here in the way of coffee shops.'

'No, and if people don't start coming in here there might not be for much longer!' He scratched the back of his head. 'I thought I was filling a gap in the market. Turns out that gap was there for a good reason.' He laughed, hollowly.

'I dunno, I reckon I could probably fund this shop single-handedly, y'know. I drink a lot of coffee. And I mean a lo-hot of coffee.'

'Are you one of those people who's like Oscar the Grouch pre-coffee and Elmo post?'

'Something like that. But I think you need to update your references. *Sesame Street* is a little dated.' Luna pulled a chair from one of the tables over to the counter and perched herself on it, leaning her elbow next to the cash register.

'*Sesame Street* is still on the telly!'

'You sound like an avid viewer.'

'Unashamedly!' He beamed. 'Who would you have said, then?'

'Voldemort and Luna Lovegood? Darth Vader and Jar Jar Binks?'

'And *Star Wars* isn't dated?' He raised a bushy eyebrow.

'Kylo Ren and Rey, then,' she said as if she were a know-it-all schoolkid.

'Nah.' He shook his head. 'I'm sticking with *Sesame Street*. That's where it's at.'

Luna smiled and felt herself batting her eyelids and wondering what he was thinking, in general, but also, what he was thinking *of her*. What was it about this man that had Luna not only weak at the knees, but wanting to share and flirt and be all the things she hadn't expected herself to be on this island? All the things she hadn't felt quite capable of just yet? Luna certainly didn't have the answers but there was a little fizzle of excitement in the pit of her stomach at the prospect of finding out.

'So, what'll it be?' he said as he whipped up a tea towel from under the counter and threw it across his left shoulder, like a warrior preparing for battle. 'Flat white?'

'Impressive.' She nodded. 'Are you part barista, part psychic? Are you able to tell everyone's exact coffee

243

order the moment they step into the shop? Just by looking at them?'

'What can I say? It's instinct.' He smiled and the coffee machine began to whir.

Luna had never really found conversation easy. Small talk wasn't her bag and she didn't really ever engage in 'chat'. She spoke to people when she felt discussion was necessary and advice needed to be given or received but she didn't often call anyone just ... because. Lottie used to call her nearly every day and Luna did enjoy listening to her rant and rave down the phone. However, Lottie often had to check Luna was still there every five minutes because her end of the line might as well have gone dead for all the talk Luna contributed. Beau was an entirely different story, though. Luna found herself asking questions and actually listening intently to the answers and it felt *effortless*. As if she'd had a thousand conversations with this man and there was such a familiarity that they seemed to share, as if they'd known each other for years. They'd finish each other's sentences and pause in just the right places when the other had something to say. Lulls in their dialogue just didn't exist because one topic flowed seamlessly into the next and Luna seemed insatiable when it came to knowing more about Beau and it seemed the feeling was mutual.

'I know it's hardly Piccadilly Circus in here but even so, I should probably finish looking through the CCTV footage ... but can I see you tonight? For dinner?'

'Not drinks? But I handled my booze so well last time . . .' Luna couldn't believe she felt okay joking about a memory that had made her squirm and blush only yesterday. Now, though, she'd say almost anything to see his smile. 'Yeah . . .' she nodded, unsure of why she felt so sure. 'Yeah, I'd love to, actually.'

'You sound . . . surprised?'

'I am, I suppose. Not that you've asked me. Not that I expected you'd ask! I'm thrilled you've asked! I'm not explaining myself very well.'

'Deep breaths . . .' Luna thought he was mocking her but his face was soft and kind and patient, no mockery in sight.

'I don't usually say yes. To anything. I say thank you but no, absolutely not then I run away and hide at home with my books and my intolerance to human interaction. I've always been quite solitary but my desire for solitude has increased dramatically over the past few years.'

'Hence . . .' he gestured outside, 'Ondingside?'

'Exactly. But . . . I dunno. Today feels . . . different.'

'Any reason why?' He tilted his head in a puppy-like fashion.

'No.' She shook her head. 'I think I'm just feeling brave today,' she said, feeling a warm glow radiate from within her. Luna could see Beau's chest puff up but he looked down at his hands as he swirled a silver jug of milk and tapped the bottom of it on the counter.

'Well, I count myself extremely lucky. Let the sixteenth

of July mark the joyous day on which ...' He looked up and pointedly raised his eyebrows.

'Miss Lark.' She was feeling brave but maybe not *that* brave.

'No first name? Or is it Miss?'

'That would make me Miss Miss Lark.'

'Why not.' He shrugged and began again, concentrating on the coffee once more. 'The sixteenth of July marks the joyous day on which *Miss Miss Lark*,' he glanced up at her and winked, 'was brave enough to accept my humble invitation to dine with me this evening at ... seven?' he said as he placed her flat white on the counter in front of her; a frothy number seven was written in the foam.

'Seven sounds perfect,' she grinned. She felt the back of her eyes prickle a little and before she embarrassed herself and got emotional over the very simple act of being asked to dinner, she took up the coffee and sipped it, swallowing past the little lump in her throat. 'Although,' Luna gave a little cough, 'it seems that there's a little bit of debate as to whether today is actually the sixteenth.' Luna rolled her eyes, casting her mind back to the way Jaxon called her 'babe' and she shuddered.

'Excuse me?' he laughed.

'Some guy turned up at the inn today claiming that today was actually the twentieth.'

'Blimey, was he drunk?'

'No, but he will be by now! He was drinking the bar

dry when I left. Poor Mrs McArthur probably won't say anything, though. She woke me up searching high and low for a doctor to give him the once-over. Make sure he didn't have hypothermia or concussion or god knows what else.'

'He'll be full of whiskey, pie and chips and in a room free of charge, by now.'

'I think he was just a bit of an attention seeker, to be honest.'

'Y'think?'

'Well . . . yeah.' She shrugged. 'Either that or he's mad.'

'Or he's right!'

'You really think four days have gone by without anyone noticing?'

'Stranger things have happened!'

' . . . have they? Name one.'

'It rained seaweed in Gloucester once.'

'What?'

'And it happened again exactly one year to the day afterwards.'

'Okay. That is weird. But definitely not weirder than a whole island skipping ahead four whole days!'

'True. He's probably just looking for attention, then.'

'Why don't you sound convinced?'

'I dunno. I have felt a bit . . . odd today. Like something isn't quite right.' Luna hated to put stock into Jaxon's story but she had to admit that she'd woken up feeling like an entirely different person. Her outlook on life had changed quite dramatically from the way she remembered feeling the night before and things that had once felt almost painful now seemed like a breeze. She would love to put it down to Ondingside's fresh sea air doing her good but now that she really thought about it, she knew overnight one-eighty in outlook wasn't normal. At least, not for her. 'Yeah, I suppose I have felt a little ... different. But it's just been such a good kind of different that I guess I've just been too busy ... enjoying it.' She bunched up her shoulders near her ears and enjoyed the way Beau scrunched his nose up at her clear happiness.

'I woke up feeling pretty warm and fuzzy myself, to be fair. But that doesn't explain why things have been moving about and going missing in here. I can live with feeling more positive than normal but cash missing from the register? Keys being in a different place to where I left them? That's the frustrating part.'

'You don't think that had something to do with Jaxon suddenly appearing, do you?'

'Jaxon?'

'That guy at the inn.'

'You're on a first name basis with the drunken story-teller?' He folded his arms.

'Only one way.' She couldn't help her lips from turning up at the corners. *Is he jealous?* she laughed in her head. 'I'm just Miss Lark to him. I'm Miss *Miss* Lark to you. Big difference.'

'I'll take it. My CCTV footage doesn't show anyone else in this shop except me, today.'

'What about last night?'

'I didn't get that far. *Someone* interrupted me by coming in and buying the first coffee I've sold in about three days.'

'Who came in three days ago?'

'Wendy from next door. Owns the second-hand bookshop.'

'Wendy?' She folded her arms across her chest, mimicking him. 'Wendy sounds like a first name to me!'

'Well, if you told me your name we'd all be equal. So, *now* whose fault is it?'

'Touché. Maybe I'll stop coming in for coffee then, if it makes looking at the CCTV any easier ... ?'

'If cash keeps going missing from the register then it doesn't matter if you come in or not. You don't fancy ... looking with me, do you?'

Luna stared at him blankly, weighing up how she felt about spending even more time with this man whose company felt so safe and familiar. She wanted to shout 'YES! I'LL SPEND THE WHOLE DAY WITH YOU, STRANGE MAN WHO I'VE HARDLY MET BECAUSE I LOVE HOW I FEEL AROUND YOU!' But poor Luna just couldn't quite figure out how to say that in a way that wasn't loud or sudden or that didn't make her come across ever so slightly insane. Sadly, she took just that little too long to answer and Beau took her fixed stare as an answer in itself. He quickly stood and wiped his already clean hands on his tea towel. 'Sorry, you've already agreed to dinner!' He gave a little high-pitched, strangled laugh. 'I shouldn't push my luck.'

Luna, admittedly, felt a little wave of relief that it would only be dinner. As much as she would have loved spending the day with Beau, too much too soon did make her fearful and she could already feel the familiar self-doubt seeping into her mind and spreading its tendrils through her thoughts. *You're not good enough for him, Luna. Wait until he hears about all of your emotional baggage, Luna. You're better off alone, Luna.*

'I'm only worried that you'll get fed up of me and very quickly retract your offer of dinner,' she mumbled, reaching for a black plastic lid on the counter and fitting it onto her coffee cup, sad to hide the number but not trusting herself to be able to drink the hot beverage without spilling it down herself in one way or another.

'I wouldn't!' he said hurriedly. 'I know I wouldn't. But dinner's good. Suspense. Exciting. Seven.'

'Seven.' She nodded.

'Okay.' He grinned.

'Okay.'

'Brilliant.' he said with a small thumbs-up.

'Great.' She giggled as she backed towards the door.

'Good.' He leant forward and missed the counter by a millimetre with his elbow and slipped. 'Seven.' He recomposed with a nod and a blush.

'Seven.' She waved and floated out of the shop.

Eighteen

Ten steps out of the door and to the right of Beau's shop, Luna felt that strange prickle of the hair on her neck beginning to rise and she heard an unmistakable intake of breath.

'You're Elle J. Lark,' breathed a woman's voice. Luna hadn't even turned around.

'I am,' Luna replied, spinning to see a woman dressed in a long-sleeved, floor-length floaty silk dress, her matching slippers poking out from underneath the fabric in the snow. The woman was holding a watering can in one hand and her bump with the other.

'Come in! Come in! Out of the snow! Out of the cold!' she said, disappearing into her shop with a ring of a bell. Luna shuffled back past Beau's window and as she looked through the glass, he pointed to the bookshop she was about to enter and mouthed, 'Wendy!' She gave him a thumbs-up for the heads-up.

'I can't believe it. I just can't believe it. You're you.

You're actually you! You're Elle J. Lark. I'd recognise your headshot anywhere.' Wendy conveniently had Luna's latest novel on the shop counter which she whisked around and then, hauling herself up onto a stool with great difficulty, she peeled back the cover and showed Luna her own awkward author photo.

'Yes, I am me,' Luna laughed. 'You're reading my novel now?' Luna took the book from her and closed it, having had enough of staring at her own grimace.

'I can't get enough. I've read everything. All of them. I want more. More, more, more.'

'Well, hopefully you'll get it! I'm contracted for two more novels but ...'

'Writer's block?'

'Something like that. It's more just the ideas. I'm sure words will come when I've got one but I seemed to have completely run out of any inspiration.'

'And you came to Ondingside to find some?' One of Wendy's eyebrows disappeared up underneath her headscarf that was pulled tightly across the front of her hairline and then tied underneath a pile of flaming curls.

'I just needed some quiet. London's noisy. In every sense.'

A look of concern flickered across Wendy's face but she seemed to think better of it and changed tack. 'D'ya wanna hear something funny?' She leant as far as her bump would allow her to across the counter. 'I set up a table and chair in the back of the shop this morning. I have no idea why, but when I woke up this morning, I had this funny idea that that was a really good idea. And I was right. It's now a quiet, peaceful space for a potential customer to sit and peruse some of the books on offer.' Luna looked past some of the many plants and she could see that a table, two of its legs propped up by paperbacks, and two mismatched chairs were indeed sat between the shelves that lined the walls.

'That is a lovely idea.' Luna nodded.

'Don't you get it?' Wendy hissed excitedly, but Luna blinked blankly. 'It can be for *you*! To work! To write! Imagine that. An actual author, writing their next novel in *my* shop! And not just any author . . . YOU. My *favourite* author!' Wendy would have bounced up and down in her seat if her ginormous bump would have let her and so instead, the excitement fizzed around her, electrifying the air. 'I promise I won't get in the way and you can send me next door on a coffee run whenever you like. Beau will be thrilled with the business. I'll be good as gold. I swear.' She crossed her heart and probably hoped to die of fangirling.

'You had me sold on this idea when you said "quiet, peaceful space"!' Luna laughed and caught Wendy's hands as she almost wobbled off her stool. 'Are you sure I won't be a bother? I won't be putting people off coming in and looking around?'

'You're the first person to come in and look around in absolutely forever. Honestly. A famous author using my shop to write a novel is probably the biggest selling point I have right about now. I might even make posters.' Wendy saw Luna's eyes widen. 'I won't make posters. No posters. I would ask you to tweet about the shop in exchange for a writing space but my phone's been playing up today.'

'Mine too. I keep checking it even though I know there won't be anything there.'

'I'm a slave to the 'gram.' Wendy sighed, flipping her phone over on the counter, its blank screen glaring up at her.

'Twitter's my vice. I wish I didn't but get such a buzz out of hating Piers Morgan. Actually, scratch that, I get a buzz out of Piers Morgan making me feel like I'm an amazing human being in comparison. I'm actually starting to miss him and that's something I never thought I'd say. Ever. In a million years.' Luna, too, checked her unchanging phone. Old habits did indeed die hard.

'Weird how both our phones are being funny,' Wendy said with a little scrunch of her shoulders that seemed to say *isn't it fun that we're bonding.*

'I think it's the whole island. The weather's really caused a bit of chaos.'

'How so?' Wendy's lips scrunched together into a delicious smile and she leaned into what might be gossip. Despite wanting to fling thoughts of Jaxon and his idiocy as far out of her mind as possible, Luna knew it was futile. Whiskey-swilling Jaxon, with his leather jacket and bad manners, had well and truly rubbed Luna up the wrong way and so she might as well embrace the rage he'd ignited in her.

'This total twat turned up at Nobody's Inn this morning.' Luna took a moment to enjoy her outburst and Wendy's magnified pupils dilated. 'Walked the train tracks here and gave Mrs McArthur the fright of her life.' She revelled in the fact that she could name places and people and not have to explain where and who they were. She loved that Wendy would already know, which made her story so much easier to tell.

'What's that got to do with the weather?'

'He claimed that today is the twentieth of July.'

'What do you mean?'

'He said today wasn't the sixteenth. It's the twentieth. Said the trains have been down for about four days but I tried to explain to him that I came here by train yesterday.'

'Wait, wait, wait. Some guy walked the tracks from John o'Groats to Ondingside?'

'Because apparently the trains aren't running.'

'Because the weather's been this bad.'

'And it's been this bad for four days.'

'Riiiiiiiiiight.'

'I know.'

'Where is he now?'

'Probably tucked up in a bed in the inn having a lovely time being waited on hand and foot by poor gullible Mrs McArthur.'

'Is he actually, y'know, *all there*?' Wendy whispered. 'Maybe he actually does need a bit of TLC?'

'Honestly, if you'd met him . . . he's bad news. If someone's capable of being that much of an arsehole, all they need is a kick up the backside.'

'What does he look like?'

'Scraggly hair, hoodie underneath a leather jacket . . . think Poor Man's James Dean.'

'You're not doing much to put me off here, Luna . . .'

'Sorry, did I not mention what a total arse he was?'

'Mmm. They seem to be my type, sadly.' Wendy absentmindedly put a hand to her bump.

'I'm sorry.'

'Don't be. Just don't introduce me to this . . . this . . .'

'Jaxon.'

'He even has a bad boy name. Keep him away from me. I'll take one look at that leather jacket and I'll do anything he says.'

'Why?'

'For some reason, in my handful of experiences, I get bored with nice guys. I seem to always stay with bad ones, the ones who keep me guessing and keep me fighting for their affections. It becomes a game, I guess. I want to be the one that changes them, the one they finally settle down with, and I felt like I couldn't quit until I'd done what I had set out to do.'

'That's horrible.'

'I know. I do know that. But when I'm mixed up with

someone like that it becomes like a drug. It's hard to quit. I'll always say to myself "when they do ten bad things, I'll leave". They get to nine and I'm thinking this is it, y'know? This is it, it's actually gonna happen.' Wendy moved her clenched fists in circles, like she was ready to fight the thin air in front of her. 'Then they do something good and win me over, the counter resets to zero and I'm back at square one.' She slumped, dropping her hands onto the counter with a bang. 'When it was just me, it didn't really matter that I was being reckless and stupid. I'd be heartbroken for approximately two days when they inevitably cheated or ran off and then after a night with Ben, Jerry, and their uncle Häagen-Dazs, I'd be on the lookout again. Now that I have this little one,' she rubbed her bump with both hands, 'the risk just isn't worth it. I'm not even really looking for anyone now. Not even nice ones. I think we'll be fine just the two of us for a while.'

'Now that I'm living here, I can help out, too ...?' Halfway through saying this, Luna realised how over-familiar she was being and phrased it as a question instead of asserting the sisterly authority she seemed to be feeling. Who did she think she was, imposing herself and her probably unwanted help on a total stranger?

'Really?' Wendy sat up straight.

'Only ... only if you wanted? You're letting me use your shop to work in so we'll be seeing more of each other anyway. When the little one comes I'd be happy to help.' Wendy's face broke into a grin and Luna could see through her thick glasses that her eyes were shining. 'When are you due?'

'Umm,' Wendy tried to shake the wobble from her voice, 'my due date is the seventeenth, so anything can happen at this point!'

'That's tomorrow! Oh my goodness, what are you doing working?!' Luna had a sudden vision of Wendy bursting and a baby flying out from between her legs and Luna having to do her best to catch the poor little mite.

'This is hardly working, now, is it?' Wendy laughed, throwing her hands up to her desolate shop. 'I've brought more plants through that door than customers have walked through it. No one comes in here so I basically just sit in an armchair in the back reading. I'd only be doing that in the flat upstairs if I wasn't down here so I may as well do it down here and at least have the potential to earn a bit of money.'

'Beau next door said the same thing. Maybe you should team up! Book slash coffee shop.'

'That's not a bad idea, but I think Beau thinks I'm a bit strange. We grew up on the same street and he still looks at me in the funny way he did back then. Never said anything, though, which is more than most boys his age did around that time.'

'Nah, I'm sure he doesn't think that,' Luna lied. 'Well, I'll make a start by buying a cactus, please.'

'You actually want to *buy* something?'

'You need to work on your salesman skills.'

'Sorry.' Wendy dramatically cleared her throat. 'Welcome to my shop of dreams and hopes! Every plant will bring you joy and every book will fill you with wonder!' Wendy woodenly gestured to the plants and books with a large grin plastered on her face, her eyes unblinking.

'Needs work, but it's a start.' Luna laughed. 'I intend on buying a house on the island to live here permanently and I believe that every home should have a houseplant. Everything I've ever tried to grow dies within about fifteen minutes of me owning it but I used to love my ex-fiancé's cactus and that thing was sturdy as a rock. Might as well have been a rock, actually. So I think cacti is where it's at. One prickly green thing please.'

Luna took her prickly green thing to the table in the back of Wendy's shop and felt a little fizz of excitement at the idea of setting up in her new 'office'. Now she wished she'd packed her bag a little more efficiently. Her laptop, notebook and pen were really all she needed but Luna liked having an array of stationery within reach, just in case. In reality, Luna felt a little scared at the thought of absolutely no way of procrastinating. She had a habit of writing a hundred words or so and rewarding herself with a fifteen-minute scroll through Twitter. No reception or 4G meant no Twitter. (Although she did write and attempt to send another message in Lottie's direction just in case, which said *All fine here. Please don't think I'm ignoring you*!) No pencil case meant no doodling, sketching or writing letters to her past self on scented parchment. She also hadn't brought her diary which was another brilliant way to justifiably pass the time. Putting dates in her diary from past events and scrolling through her emails to find the dates of future ones was *important* and no one could possibly tell her off for doing that instead of writing. Luna would be forced to actually face the blank page without all of these things close at hand and the excitement of a new office very quickly dwindled. *Tomorrow?* questioned the little gremlin in her brain who spouted all of her most indulgent ideas. *I could start tomorrow?* Luckily, she was a rational, logical and (sometimes) productive person and she knew she was highly capable of starting and finishing a novel. She had done it five times before and she would probably do it five times again in her lifetime.

Luna opened her notebook and flicked through the pages until she found the next blank page and began to write the date. She slowed as she swirled the 'Y' on the end of July and then stopped altogether. She rolled the previous page over and stared at the date in the corner.

July 16th 2019

It was definitely her handwriting. The notes below it were certainly hers, too but she had absolutely no recollection of writing them. She flipped back a second page. The same date sat in the corner. Feverishly, she pulled back page after page dated July 16th 2019 in her own handwriting.

'Four pages.' She breathed through her dry mouth.

'What was that?' Wendy called over a row of ferns.

'Nothing,' she croaked. 'Nothing!' She said a little louder. 'Oh my god!' she whispered, clutching her head, still staring down at the scribbles in her handwriting that she was sure she had never scribbled. 'I'm going mad. I must be ... either that or ...' No, she refused to believe Jaxon was right. How could he be?

'Wendy.' Luna closed the notebook and stood up so abruptly that the chair squeaked against the floor. 'Wendy.' She walked to the door, knocking several plant pots as she went. 'I'm just popping next door for another coffee.'

'Oooh, I'd love a—'

But the bell rang above the door and Luna had already gone.

Nineteen

The Notebook

Luna crashed through the door of the coffee shop. The bell rang so furiously Beau jumped even though he watched her storm through the door and charge towards him.

'Look at this,' she said dropping the notebook onto the counter.

'Hey, is everything all right? You look a bit—'

'Open the notebook and look at it.' She hadn't even thought to put her coat on before she left the bookshop but her blood was pumping so vigorously around her body that she didn't notice the chill.

'This is yours?'

'Yes.'

'I don't really know how I feel about reading your

diary, Miss Lark.' Beau pushed it towards her but she rolled her eyes and slid it back.

'It's not my diary. It's my *journal*.'

'There's a difference?' he asked. She closed her eyes and clenched her jaw.

'Beau ... just open it,' she said and Beau gave a little sigh.

'Oookay.' Beau opened the notebook with suspicious, narrowed eyes but his lips were still turned up playfully. The book naturally fell open at the latest entry.

'The date. Look at the date,' Luna said past her fingers as she chewed her thumbnail.

'It's today's date,' he said with a dismissive shake of his head.

'Now go back a page,' she said as she turned the page for him.

'It's ... well, that's odd.' He picked up the book. 'Were you drinking last night?' He laughed but then he flipped back another page and his smile slipped. 'And ... the night before?'

'And the night before that? And before that? Beau ... every page for the last four days is dated as July 16th.'

'Why?' he asked, laughing again.

'I don't remember, Beau. I can't remember writing any of that.'

'Lots of people's memories go when they get hammered.'

'Beau, I haven't been drinking. Just because the first time I met you I was legless doesn't mean that's a usual occurrence. I need you to take me seriously right now.' Luna could feel her knees starting to shake. It was a mixture of urgency and frustration and she was starting to wonder if maybe coming to Beau for whatever reason she felt was a good idea, was actually a mistake. After all, she didn't really know him at all ... or did she?

'Okay, hold on. You need to back up for me a little bit.' Beau ruffled the back of his hair, his eyes wide and his eyelids flapping wildly. 'Has that Jaxon fella got to you? Has he made you start believing in that tall tale of his you told me about?' Luna could hear venom creeping into his voice and she felt the sting of his abrupt jealously. His attachment to her made little sense within the context of the reality they knew. *But if Jaxon's right,* she thought, *maybe Beau and I have more history than we know.*

'I haven't seen Jaxon since this morning. He hasn't said anything to me since. I sat down in Wendy's shop, who, by the way, I think is awesome, I opened my notebook to start work and was faced with four days' worth of notes I have no memory of. All apparently made on the same day. Your name makes an appearance several times.' She thought maybe that would make him smile, but his face remained serious and unchanged.

'It's not possible.' Beau shook his head and slid the notebook back to her again, this time with a defiance that made her clench her fists.

'I know it isn't. Understand that this morning, I

265

thought Jaxon was either a raving lunatic or a sociopathic attention seeker. He still could be one of the two but the point is, we don't know.'

'What's made you change your mind?'

'I haven't changed my mind, Beau. The evidence has changed. Before this,' she gestured to the notebook, 'we had nothing to support Jaxon's story. Now ...' She started to feel the futility creeping into the conversation. Then she had a brainwave. 'Remember when you said you'd woken up feeling differently today? Maybe there's a reason.'

'Yeah, I think the reason is I had a good night's sleep and ...'

'And what?' Her heart buoyed with hope.

'And ... I've just had a good morning.' It sank. 'It can't be anything more than that. It certainly can't be because of whatever Jaxon was spouting.' He scoffed. 'What was it? That today's actually four days later than we think it is? C'mon ...' Beau picked up a tea towel and started wiping down his already very clean coffee machine that he'd already wiped down twice that day.

'Humour me for a second.' She followed him and placed the open notebook on the top of the green machine and she pointed at his name in her handwriting on the bottom of the page five entries ago. 'What if the reason you and I woke up feeling so different because there have been four days in between now and what we think was yesterday. What if ... what if we've met before?' He looked at her

266

then and she could see there was a small hint of softness returning to his eyes.

'I would remember that,' he said delicately.

'I thought I would, too. But according to my journal we've met every day for the last few days and every day our meeting has made enough of an impact on me to write about it. And I never write *anything* these days! That has to mean *something*?' She leant her arms on the machine and her chin on the backs of her fingers. Beau stepped back and leant against the opposite counter top where cartons of oat, soy and coconut milk stood behind him in a neat row.

'What could even possibly happen in four days?' he asked, tucking his fingers under his armpits.

'I don't know, but if Jaxon is right and that's true, then evidently quite a lot.' Luna braced herself for what she wanted to say next. Part of her prayed Beau would interrupt her but she knew if anything could convince him that something had certainly changed within her, it was this. 'I've never felt like this,' she admitted, quietly and all at once. Every nerve ending was tingling.

'Like what?' he said, a little too unimpressed for what had felt like quite a momentous statement for Luna.

'... happy?' She shrugged. He raised an eyebrow.

'You've never felt ... happy.'

'I've felt happy but I've not had an easy few years, put it that way.' A silence ballooned between them.

'I dunno,' he said, finally puncturing the atmosphere

as he fiddled with something on the floor with the tip of his shoe. 'It's still a big leap to make. Sometimes people just . . . feel differently.'

'I don't think it's that simple.' Luna lifted the book to look through its pages again, hoping that something might jump out and jog her memory.

'Sometimes it is, *Miss Lark*.' Beau almost hissed her name and she picked up the notebook from the counter and held the open book to her chest, suddenly feeling a little foolish at putting her writing on display, even if she did feel so detached from it. Beau put both of his hands on the table and as they shifted, Luna could see his palms were leaving sweaty marks on the counter. Was she making him nervous or anxious? Upset, even? He inhaled deeply and she could hear the shake in the sound. He closed his eyes for a moment and Luna wondered why it was that he felt he needed to compose himself.

'Sometimes,' he said softly, his eyes still closed, 'you find that people have a quick change of heart or mind. They realise that their outlook on life has been entirely skewed and then all of a sudden it gets clicked back into place. It's not because there's an outside force that's made them feel that way, as much as you wish that were the case. It isn't a change in weather that makes you think they'll come back when the seasons change. Sometimes people just . . . change their minds. Just like that and without warning. They inexplicably feel differently and there's nothing you can do about it. That's just the way life goes.'

He opened his eyes but he didn't look at Luna. He kept his head tilted down and away from her and it pained her to see him look so forlorn. That emotion didn't sit right on his cheerful features. He turned away from her and continued wiping down every already clean surface he could find and when he sniffed more than once, she knew he'd made himself emotional. Luna didn't know why but she wasn't stupid. She knew there was a story to Beau's sudden speech and maybe his happy, carefree nature stood in front of a lot of hurt that hadn't really healed.

'I agree,' Luna said, keeping her voice low. 'People can be fickle. People do just up and leave at a moment's notice and give very little explanation as to why ... but not me. I have never been fickle and I have never been sudden. I keep myself to myself which means I know me better than anyone on this planet and I *know* I wouldn't just wake up and ... and *be different*. I don't *do* different.' Luna felt a heat flush through her system and her eyes started to sting. Yesterday, she would never have started a speech let alone get this far through so she swallowed past the lump that was forming in her throat and continued. 'I don't like change and yesterday, whenever we think yesterday was, I would never have walked into a quiet coffee shop and risked having to have a human interaction or a conversation longer than a few seconds, let alone sit and chat for the best part of an hour to a complete stranger. Not through lack of capability but through a lack of trust and an even bigger lack of a desire to be close to anyone or let anyone close to me. I've learnt that the closer people get, the harder it is when they inevitably leave and so I've made a huge effort not to let that happen. And yet ...' She gestured around the empty shop where the silence surrounding them felt close and suffocating, 'here I am. Spending time with you minutes after we've just been reunited after an incredibly embarrassing first encounter, that I was even happy to joke about by the way, and I've just been next door and enjoyed Wendy's company so much that her bookshop has now become my office! It's not normal!' She laughed through a sob. 'This isn't me. This is a much nicer, kinder, calmer, more carefree version of me that I don't believe I've ever met before and, for me, that kind of change doesn't happen overnight. Not after everything I've been through,' she finished with a small but definite nod.

Beau had avoided her gaze for a while but when he eventually lifted his eyes to meet hers as she spoke, Luna could see he seemed to be as moved as she was by her own sudden passion. 'I may have found some "get up and go" but that doesn't mean I'll get up and leave. They're two very different things, Beau.' She half smiled at him as a tear escaped. She quickly wiped it away, inhaled quickly and huffed out the breath as she opened the book back out on the top of the coffee machine. 'So.' She smiled properly now. 'What do you think this all means, eh?'

Beau pushed himself to standing from his slouched position, screwing the tea towel into a tight ball in his fist as he turned away from her. 'It means whatever you want it to mean. But I can't risk believing in some drunken thrillseeker's bullshit just because I woke up feeling a little happier than I did yesterday. That's obviously not reality. Reality is that people change and people leave and the sooner you learn that the easier it is to swallow life's bitter pills.'

'Are you kidding me?' she whispered, but he didn't turn around. 'Are you actually *kidding* me?' she said, hitting the top of the coffee machine, causing the beans to rattle about in their perspex compartment. Luna couldn't understand her own anger. Why was she *so* furious at him? Sure, he'd rejected her brave speech and she felt extremely hurt that she'd offered him her friendship and told him she wouldn't disappear at a moment's notice and he'd quite literally turned his back on her ... but even she could feel that her anger seemed disproportionate to being snubbed by someone who was a stranger.

Was this yet even further proof that Luna and Beau had indeed met before? Luna was livid and the only way she could explain her seemingly infinite anger was if she actually knew Beau a lot better than she thought she did and his cold actions were out of character. Luna snatched up her notebook and dramatically slammed it shut before storming out into the snowy street, slamming the door to the coffee shop behind her, too. Luna didn't offer friendship to anyone, let alone someone she'd (allegedly) just met. So if Beau didn't understand what a momentous occasion that was for her nor have the decency to let her down gently, he would find that not only had he lost his only customer but also the only potential candidate for a friend.

Luna's rage carried her all the way back to the inn. There was nothing like the fire of anger to keep you warm against the chill of freshly fallen snow. She felt like she could have melted the snow in her wake.

'Where is he?' Luna said as she flung the front door to the inn open wide. She kicked snow and sludge off her boots against the door frame.

'Who, my dear?' asked Mrs McArthur, jumping at the noise of the door banging shut behind Luna who was now marching towards the front desk.

'Jaxon,' Luna spat. 'The man who barged his way into this inn this morning and had you beating down my door.'

'He's at the bar,' Mrs McArthur said with wide unblinking eyes that took in Luna's seething state.

'Should have guessed,' Luna grunted and swiftly turned towards the bar.

'Sweetheart,' Mrs McArthur cooed as she reached over the counter, caught Luna's icy hand and rubbed her thumb in calming circles, 'is everything all right? You don't seem like yourself.'

Luna wanted to reassure Mrs McArthur but there was

no denying that she was indeed not like herself. Luna was actually entirely unsure of who 'herself' was now. Jaxon was sat on his own with a swiftly emptying bottle of whiskey in front of him and a quickly filling glass. Luna reached over the bar, picked up an empty glass and marched across to interrupt Jaxon's binge.

'Take a look,' she said, feeling satisfied as the notebook's leather covering slapped against the wooden table. Unstartled and unfazed, Jaxon swigged from his glass and poked the pages open with a grubby finger and a grimace, as if she'd placed roadkill in front of him.

'Have you written me a poem?' He smirked as his eyes flickered across Luna's cursive handwriting.

'Look at the date,' Luna said through her teeth. She tried to stay calm but the bottle shook as she poured herself a small glass of whiskey. His eyes drunkenly swayed up to the right-hand corner of the page.

'I've already told you today isn't the sixteenth.' His concentration returned to swilling his drink around in the glass, its amber contents rising and falling in his practised hand.

'*I know*. If it is, it has been the sixteenth for the last four days, according to ... well ... me.' Luna flipped the pages back one by one until his attention finally swung back to the book and his eyes widened. He swivelled in his seat, the glass clattering against the table as he almost dropped it and he picked up the book with both hands.

'Well, well, well. Finally realised I was right, then?'

His hazy eyes started to focus a little more and he looked from date to date.

'You didn't give me any evidence this morning.' She shrugged, slowly sipping her whiskey. 'Now that I have it, I believe it. At least, I think I do. Either you and your story are correct or I've gone mad but either way, something's not right.'

'So what's the plan, then?' He closed the book and poured himself a celebratory drink.

'The plan?'

'We're at the precipice of history here, babe.' His voice raised and Luna could feel Mrs McArthur lurking in the doorway, watching them with eager, worried eyes.

'Don't call me that.' She took another, longer sip.

'Something big is happening on this island and we could be the ones to uncover it. Listen, I'm camping on the tracks tonight to watch the island from a distance and see if there's anything freaky going on. You coming?'

'Are you serious?' she asked, but by the look of his unfaltering expression, he was. Camping out in the snow felt like the last way Luna wanted to spend her evening. Especially with someone who made a point of trying to intimidate her. However, part of her was so intrigued that a 'yes' almost slipped out of her mouth before she'd really thought it through.

'No,' she said, finally. 'You need someone on the inside. Things might happen here in Ondingside that you can't witness from a distance. I can report what I've found out, if anything, tomorrow.'

'But it seems when you stay here, sweetheart,' he opened her notebook again and tapped her own repetitious writing, 'you can never remember anything.' As annoying as he was, he did have a point.

'I'll write myself a note or a letter or something? To explain it to myself. Or I can use my phone to make a video, tonight? I reckon no one will be able to convince me of what we think is going on except myself.'

'Yeah, that sounds about right,' Jaxon agreed, downing double as much as Luna had poured for herself in the first place.

'Who even *are* you?' she said, her face crinkling as she watched him swallow such a potent liquid without so much as a wince. She could practically hear his liver screaming.

'I told you, I'm a storm chaser.' One of Jaxon's eyebrows raised and for a moment, Luna's breath caught.

'I know you're "Jaxon the Storm Chaser", but . . . don't storm chasers have like . . . teams, or something? People to look out for each other so that you're all safe? Or are you a "lone wolf"?'

Luna wasn't often sassy; it was probably part of this change she was feeling but also partly because of the fiery whiskey that was sliding down her throat. Despite her newfound sass, she still had to look away from him once she'd said it.

'Something like that,' he said, looking wistfully out of the window.

'Aren't you supposed to have equipment? Cameras? Radars? Or is this just a hobby?'

'We're not the cast of *Twister*, honey. I don't do this for science,' he sneered.

'What do you do it for then?'

'I dunno. Fun,' he said with an over-pronounced 'F'.

'So you're an adrenaline junkie?'

'Sure,' he huffed.

'Isn't it dangerous?'

'Isn't that the fun?'

'It sounds like you have a death wish.'

'Says you, here in the middle of potentially the most exciting freak weather conditions the Earth has ever seen.'

'I didn't come looking for it. Seems like *it* found *me*.'

'So why *did* you come here?' he asked, leaning closer so that she could smell the smokey scent of booze on his warm breath.

'Is that any of your business?' she said, leaning back.

'No.' He shook his head. Luna was sure he'd continue to pry. She'd become accustomed to people pushing and prodding when she didn't give them the answers they were looking for and so she was surprised, maybe even a little disappointed, when Jaxon didn't. 'I'm just saying, this place is boring as shit. Everyone here is ancient. There's absolutely nothing to do unless you like reading and knitting. The silence is the most annoying thing about this place. Doesn't it drive you *mad*?' he said, swiping his hair out of his eyes.

'Maybe I like reading and knitting,' she said and he smiled at her then. A smile that wasn't necessarily warm, lopsided or particularly kind but it made her stomach flip all the same. Luna wondered if this was the sort of smile that would win over Wendy despite the amount of heartache that had come before it. Jaxon certainly seemed like the heartbreaking sort. 'Anyway. Ondingside is clearly more exciting than it looks.'

'Ah, yes, but the question is,' he sat back now and Luna found herself leaning towards him, 'are you?'

Twenty

Train Tracks

Jaxon was indeed well equipped for such an extraordinary camping trip. He had parked his car at John o'Groats station, and in the boot was a hiking rucksack filled with several thick blankets, heat packs, a pair of binoculars, a tent, thermals to go under his clothes, extra socks and gloves and a portable charger for his phone on which he planned to film the island from his makeshift campsite. He had it all planned out. After carefully but quickly scaling the tracks back to his car, he grabbed a meal deal from a local shop and scoffed it down pretty quickly. He stocked up on Pringles, Starbursts and cans of Diet Coke to go with the bottle of whiskey he'd snatched from behind the bar at Mrs McArthur's inn and he changed into his thermals in the back seat of his car. Jaxon donned his helmet with attached headlamp and although tired and tipsy from the booze, he made his way back towards Ondingside.

He had always been good at sneaking in and out of restricted areas and bragged about his ability to blag his way past bouncers, ushers and security. He always saw barriers of any kind as a welcome challenge to improve his skills; however, even he had been surprised at how deserted John o'Groats station seemed to be and how little anyone was doing to prohibit him from climbing on the tracks. The station was closed for business and that, it seemed, was that. It made his task much easier, but he did love a challenge.

As Jaxon walked the tracks, loaded up with equipment like a donkey, his thoughts and his heart began to race. Memories swam in his mind's eye of the last time he'd visited the island – less than a year ago when his friends realised that Ondingside would be the cheapest place for a stag do for a bunch of storm chasers with no money. It was technically abroad considering they had to go 'over seas' to get to it, booze was cheap and they could all bunk together in one or two rooms for the weekend. Said Stag wasn't too thrilled at first but stopped complaining when he realised just how far and how drunk a tenner would get him. The weekend went as disappointingly as they had expected, though maybe not for all of them. Jaxon's relationship with Bella had always been on and off with the ons being as disastrous as the offs. The trip to

Ondingside had coincided with one of their biggest rows and Jaxon had been looking forward to a night of getting drunk. He definitely hadn't anticipated how awestruck he was going to feel when he met the red-headed bookworm reading at the bar. She laughed when he wasn't trying to be funny and he loved that it was she who had suggested going back to his room. She knew what she had wanted and she wasn't coy about getting it and Jaxon had been bowled over by her playful boisterousness. The night they had spent together had been unlike anything he'd ever had before and he realised the closer he got to her, the closer he wanted to be ... which terrified him. So much so that he woke before she was done dreaming and left on the first train. Back to Bella and back to what was comfortable and convenient. Back to the destructive kind of love that beat him down and left him broken. It was the kind of love he felt he deserved.

Memories of the girl with the hair and the book at the bar often clouded his head like her perfume had done as they had lain tangled in his cheap room and he let those memories torture him. The idea of seeing her again now that Bella had gone for good gave him a hope he'd never dared let himself feel and ever his fear wasn't able to douse the flame. It drove his feet further and further back to the island, and back to her.

Jaxon wondered where the best vantage point would be as he carefully picked each step along the tracks, the sea spray often splashing into his eyes as the waves collided in the darkness below him. But it didn't take long to figure out, as the light of his headlamp showed him when his feet suddenly hit snow. Jaxon hadn't noticed in the darkness on his route to the island nor when he had been walking away from Ondingside but now that he was making the journey once more, his vigilance turned up to its fullest, it became abundantly clear that snow began quite abruptly. As he walked on the clear stony tracks, he could see up ahead as he raised his head and the lamp upon it that there was a distinct line between stone and snow. Jaxon carefully pitched his tent a couple of feet back from the frosty white edge and settled in underneath the blankets, his binoculars poised, and waited.

Hours passed and Jaxon could feel his hope beginning to dwindle. Not even so much as a drop of rain had fallen from the sky. The sea spray had tricked him many a time as it splashed up and hit his skin. The binoculars would spring to his eyes but would show him nothing but clear air. The sea kept roaring and seemed to become more violent as the hand ticked closer to midnight. Jaxon could feel the wind filling up the tent, threatening to snatch it out from over him and although he was underneath at least ten layers, the nip of the air still managed to make his skin prickle and the hair on his arms raise.

Jaxon had opened the camera on his phone so that if anything should happen, it would already be in position to film but so far, there had been nothing camera-worthy in the slightest. At eleven fifty-eight, Jaxon was about to begin packing it in and packing up but as if in answer to his resignation, everything went still. The extreme change in atmosphere caused Jaxon to hold his breath for a second and he felt calmer than he had in years. It was as if the world threw itself into slow motion. The sea stopped its roaring and splashing and, instead, purred softly and rocked gently underneath Jaxon's tent. The entire island stood still. All the lights of town stopped their twinkling, the trees stopped their swaying and all life hushed, as if Jaxon held the remote control to Ondingside and had accidentally hit mute. Jaxon inhaled the misty sea scent. As he exhaled, the clock struck midnight and it began to snow.

'Holy shit,' Jaxon breathed as he watched the snow-flakes begin to tumble from the sky over Ondingside and Ondingside alone. Like a sieve sprinkling icing sugar directly over a Victoria sponge, the sky dusted only the island with its chilly delights and nowhere else. Jason watched, mesmerised by the snow as each flake twirled in the breeze and landed only a few feet away from him. Each tiny speck floated downwards to join the ever-growing army, already in formation from the (apparent) many nights before, although the warriors dared to come no further, as though they were attempt-ing to build a shield against the outside world, walling in the residents of the island. Ondingside had become a lifesize snow globe. It seemed it had been picked up and turned on its head and fiercely shaken, along with the lives of the people within it. For a few minutes, despite being at a safe distance from the snowfall, Jaxon had completely forgotten why he was there. His binoculars sat unused in his lap, his phone still locked in his hand, the camera pointed towards his jeans, and any trace of a storm-chasing, blizzard-hunting, adrenaline junkie bad boy had entirely disappeared. The Jaxon who now sat engulfed in blankets, who was transfixed by the sky and its beauty, was merely a boy. A boy who simply loved the snow. A boy from the mainland who, once upon a time, fell in love with a girl on the island and had returned not for storms or sea or snow ... but for her.

Vlogging was something Luna had been made aware of but not something she was particularly practised at or keen on pursuing. Her editor often brought up how helpful it would be if she could announce her new publications via the medium of YouTube but Luna just wasn't able to bring herself to switch on the camera. It was far too exposing. She liked to write and release her words into the wild but putting herself in the public eye was absolutely not for her. This video, however, was for her eyes and her eyes only. She thought about writing a letter but she couldn't be certain that she would believe a letter tomorrow. Letters and writing could be forged. No, Luna was sure she would be more likely to believe a video in which she could plainly see herself.

Luna had worked herself up all evening to making this video. She'd even put off taking off her make-up and changing into her pyjamas but it was getting late now and she knew this had to be done. She perched her phone on the pile of novels she'd packed in her case and leant it up against a box of tissues that had appeared in the room. She turned her camera onto selfie mode and sat in the desk chair, staring at herself on the screen. Before she overthought it, she pressed the big red button.

'Hi ... Luna. Erm ... I'm you. You're me. Obviously.' Luna didn't know how people did it. She felt so awkward and her palms had quickly become slick with sweat. 'If you're watching this you may or may not remember film-ing this video but it's really important that if you don't remember making this video that you listen to me ... you ... very carefully.' Luna tried to swallow, but her throat was dry. 'You will think today is the sixteenth of July but ... it isn't. At least, I don't think it is. Tomorrow or ... today for you, is actually the twenty-first of July and this isn't your first day in Ondingside. It's your sixth. I don't know why this is happening or what you've been doing to fill each day that's come and gone on the island but something weird is going on and right now, we don't quite know what it is, we just know something's not right. "We" being me and ... and this guy called Jaxon.' She shook her head. How did she explain who Jaxon was to a version of herself that had never met him? 'He's from the mainland, he arrived yesterday and he's unbelievably annoying but he's definitely onto something. He's been tracking the blizzard over Ondingside and . . . ' Luna felt like lightning had struck her brain. 'The blizzard. Oh my God, it's the snow! Yesterday, it hadn't snowed here at all but it snowed overnight and when I woke up I couldn't remember being here before. But what if it's snowed every night? That means every night I've woken up thinking it's the same day. But it isn't the same day. Oh my God. Oh . . . my . . . God. You need to find Jaxon. Immediately. Knowing him, he'll be downstairs in the bar. Look for the scraggly guy that smells like booze in the leather jacket.' Luna stopped the video rolling and saved it with shaking fingers. She opened up her notebook and used her phone as a paperweight to keep the pages open.

WATCH THE MOST RECENT VIDEO ON YOUR PHONE BEFORE YOU LEAVE THIS ROOM, she wrote. ONDINGSIDE IS NOT WHAT YOU THINK IT IS.

She threw on her coat and shoved her feet in her boots, not bothering to tie them properly as she ran out of the door, down the stairs and into the cold, nighttime air. Although not able to see it clearly, she could hear the sea roaring louder than she'd heard it before. The waves crashed together like reunited lovers and threw themselves onto the snowy banks. The inky black sky looked calm and still but the absence of the stars and the moon made Luna feel more nervous than she could explain.

When she'd looked at her phone before she'd left her room it had been 11:58. Luna was often in bed before ten-thirty and asleep long before midnight ever struck. She would have been the fairy godmother's dream. However, this night she'd been so anxious about making a simple video for herself and about what would happen when she awoke without a single memory of everything she'd discovered, sleep wasn't something she was entirely keen to do. Luna had to admit that she was also a little worried about Jaxon on the tracks on his own. Especially when the sea sounded so fierce. She wondered how equipped Jaxon actually was to face such severe weather conditions and whether he'd be okay. Now that she was filled with her own worry, she felt a little guilty for thinking Mrs McArthur had been overreacting when Jaxon had arrived covered in ice and snow and proceeded to thaw out in her hallway. Luna's train of thought was halted entirely then as the end of her nose became suddenly icy. Then her cheeks, and the tips of her ears followed. She looked skywards and the black sky had become speckled as snow poured down from it, onto her world below. She blinked as snowflakes caught in her eyelashes and her mind became foggy.

'This is my sixth day in Ondingside. Today is the twenty-first of July,' she chanted, feeling panic start to rise in her throat. 'It's my sixth day in Ondingside and today is ... today is ...' It became harder and harder to think straight. She clenched and unclenched her fists.

'Today is the twenty ... twenty-first of July. This is my ... my ...' Luna felt like all of her thoughts were scattering like a line-up of pool balls that had just been walloped hard. They all skittered this way and that way, some dropping down the holes and disappearing entirely. Luna shook her head, trying to clear the fog but instead, all she did was spread it to the furthest corners of her mind. She squeezed her eyes shut and took a deep breath but when she opened her eyes, everything seemed different.

Luna looked around her.

'Why am I ... ?' She shivered and looked down at her cold ankles where her boots were undone and letting in the icy air. Not only was it snowing but the ground was also thick with it and she wondered how long it had been falling. It was inches deep and she was amazed at how much snow had built up in what must have been such a short amount of time. She looked up at the falling flakes and thought how odd it was to be seeing snow in the middle of July. Even so, she couldn't help but smile at how beautiful it and also at how excited she was about her first day in Ondingside.

The silhouette got taller and larger as it came closer and Luna stood to greet it. She had so many questions that she wished to ask this being. How did it come to be so sure? Why was it here and could it help her find the way out that she was incapable of finding herself? As she practised these questions in her head, the snow began to fall slower and slower, letting the figure come into focus. As its hazy, blurred outline sharpened, it became more womanly. Luna hadn't noticed the clear shape of a bust, a waist and hips and of hair tied tightly in a braid that swayed back and forth as she walked towards Luna. The snowflakes stopped falling entirely, some frozen in mid-air, and Luna's breath caught in the back of her throat when the woman's face became clear. It wasn't her but at the same time it very much was. Her eyes were vibrant and lively, her hair brushed and well kept. Her shoulders were back and her chin lifted to face new challenges. It looked like nothing could knock this woman over. Luna pulled her own shoulders back, lifted her own chin and finally faced herself.

Twenty-One

Day One . . . . again

July 21st 2019

Beau awoke in the flat above his shop – although calling it a flat, he felt, was extremely generous. A bedroom with mattress on the floor, a kitchenette that contained a sink, a cupboard and a mini fridge and a bathroom with a toilet and a shower so close in proximity that he could shower whilst sitting on the toilet wasn't his idea of home. He couldn't even call it a stepping stone, considering business was drying up fast and he had no intention of moving anywhere that the market for a swanky, borderline pretentious coffee shop was infinitely larger than Ondingside. Even so, he swung his legs around off the mattress and prepared to muddle through yet another very disappointing day in Ondingside. A place where there was very little left for him and yet he was still trying to squeeze every little bit of life out of it, to no avail. Everyone born on the island with even a shred of ambition had moved away, if not to the mainland, further than Beau could dare to imagine. Even his parents were more ambitious in their retirement than Beau was at life in general. They had dropped everything and moved to the south of France and whilst they made a point of badly navigating Skype every night to speak to their son, they very rarely came back to the island and Beau never left it. Whether it was fear of what was ahead or fear of bumping into what came before, he couldn't think about it for long enough to figure it out. Beau felt it was best to plough on and make the most of what he was lucky to have and wanting anything more would be selfish.

Ondingside was a place where nothing really ever changed for anyone; however, something did feel different. A little off and a tad awry. In his stomach sat an especially large knot that he didn't remember tying. The day before had been relatively normal and he didn't recall arguing or even disagreeing with anybody. The only thing out of the ordinary was ... no. Nothing. Something was certainly wrong because he felt so right. More right than he had done in a long time which in turn made him anxious. He wrangled with the feeling, trying to pry at its tangled rope, but nothing came loose and

he knew he'd spend the day trying to understand why he
was smiling for seemingly no reason at all.

Luna paused the video halfway through her fifth watch. For a while she was certain it was a hoax. Someone playing a strange joke on her that she was unable to explain – but then, who could explain if not her? She was absolutely certain she was watching herself, that much was clear. It was her face, her voice, her expressions and her mannerisms. There was no way to fake or forge it. But how could she have recorded a video and have no recollection? Luna on the phone most have been telling the truth, no matter how truly crazy it sounded. She had opened the curtains and the snow had built up significantly. Prior to the snow falling the night before, Luna couldn't remember getting outside nor why she was there. The last memory she had was of setting her alarm and lying down in bed. Had she been sleep-walking? Had she been sleep-recording-videos-on-her-phone too? Sleep-writing-ominous-notes? There were far too many questions and far too few answers. One thing she did know was that she needed to find Jaxon.

No signal but I hope when this message goes through, you know that I've been really missing you, she wrote out in a text to Lottie. Just before she pressed send, despite knowing it would just bounce back, she noticed the edge of another text at the top of her phone screen. She scrolled down and more and more texts to Lottie showed up. Texts she had no recollection of writing and each one increasingly affectionate towards her old friend.

Don't worry about me, they began.

Don't think I'm ignoring you.

I've been really missing you.

'Miss Lark, there's a man in the bar who arrived this morning and he seemed to be looking for you,' babbled Mrs McArthur as Luna descended the stairs. 'I didn't tell him that you were staying here but he refused to leave until he'd seen you. I thought about calling the police but I didn't know if you knew him and I've been humming and hawing all morning about whether I was doing the right thing by doing nothing and I—'

'Mrs McArthur …' Luna took hold of the woman's shoulders and rubbed her thumbs in calming circles, a gesture that surprised both of them. 'I'm actually looking for him myself … I think.' Luna looked to her left and she was certain the man nursing a stiff drink was Jaxon. He was just as she herself had described him. Mrs M relaxed under Luna's hands and she left her with a reassuring smile. With that one interaction Luna knew something certainly wasn't right. Luna didn't comfort people. She wasn't cold or hurtful but she certainly wasn't warm and affectionate, despite never having written a character who didn't have either of those traits. That was the sort of person she longed to be but didn't quite know how. Taking charge of a situation felt uncomfortable and she worried far too much that she might be doing the wrong thing. She would hesitate just long enough for someone else to step in and guide the way. But today was different. Today Luna felt a swelling sense of authority and she put her best foot forward as she marched towards the man in the leather jacket.

'Jaxon?' His head flopped up to her, his red eyes accentuated by the dark circles underneath them. He smelt of sweat and whiskey with a slight hint of salt and vinegar crisps.

'Hello again,' Jaxon said cheerily, trying to right himself in his chair.

'Again . . . ?' she repeated.

'You don't remember . . . ?' He tried to shake himself sober, his bleary eyes clearing a little.

'Not a thing.' Luna shook her head. 'I remember going to bed and then suddenly, I was outside watching the snow, wondering how I got out there. But I found this, this morning.' Luna pulled the note that she had left for herself and slid it towards him as she sat in the adjacent chair. She also handed him her phone, the video prepared for viewing.

'. . . *he's unbelievably annoying but he's definitely onto something . . .*' said the Luna in the video.

'Whoops! Sorry!' she said with a breathy laugh. 'Although, I don't feel too bad because I don't remember saying it and that doesn't really feel like it's me so ...' She shrugged.

'No hard feelings. I promise,' he said. For a moment, Luna was impressed with how quickly he had seemed to sober himself but then felt a little uneasy at how practised he must be at functioning at a certain levels of intoxication. 'I'm amazed you actually pulled this off.'

'Yeah, well. I must have known I wouldn't believe anyone other than myself. Least of all you,' Luna said, her lips squeezed tightly into a smile.

'So, it *is* the snow,' he said, thumping the table with his fist, a grin spreading across his face.

'I ... I guess so,' she said, taking her phone back and looking at herself on the screen.

'Well, you better start believing it because this time, I have proof. Check this out.' Jaxon pulled out his own phone, scrolled for a moment and pressed play before turning the screen to her. The video took a moment to focus but then the orb of snow around the island finally sharpened. She could see where the snow stopped on the train tracks and where the snow refused to fall and then Jaxon's knees where he was sitting cross legged.

'What's that sound?' Luna put the speaker to her ear and could hear the distinct sound of someone sniffling. 'Were you crying?'

'No.' Jaxon quickly snatched the phone away from her

and scrambled with all his fingers to hit the right button to cease the noise. 'It was cold. My nose was running.'

'Were your eyes streaming too, by any chance?' Luna rested her chin in her hand. Luna wondered if her stomach had felt fluttery when she'd first met him too. Despite the haggard appearance, Jaxon was quite an attractive man. His eyes were a dulled blue that would probably look a lot more striking were they less bloodshot and if he wasn't squinting against the light. He had a good head of hair that would look quite smart when brushed and not sticking up in all directions and although quite a detour from the type she usually went for, Luna even found herself jumping on board with the leather jacket. He looked like a very tired James Dean. She felt a familiar squeeze in her chest but something was telling her it was misplaced. Like that feeling when you cheer when your team scores, only to find out it was an own goal. Or when you celebrate potting one of your colours on a pool table only to see that the white ball has followed it down. Luna quit batting her eyelids and tried to get a grip. She didn't want to add to the ever-growing list of things that didn't seem quite right.

'The point is, the snow is only falling on this island and nowhere else. You said last night you remember going to bed and then suddenly you were outside in the snow?' he asked, his eyes now wide and wired. Luna nodded. 'So that must be a memory from the sixteenth. The actual sixteenth. What do you remember?'

'I arrived here by train on the fifteenth of July. I got into bed and I remember setting my alarm for ten the next morning.'

'And then what?'

'And then I went to sleep.' She shrugged.

'Nothing else?'

'No I just laid down and closed my eyes ...'

'But then next thing you know it's still dark and you're outside in the snow wondering how you got there? It *has* to be the snow. The snow is making people forget. Can you believe it?' Jaxon stood up, sliding his chair backwards with a screech. He started to circle the table, his footsteps quick and unsteady. He reached out to hold onto the backs of chairs to help himself walk on his uncertain legs.

'Is that ... usual ... for snow?'

'Obviously not,' he said, his voice deepening in a mocking sort of way. 'But that *has* to be it. It's the only thing that seems to have changed here. Every morning you wake up and you're surprised to see the snow. Because it wasn't snowing when you arrived, correct?' Jaxon took his hand off a chair to point at her and he stumbled with his next step.

'Correct,' Luna said reaching out to him but he had managed to recover relatively quickly and so she looked away, pretending she hadn't noticed.

'Exactly. The snow is the one thing that's different to when you arrived. It snows here every night and everyone forgets the day they've just lived through.' Luna couldn't argue. As absurd as it sounded, Jaxon was right.

'Making every day the same day!' she said, placing a cool hand on her hot forehead. 'Oh my God, that's why we've all been thinking it's the sixteenth for ages! According to our memories, it is!'

'But the outside world is living on. Without you. You've lost four days of your life without even knowing about it.'

'All right, Jaxon. I'm kind of freaking out enough about this without your dramatic commentary. I get it.' Jaxon finally sat back down, his racing thoughts having crossed the finish line and started to slow. 'So what are we supposed to do?'

'What do you mean?'

'Well ... we can't stay on the island for a start. I don't particularly want to become the cast of *Groundhog Day*.'

'Fair point. Then leave.' He shrugged, reaching for the whiskey bottle but Luna, with her reflexes unhindered by alcohol, moved the bottle away from him.

'But the only way out is by walking the tracks.'

'Yeah.' Jaxon stared back at her.

'I know you've proven it's doable but there are other people on this island. Elderly people, wheelchair users, pregnant people ... not everyone will be able to navigate them as well as we can.'

'So ... ?'

'What do you mean "so"? There. Are. People. On.

This. Island. We can't just leave them behind to live out the same day over and over and over and over.'

'Why not? The weather isn't my responsibility. An island full of weirdos isn't my responsibility.'

'Are you kidding? Is this some kind of joke? Or part of the leather jacket-wearing, whiskey-drinking, motorbike-riding, bad boy persona?'

'I don't ride a motorbike.'

'We may not have a responsibility to help other people but ... don't you think it'd be morally wrong to leave all these people behind in a place that is *literally* cutting their lives short? According to the video I left for myself, it's only been five days. But what happens when months go by and people start visiting family or people on the mainland start to wonder why they've not heard from their friends on the island?' A sudden thought struck Luna's brain and her heart plummeted to the soles of her boots. 'What if someone on the island really is pregnant and they have their child here? Do they wake up the next day not remembering that they've given birth? Does their child then grow older and older with the mother not ever remembering that she's had it? Do mother and child miss out on god knows how much bonding time?' Tears sprang to Luna's eyes and she was taken aback by just how affected she was by the thought. The idea of a mother not remembering her own child was tragic, and Luna felt a deep personal connection to the story but couldn't explain why. 'I'm not pregnant, or married, nor am I unable to leave this island. I have zero attachments and I could go back to the mainland now if I wanted to. But even I have already seen a huge change in my own life. I'm a totally different person to who I was when I went to sleep on the fifteenth. From my point of view, I've woken up as a better version of myself. I feel brand spanking new – but then there are moments . . . ' Luna's mind fumbled for a way to explain how she felt.

'Moments?'

'Something someone says or does triggers off the beginnings of a memory and I start to feel . . . something. Just as I think it's on the tip of my tongue and I'm about to remember why I'm feeling how I'm feeling, it fades like smoke.'

'What do you start to feel?'

'I feel like something's missing. Or some*one* is missing? It's like there's a hole that I need to fill but I don't know what shape the hole is nor what to put in it. Am I making any sense? At all?' Luna caught sight of Jaxon's bemused expression.

'Vaguely,' he said, nodding his head this way and that.

'Enough to convince you that something has to be done? That we can't just up and leave without, at the very least, warning people about what's going on?'

'I dunno, babe.' He leant across the table and took the bottle back but surprisingly, didn't pour himself a drink. Luna folded her arms across her chest and huffed.

'What do you want me to do, babe? Walk the streets with a megaphone?'

'That would cause mass hysteria! And ... and don't call me babe,' she said, wondering why she was protesting something that had made her nerve endings fizz.

'Well, what then?' He pulled the collar up on his leather jacket and folded his arms as he rested back in his chair.

'Miss Lark ...' Mrs McArthur's voice rang out from the doorway. 'There's someone here and I think they might be looking for you.'

Standing in the reception area was a man Luna recognised immediately. His soft features and cuddly frame were unmistakable if his coffee-coloured eyes hadn't already jogged her memory. *Beau. He worked at the Green Arrow. You threw up in his pint glass,* she reminded herself. She thought she'd be feeling a deep sense of shame, her insides cringing at the thought, but instead, she felt a glowing warmth rise from within her. Still, it was tinged in an annoyance that she just couldn't shake.

'Beau,' she breathed, clutching her notebook under her chin.

'Miss Lark,' he said, beaming.

'I'll let you two get ... reacquainted.' Mrs McArthur said with a wink that Luna tried to erase from her mind immediately so as not to cringe further for fear of her insides imploding. Beau and Luna looked at each other, heat filling the air between them so it almost blurred like the air above an open fire.

'What do you know?' he asked, quietly, looking past her into the bar at Jaxon who was busying himself with whiskey but Luna knew he was undoubtedly listening.

'I know that something's not right and that I probably know you more than I think I do.' Every muscle in Beau's body seemed to relax as her words reassured him of his own sanity. 'What do you know?' she asked him back.

'I know that we *definitely* know each other more than we think we do and I have the evidence to prove it.'

'Excuse me?'

'Do you have some time?'

'I can make some time,' she nodded, unable to keep her lips from curling into a smile.

Luna was acutely aware that this was not a date and she kept having to inwardly berate herself when she found herself wanting to reach for Beau's hand or laugh too hard at his admittedly groanworthy jokes. She felt like a mess. Her emotions were entirely out of sync with her memories. To feel like there's history with someone when you have no memory of that history was disorientating to say the least. Especially when it came with an unexplained sense of anger. The lovey-dovey, weak at the knees thing Luna felt just about well equipped enough to deal with. It was a lovely feeling she'd not felt in a long time and if Beau was somewhat responsible for this big change in her personality then she owed him a very large thank-you. However, the sense that someone had wronged you but not being able to put your finger on exactly how and why was infuriating. They reached his coffee shop and Beau led her to the door behind the counter.

'I don't think I've ever been behind the counter of any shop. Ever,' Luna said, ducking her head under the counter and coming face to face with bags and bags of coffee beans and silver refrigerators.

'Eh.' He shrugged as he rattled the keys in the lock of the door. 'It's like a magic show. Once you've seen how the tricks are done, the show loses its charm.'

'Are you saying you're a magician?'

'Dunno. Can you remember how good my coffee was?' He looked over his shoulder and smirked.

'Nope,' she chirruped.

'Then no. Clearly not a magician. But what I'm trying to say it back here it's all book-keeping, inventory and a clothes horse covered in my boxer shorts. Out there it's lovely decor and caffeine.' Beau opened the door and gestured for her to enter where there was, in fact, a clothes horse at the back of the room on which hung his damp laundry.

'Okay. Point taken. I choose out there,' she said, sniffing the slightly stale air.

'Good choice.' Beau closed the door behind them and sat in front of the open laptop on the desk and typed in his password. Without looking up at her he reached behind him and pulled over a stool. 'Take a seat. You might wanna be sitting down for this,' he said as he fiddled with wires and clicked seemingly a thousand buttons on the screen before finally, a video player popped up. 'This morning, I opened up the shop and when I checked the cash register, there was much less in there than I expected there to be. Also, my keys were in a totally different place to where I'd left them last night, there were clothes in my laundry basket upstairs that were definitely hanging in my cupboard yesterday, all the food in my kitchen is either half gone or the wrappers are in the bin ... I just couldn't figure out what was going on. So, I thought I'd check the CCTV. See if there was anything suspicious going on.'

'Let me guess ... the date on the CCTV is different.'

'Yeah! I've got these cool little cameras that cost me an arm and a leg but they work without internet if there's none to be had and link to my phone on 4G so I can watch it live. I make a point of emptying the SD card everyday just so it doesn't get full and stop recording but I've had to do that today anyway seeing as all internet seems to be down. The thing is, when I opened up my CCTV folder, there are files dated up to five days from now. The latest one says the twentieth which would make today—'

'The twenty-first,' Luna finished.

'How did you figure it out?' He pulled the laptop screen a little closer. Luna finally pulled the notebook away from her chest and opened it up to the entry from five days ago.

'Apparently, I've been making notes every evening and I guess the habit of dating my work never left me after school.' She watched as Beau flicked from page to page and she could see the flicker in his eyes when he caught his own name scrawled in her handwriting on the majority of the pages.

'Beau can do one?' he read and, luckily, laughed.

'I'm not going to say sorry because I don't remember why I wrote that but quite frankly, you probably deserved it,' she jibed. 'Speaking of ...' She looked down at her glistening palms. 'I feel like maybe ... I'm pissed off at you, right now? And it's really bothering me.'

'And you have no clue why?' he asked, scooting his chair towards her, his face filling with concern. She shook her head. 'Well, maybe I can help ...' Beau fully opened the laptop up and pressed the space bar. 'This is five days ago.'

Luna watched herself enter the coffee shop behind Beau, wearing her blue coat. Only ten seconds in, Luna could see a whole posture and demeanour that was alien to her now. She was hunched and shrunken in on herself, her hands wringing and her head down.

'You spent a grand total of ten minutes in the shop and that was with a lot of coaxing from me. For the next couple of days you only spend around ten to fifteen minutes in the shop but then you stay for half an hour and then yesterday, you stayed for a couple of hours and then I asked you out to dinner and ... you said yes.'

'I said yes?' she gasped.

'All right, don't sound too surprised! I can play it to you if you want.' Luna didn't want to admit that she needed proof but ... she needed proof. Together they sat and watched from the beginning to the end of their story that they couldn't remember. All the coffees he'd served and the different latte art he'd drawn. From Luna's awkward one-word answers up to their sprawling conversations. From the declination of her name to the freely given details of her childhood. She'd kept a firm hold on her family history and her name but Luna had lost count of the many things she never would have expected to tell someone that she'd ended up telling Beau. Considering every new day they watched was a clean slate in which they met for the first time, Luna was sharing thoughts and feelings she'd usually only feel comfortable sharing with the likes of Lottie, certainly not a stranger which technically, Beau was.

'You know that feeling when you meet someone and after a couple of minutes you feel like you've known them your whole life?' Luna said, still staring at the screen as the final video came to an end.

'This feels like that times a hundred, right?' he said, glancing sideways at her, and she nodded.

'Well ... I guess it feels like that for us because it's kind of true.' Luna turned her head and met his gaze. 'At least now I know why I was annoyed at you.'

'Do you hate me?' His eyebrows turned up in the middle, framing his big, swimming eyes.

'Only a little bit. I'd hate you a lot less if you apologised.'

'I'm sorry,' he said without hesitation and Luna's head snapped round to him. 'I really am. Although, I don't think you can blame me toooooo much for not believing you. It's a pretty tall tale.'

'"Tall tale"? How old are you, seventy-two?'

'No, but I grew up around old people, what do you expect?'

'Fair enough.' She laughed. 'And yeah, I get it. If I were you, I wouldn't have believed me either.' Then she had a thought and said it before she had a chance to overthink it and talk herself out of saying what she felt. 'I think I'm more annoyed at how you spoke to me, though.'

'Yeah, having a recording of the things I said and the way I said them really makes me realise just what a wanker I was. And I'm sorry. Again.'

'I don't think I've ever been apologised to this much.'

'I would stop, but you keep giving me things to say sorry for!' He pulled his sleeves over his hands and folded them under his arms.

'There's obviously something about you that I don't know that made you say those things. You've clearly been burned by someone and it's made you closed off.'

'Says you!'

'I know, I know.' She nodded slowly. 'I'm the queen of closed off. But I guess the difference is ... I'm open about being closed off. I don't think anyone has ever been under the illusion that I'm a sharing and caring person that always says what's on her mind. You, on the other hand ... Mr Come-Into-My-Coffee-Shop-And-Let-Me-Ask-All-The-Questions-But-Give-You-No-Answers.' She bashed her shoulder into his and he had to unfold his arms to steady himself.

'Huh. I never thought of it like that.' Beau squeezed his hands between his knees and looked down into his lap. Luna saw a flicker of the hurt boy who was underneath the cheery exterior and she wondered how long he'd been hiding it all. It seemed he had been sweeping his emotions under the carpet but now the carpet was three feet off the ground.

'At least I was being honest about being cold and miserable.'

'Yeah, I suppose out of the two of us, I am the fraud.' He smiled, sadly, still staring at his hands, unable to make direct eye contact for fear of letting his cheerful mask slip, even just for a moment.

'And look ... it's cool if you don't wanna talk about it. I never talk about anything and would much rather people didn't dump their emotions on me but ... amazingly, I'm actually offering.'

'You're asking me to emotionally dump on you? Is that a kink or ... ?' He turned his head towards her, a smile creeping onto his face.

'Beau ...' she warned.

'All right, all right.' He looked back down at his hands in his lap and squeezed his eyes shut. 'I don't wanna get too into it, but ...' he inhaled deeply and exhaled hard, 'The reason I've never left this island is because when I was seventeen, I fell in love with this girl and I mean . . . I fell in love *hard*. She was The. One. Capital T, capital O. We were together for years. When I was about twenty-two, she got a job working on the mainland and would come home to me each weekend a little more distant than before. Eventually, she left and never came back. No explanation. No goodbye. She just never came home. I tried to get in touch but . . .' He shook his head. '. . . I think ghosting is the term these days.' He laughed, hollowly.

'I don't think it counts as ghosting when you've been together for years and years. Ghosting is when you meet on Tinder, go on a couple of dates and they don't know how to say they don't really fancy you so never call again.'

'What is this, then?'

'Arseholery.' Beau snort-laughed but hung his head all the same.

'I'm sorry that happened to you,' Luna said, nudging her knee against his.

'Yeah . . . well . . .' He scratched the back of his head.

'But you do know the mainland is a lot bigger than this island, right? By like . . . millions of people. The chances of you bumping into her are so small that it's not even worth worrying about.'

'That's not why I've never left,' he said, wincing.

'Then what is it?'

'She was always a big fish in a small pond here,' he

310

said all at once. 'I've always just been ... a fish in a pond. Nothing too big, nothing too small. I think I'd drown out there. I can't even successfully run a business on an island the size of a peanut. What chance do I have out there?'

'Beau, the reason this coffee shop is failing is *because* this island is the size of a peanut. There's no gap in the market for hipster coffee on this island when the meaning of "hipster" to anyone over the age of fifty is trousers that sit on your hips instead of your waist!' Luna was fed up of simply nudging his knee with hers or bashing her shoulder against his. She wanted to take his hands or wrap her arms around his shoulders. 'Your coffee is amazing. It would be a strong contender out in the land of caffeine fiends. Or caf-fiends, if you will.'

'Nice.' He nodded his approval.

'Author.' She winked and smirked. 'Life on this island is slim pickings if you have ambition. And you do have ambition, Beau. You *are* a big fish in a small pond. Fear is stopping you. I came here because I wanted to run *away* but you should be running *to*. There's nothing for you here except an empty shop and disappointment.'

'Blimey, don't hold back, will you!'

'Well, instead of being open and honest about how I'll never be open and honest, I'm just trying to be open and honest ... full stop.' She smiled, only half joking.

'So, how *do* you feel?' Beau asked. A tingle of panic shot through her and she felt a white heat burning in her chest but she breathed deeply and thought about his question. How *did* she feel? She had definitely surprised herself because she wasn't as terrified about the entire situation as she thought she would be but she wondered if that was because she had Beau. Luna had felt abandoned and alone in recent years. In moments when she had needed someone to turn to, she had found that the people she wanted the most weren't there and so she found that she'd just stopped turning at all. Luna had stopped looking for help when she needed it and had taken it upon herself to always fix her own problems, even when they were impossibly large for one small human to manage alone.

However, the weight of all her own burdens, the big and the small, had started to accumulate and her back had begun to bend and break. The tragic loss of her family. A marriage that didn't even begin. The slow but sure shrivelling of her creativity. It had all become too much and running away from everything and everyone had seemed like the only plausible option for the time being. That was, until she actually ran away. It's a wonder what a little bit of snow and a lot of memory loss can do for a person's outlook on life. The memory she had of how she had felt when she had laid down in bed on the night she had arrived, lonely and admittedly a little scared, was a world away from how she felt sat next to Beau with his knee rested against hers. Luna felt like nothing was so terrible or so difficult that it couldn't be overcome. She felt happy to have him next to her, talking.

She felt – she just felt happy. A spark had been reignited and she could start to feel the heat of it, radiating outwards, melting the ice that had been building up inside her for too long. In amongst something quite big and confusing that seemingly had no solution, she felt foolish and almost schoolgirlish for only being able to think about how close Beau was sitting, how she could smell the coffee on his breath and how much she wanted to cup his face in her hands and be as close to it as possible.

'I feel like I came here to run away from everyone and instead I ran straight into the one person I needed to find,' she said, taking the plunge and turning towards Beau. She put a cold hand on his warm knee and slowly, gently, brushed his hair away from his face with the other and rested her forehead against his, holding his chin in her fingers.

'And who was that?' he whispered and just before she tilted his head and pressed her lips against his, she whispered back:

'Me.'

Twenty-Two

Over The Rainbow

'So, what exactly is a storm chaser again?' Beau struggled to keep up with Luna's fast pace as she marched back through the snow to the inn.

'Storm chaser. Does what it says on the tin.' She shrugged.

'But what's the point in chasing a storm? Doesn't seem very safe ...' Beau stumbled over a twig hidden under the snow but just caught himself before he hit the ground.

'From what I can gather, I think that's the point. Adventure. Seeking thrills. All that rubbish.'

'How does he earn any money?'

'By the looks of him, I think it probably costs him more money than he makes. I also don't think he cares.'

'Doesn't sound like I have much to worry about, then,' Beau mumbled.

'What?' Luna looked over her shoulder at Beau's reddening face.

'Just saying I'm worried about what's going to happen. You know, with the snow and the, erm ... the island and stuff ... '

'I doubt Jaxon will have thought up some kind of plan but I'm sure together we can figure something out.'

Jaxon was in exactly the same place she'd left him except now he had abandoned the empty bottle of whiskey and was holding a half empty bottle of gin. He was also almost horizontal, slouched far down in his seat and with his feet up on another chair under the table.

'Do you even have a liver?' Luna said as Jaxon reached under the table with his foot and kicked out a chair for her to sit down. 'Jaxon, this is Beau. He's figured out what's going on too and has even more evidence. CCTV evidence. We have enough proof to prove what's going on now.'

'Great. Go on, then.' He waved a hand towards the door.

'We need you,' Luna said, grabbing the neck of the bottle before Jaxon poured himself another drink. Luna couldn't fathom how he was still able to hold a conversation with that much alcohol running through his system.

'Oooh, I feel special,' Jaxon mocked in a high-pitched voice.

'What's your problem?' Beau said. Jaxon hadn't looked

at him yet but now his eyes slowly slid towards him as he took his feet down and pushed himself straight, trying to get a little bit of height over Beau. Although wobbling slightly, Jaxon's face had turned serious, his sunken eyes glistening with an unpredictability that made Luna uneasy.

'My problem is people like you always trying to do what's right. What's wrong with a little bit of chaos for once? Chaos brings out the best in some of us.'

'Could you let us know who you're referring to? Because surely you can't be talking about yourself?' retorted Beau.

'Jaxon, we do need your help. You're the only one who's been on the mainland since it started snowing here. You're the only person who can actually vouch for the story. You have the video of the view of the island from the train tracks.'

Jaxon opened up his phone and swiped until he found the video. 'You mean this one?' He swiftly hit delete before Luna had a chance to react.

'NO!' She tried to grab for his phone but he'd snatched it away and tucked it back into his pocket. 'Why ...?' Luna breathed but Jaxon only shrugged.

'Stop trying to change the natural course of things, babe.'

'Don't call me that.' Luna gripped the edge of the table not knowing whether she was going to stay and shout or run and hide.

'You can't stop a storm, sweetheart. You just have

to ride it out.' He snatched the bottle off the table and unscrewed the cap.

'Jaxon.'

'You just have to let the chaos happen and clean up the mess that's left afterwards.' He poured the drink and sloshed it over the table.

'JAXON!' Luna yelled and finally her turned to her, his face red and his grin slipping. 'You might not be able to stop a storm once it's happening but you can minimise the damage before it hits. You can batten down the hatches and you can make sure people are safe. You may be fine with putting people's lives and in this case their minds and memories and futures at risk but Beau and I are not. Clearly, you're not with us and the only thing we needed from you, you no longer have, so you can do what you want but we're going to do all we can to help as many people as possible. Some people revel in chaos and watch the world burn and some people freeze it out, but the world keeps on turning, Jaxon. Either we're with it or we're against it.' Luna stood up and went to walk away but Jaxon wasn't able to resist having the last word.

'The world is against me, babe,' he said, downing his gin. Luna spun quickly on her heels and Beau stood too, almost ready to catch her should she fly at Jaxon like she wanted to. Instead, she walked calmly towards him and sat back down directly opposite him.

'The world is a big, spinning rock floating in the middle of space, Jaxon. It's not sentient and it sure as hell wouldn't be bothered about your drunken arse if it was. You're not special. You're just angrily shouting into the void and getting pissed off when you hear nothing back but your own echo. Well, surprise, surprise, Jaxon, no one's listening! Because it seems all you do is bitch and moan to no one. You don't actually talk to anyone who can help you because I don't think you actually want help. Sitting and drinking your cares away is easier.' Jaxon stubbornly poured himself another glass. 'But you must understand that the universe doesn't give a shit about you and your self-made drama and so the only person stopping you from being successful and happy is you. So grow up and learn how to deal with it. Or don't! I don't care! But you can't go around making life harder for everyone else because you haven't figured out how to make yours any easier.' Luna stood up and swayed, a little uneasy on her feet and taken aback by how many words she'd just spoken to another person in one go. 'At least I'll have a clear conscience when I wake up tomorrow, wherever or whenever that may be.' Luna strode away but could hear Jaxon mutter 'Bravo' as he slow-clapped her from the room.

'Are you all right?' Beau caught up with her as she reached the front door to the inn and he gently pulled her back to him by her elbow. She was shaking.

'I'm fine. Whoooo,' she sang with a grin. 'Adrenaline feels pretty good when it gets going, doesn't it?' She shook out her hands that had started to tingle.

'Don't turn into a storm chaser on me!' Beau gently nudged her arm with his fist.

'Never!' she said, returning the gesture, wishing for a little more contact. 'Self-righteous monologues are my thing.' She laughed and Beau laughed with her, enjoying a brief triumphant moment in an evening that could still go either of two ways. Then Beau's face fell for a brief moment before it lifted higher than before.

'Monologues! Oh my god, Miss Lark, I could kiss you,' he said, grabbing her shoulders.

'Okay.'

'What?'

'Monologues?' Luna corrected herself quickly, but Beau had definitely heard. She could tell by his suddenly pink cheeks and mischievous eyes.

'The school play. It's tonight. Everyone's going ...'

'Everyone's going ...' she repeated, processing his idea.

'*Everyone is going.* Nearly the whole island will all be in one place at the same time which means ...'

'It's the perfect place to let everyone know what's going on at once!' Luna said with a little bounce.

'Exactly!' Beau laughed as he let his palms slide down her arms and took her hands in his. Luna felt a tingle run from her pinky fingers all the way to her heart.

'Oh Beau, it's brilliant! What time is the show tonight?'

'Five o'clock,' he said, twisting their hands so he could look at his watch.

'That doesn't give us much time to get everyone off the

island ...' Luna craned her neck to see his watch which told her it was only quarter past one.

'Do we even know what time the snow will fall again?'

'Not exactly, but I know I found myself outside last night at midnight ...'

'Like Cinderella?'

'I guess the fairytales we know aren't all entirely fiction.'

'No, it certainly seems that way.' Beau stared into her eyes for a moment and Luna wondered if he was talking about the incorporation of magic into their own reality or whether something else was on his mind.

'So ...' She tucked a strand of loose hair behind her ear, not quite knowing how to meet his gaze. 'What do we do until we see the Munchies?'

'I think you mean Munchkins.' He laughed and this time, Luna did feel a little foolish so she kept her gaze down towards her feet. For someone so interested in fiction, she really should have seen or read what was undeniably one of the world's greatest stories. Her dislike for musicals certainly excused her from never having watched the movie, but the book? The word 'munchkins' should definitely have been part of her vocabulary.

Thankfully, Beau seemed to find her ignorance on the matter endearing. 'I guess we figure out exactly what we need to say and how best to convince people that we're not crazy. That we are telling the truth even though it sounds completely barking mad ... and then we wait.' Beau squeezed her shoulders and Luna finally gave into her urge to be closer to him. She sunk in between his arms and naturally he embraced her.

'And then we wait.'

Beau had been right when he'd said almost the entire island came to watch the school play. With the population of Ondingside being so small, almost everyone was related to at least one of the children that attended Ondingside Primary and even if you were one of the few that wasn't, no one would be pleased if you didn't come to support the children from the island. Every year, the play was held at the Town Hall, right in the heart of the island, and as Luna and Beau approached on foot, Beau clutching his satchel containing his laptop and Luna holding her notebook to her chest, they reached for each other's hand. It wasn't a romantic gesture but simply a reassurance that they had each other and that things were going to be okay, despite neither of them knowing if they were.

'Do we do it before the show or after?' Beau whispered out of the side of his mouth as he watched parents hug their children before they ran inside to join their friends.

'Before. Technically these children have put on this play five times already so we shouldn't feel bad about cancelling this one.'

'Those poor kids. Well, at least they weren't doing *Les*

Mis!' he chuckled, gently jabbing Luna in the ribs with his elbow. She threw her head back with an insincere laugh, not willing to admit that this was yet another hole in her cultural knowledge, but Beau caught her flicker of insincerity. 'Seriously?' He bent at the knees slightly to try and catch her quickly averting gaze. 'When we get off this island we're having a movie night.'

'Might need to be a movie week, by the sounds of it.'

'To be fair, though, I reckon we could skip *Les Mis*. All you need to know is that everyone dies.'

Luna gasped and bat him with the back of her hand. 'Spoilers!' she yelped, but he swatted her back.

'*Les Misérables* is over a hundred and fifty years old! If you haven't caught up by now, it's your own fault.' He laughed. Again, she found she had no excuse. As a lover of books, she most certainly should have dedicated some time to reading the brick that was *Les Misérables* but it had taken one of her more intelligent friends a dedicated two months to read it and she'd just never found the motivation to begin.

'There's Mrs Tucker. The headmistress.' Beau clutched the strap of his satchel and pointed to a tall, spindly woman in a bright pink trouser suit, looming over the children and the majority of their parents in her extraordinarily high heels.

'She looks ... terrifying.' Luna swallowed hard.

'That's probably what makes her such a great teacher. She looks scary so kids stay in line but she's actually ridiculously lovely. I learnt that after I left the school, of course.'

'You mean she was *your* headmistress? How old is she?!'

'She was the English teacher when I attended Ondingside Primary but I think she's looked the same age for about fifty years.' Mrs Tucker looked like she was around Mrs McArthur's age. A glamorous sort of sixties, maybe even early seventies. 'Pretty sure she used to wear that same trouser suit when she was teaching me Shakespeare.'

'Do you think she'll let us do our speech?'

'If we don't tell her what it's about, then yeah, I don't see why not?' The pair took a breath and made their way through the hordes of proud parents, excitable children and stressed teachers to get to Mrs Tucker, the woman who could make or break their entire plan.

'Now boys, boys, please – I'm sure the Lollipop Guild didn't hit each other with their oversized lollipops! And no, Clara-Belle, Doc Martens are not an appropriate shoe for a member of the Lullaby League! Oh, Beau! I'm so pleased you came! Are you ready to soar Over The Rainbow?' Mrs Tucker's eyes disappeared almost entirely when she snort-laughed at her own little quip.

'Very clever, Mrs T! Very clever indeed!' Luna slowly turned her head towards Beau. His demeanour had entirely changed. He laughed with a nasal *her-her-herrr* noise that she was sure she'd only heard seals make on nature documentaries when they were in danger. He swept his hair back with one hand and left it there, flexing his bicep, and he jabbed Luna with his elbow again, this time a little more forcefully to get her to stop staring at him with such disdain. 'Can't wait to see the show, just can't wait.' He flashed his teeth. 'I was wondering, you couldn't do us an enormous favour, could you?' Mrs Tucker looked at Luna for the first time, not even noticing that she had been with them. 'This is Miss Lark. She recently moved here and has begun working with me in my humble little coffee shop.'

'Oh, I hear it's doing so well!' Mrs Tucker reached out and touched Beau's arm and left her hand there.

'Not so well at all, actually, if I'm honest. Might have to go out of business!' he said with a little pout.

'Oh, that's so terrible! Is there anything I can do to help?' She now lifted her other hand and held his shoulder, stooping so that she could look into his eyes.

'Well, it's funny you should mention it! I was wondering, if it's not too much trouble, if we could give a little speech before the show started tonight. To let people know where the shop is, what times we open and close and what kind of coffee we sell, that kind of thing!'

'Well ... I'm not sure, Beau. This is a children's show, after all. What kind of children drink coffee?' She snort-laughed again, this time a little more forcefully, and she coughed.

'We were thinking we would gear it more towards the adults,' Luna chimed in. 'Tired doing the school run? Stop by Beau's coffee shop for a quick pick-me-up! Got lots of late-night marking to do? Beau's coffee will keep you awake!' Mrs Tucker looked at her blankly but Beau beamed.

'Exactly. All we'd need to borrow is an interactive whiteboard or a projector of some kind. We've, um ... got a couple of nice visuals to go along with our mini presentation. What do you say, Mrs Tucker? I'd really owe you one ...' Beau spoke softly now and gave Mrs Tucker his best puppy dog eyes.

'Fine ...' Mrs Tucker narrowed her gaze sideways at Luna before her smile returned for Beau. 'There's a projector in the hall that we're using for the hurricane! It's all newfangled technology that I don't quite understand but it looks quite spectacular. Ron has it all linked up in there if you want to speak to him. I'm sure he'll be able to sort something out for you!'

'Great,' Beau replied and Luna relaxed, not realising that she'd been tensing in anticipation of Mrs Tucker's answer.

'But you only get a couple of minutes, mind. Don't think I'm above dragging you off stage like I did when you got overexcited as Santa and did a little wee in the sleigh.' She booped Beau on the nose with her pink painted acrylic nail. 'No, boys! Please don't pull the stuffing out of our poor Scarecrow's costume! There'll be nothing left of him to perform!' Mrs Tucker strode off in her towering heels to reassemble the poor little boy whose costume was now strewn around the town hall car park. Beau groaned.

'Ouch. That must have been a real hit to your pride and your ego. Do you need me to look away for a second? Pretend I didn't hear any of that? Never bring it up again?' Luna patted him on the shoulder.

'All of the above.' Beau put a hand over his eyes and looked at Luna through his fingers.

'You were a kid!' Luna laughed. 'But I will be calling you Little Beau Pee from now on.' Luna found herself unable to breathe. Bent double, she gasped for air. 'Like Little Bo Peep. But ... but ... LITTLE BEAU PEE!' She howled. It took her several moments to compose herself.

'Are you quite finished?' said Beau, his stony face still slightly pink.

'Oof. I think so.' Luna couldn't remember the last time she'd laughed like that. 'I think I needed that!' Beau rolled his eyes at her but Luna could see his smile return as he walked towards the town hall.

Inside, the cacophony that echoed around the room was deafening. The high ceilings and stone walls made even the slightest whisper reverberate but the sound of almost three hundred people stuffed into the hall, all nattering about how marvellous or how troublesome their children were, created a din that neither Beau nor Luna could match.

'WHERE DO WE NEED TO GO?' Luna yelled.

'WHAT?' Beau pointed to his ear and shook his head.

Luna tried to mouth what she wanted to say to Beau

but it was no use. He grabbed her hand and pulled her through a door to the left of the stage when no one was looking. A few children were on the other side of the door, all dressed in multicoloured T-shirts, collectively playing the rainbow that Dorothy would cross in order to end up in the land of Oz. They scurried away as the pair tumbled through the door and closed it behind them, only shutting out a fraction of the din. Beau stopped abruptly as he caught eyes with a couple of Munchkins and Luna stumbled into the back of him. He kept his voice low as he turned towards her and the warmth of his breath sent a shiver through her.

'I need to go and speak to Ron. Are you okay handling the crowd?' He knelt down and pulled his laptop from his satchel.

'Handling the crowd?' Luna froze.

'Yeah. You do the talking and I'll get the footage set up.'

'No. Way.' She frantically shook her head.

'It'll all be okay! They're a great bunch of people!'

'Then you do it! They know you. They're more likely to believe you because they already trust you. To them, I could just be some random stranger who's turned up to cause havoc.'

'Like Jaxon?'

'Exactly,' Luna said and she caught the flicker of a smile on Beau's lips as he looked back to his bag to search for a cable.

'Well, can you set up the laptop, then?'

'Gimme.' Luna put his satchel over her shoulder and took the open laptop from him. Beau leant over to the curtain and pulled it aside. The crowd were restlessly shifting. Over-excitable children clambered on seats and people as their parents did their best to feed them snacks or show them videos and games on their phones and iPads in an attempt to keep them calm and still.

'That's Ron there.' He pointed to an older gentleman with a big bushy ginger beard. 'Always does the sound and effects for every school musical.'

'Effects?' Luna asked and Beau gave a hefty sigh.

'He always tries to add at least one poorly timed pyro to every production and usually at a time it most endangers a child. Poor little Bruce Thompson lost his eyebrows back in twenty-fifteen.'

'Well, let's hope I come back with mine!'

'I'd still want to take you to dinner if you didn't,' he said, not looking at her. 'I'll wait here until everyone goes quiet,' he added quickly.

'Why will everyone go quiet?'

'Have you never noticed when you're in a crowd full of talking people that are all waiting, there's a moment in which everyone senses the beginning of something and they fall silent at exactly the same time?'

'No, but that's probably because I make a habit of staying out of large crowds.'

'Fair enough. Now go, quickly.' He smiled. 'And good luck!'

'You too!' Luna quickly planted a kiss on his lips and scarpered through the door before she had a chance to let the giddiness get to her.

Ron was an awfully sweet man who, despite being a disaster with pyrotechnics, was seemingly a dab hand with computers. Much more so than Luna. The desk at the back of the room was covered in far too many confusing cables with different ends that didn't look like they fit in any holes, but it was a language that Ron spoke fluently. When Luna asked for his help he took the laptop from her with a hearty 'Of *course*!' and he opened up folders and apps on Beau's screen that Luna had never dared venture into on her own laptop but within moments the projection on the large overhanging screen above the stage that read ONDINGSIDE PRIMARY SCHOOL PRESENTS THE WIZARD OF OZ! turned white.

'Then if I just plug this into here . . .' Ron said, his little pink tongue sticking out of the side of his mouth as he jammed a cable into the side of Beau's laptop and what was on Beau's screen was now also being projected onto the big screen for the whole hall to see. Everyone fell silent and, panicked, Luna gently pushed Ron out of the way and quickly scrambled to open up the right video file and waited for Beau's signal to press play. Now that the hall was hushed, she was certain her heartbeat was echoing in everyone's ears as much as it was in hers.

The audience dutifully applauded as Beau shuffled onto the stage. He scanned the crowd and found Mrs Tucker's stern gaze in the stage left aisle. She gave him the nod to proceed.

'Hello, everyone!'

'Hi, Beau!' said the mass as if it were an AA meeting. The only difference was that everyone was smiling happily up at the valued member of their community.

'I'm here to tell you about two things.' He glanced at Mrs Tucker again who raised an eyebrow. 'Firstly, coffee! Most of you who know me, will know I recently opened a coffee shop on Kismet Road. So ...' Luna could tell he was nervous. His voice was three octaves higher than normal and he was hurriedly pushing through his coffee spiel. However, that may not have been nerves and rather his urgency to get to the matter at hand. 'So, if you're a parent on the school run, stop by to get a quick pick-me-up or if you're a teacher getting ready for a late night of marking, I'm open until six in the evening.' Beau searched for Luna's face and when he found it, he gave her a thumbs-up. She muted the laptop and pressed play.

'Speaking of my coffee shop. This is it!' He pointed directly above him. 'That's me up there and that's my friend Miss Lark who just moved here and this was the day we first met. The sixteenth of July.' Beau waved his hand and Luna opened the next video. 'This was the day after that.' He waved his hand again. 'And the day after and so on and so forth.' Luna opened all five files so they played simultaneously side by side. There was a small

331

hum that rippled through the crowd. 'This is legitimate CCTV footage from the cameras in my shop.'

'Might wanna check your cameras, Beau! Looks like they're faulty to me!' shouted a voice from the crowd, and a little titter rippled through the audience.

'It sure looks that way, Tom! But the reason I checked the cameras in the first place is because things kept going missing in my shop. Money from the register. My keys were always in a different place to where I remembered leaving them. I kept running out of food in the fridge and toilet paper!' He chuckled and the hall laughed with him but the laughter fell short as couples and families all suddenly looked at each other, realising they had recently experienced the same predicament. Luna was witnessing first-hand what a valued member of the community he was and she understood a little more about why it would be so hard for him to leave. Not only would he be leaving behind everything and everyone he'd ever known but also the hole he would leave would be noticeable for those who remained. 'I checked the cameras to make sure no one had broken in and it turned out my burglar was ... well ...' he scratched the back of his head and slid his other hand into his pocket, 'me! It was *me* moving my keys and eating my food and wearing my clothes. I just couldn't remember because ... because of the *snow*.' He shrugged. Luna could tell he felt like a crazy person explaining this out loud and she felt a little twinge of guilt at lumbering him with the far more difficult job.

'Keep going, Beau ...' she whispered under her breath.

'The snow? Beau, are you feeling okay?' Tom spoke up again, taking a firm position as the voice of the community. Luna couldn't help but feel irked by his confident opposition, even if she did understand it. She hated watching Beau in such a vulnerable state.

'Hear me out. I know it sounds crazy and I didn't believe it either but the proof is right up there.' He gestured to the screen, where one of the videos was paused on a frame in which Luna was gazing over the counter at Beau who looked equally as taken. It was from the final day that had escaped from their memories. She beamed at the frozen image and was sure she felt her heart swell three sizes. 'I met my friend Miss Lark, who's right back there at the sound desk if you don't believe she's real!' Beau waved and she waved back, enthusiastically. There was a rumble as people collectively shuffled in their seats to look at her and she found she was met with a few smiles but mainly puzzled faces. 'I met her on the sixteenth of July and when I woke up the next morning I had completely forgotten. Now, for those of you that haven't already had the pleasure of meeting her, she's just not someone you forget in a hurry.' *Oof,* Luna thought. That hit her right in the heart. 'Then, as luck would have it, she came back in on the seventeenth and on the eighteenth and the nineteenth. In fact, we have met for the first time every day for the past five days. Except, every day, just like all of you, we both thought it was still the sixteenth and that no time had passed at all.'

'Beau, I think that's enough of this joke now.' Mrs Tucker made her way through a row with panicked urgency, clambering over people's laps and bags causing a chorus of 'oww's and 'sorry's. Finally she made it to the central aisle but Tom stepped out from his seat to meet her and put a reassuring hand on her shoulder. He was a tall, stocky man in his mid-forties with a little beer belly who constantly seemed to be absentmindedly wrestling with his toddler. He rarely looked down at the child as he slithered like a snake through his father's legs and climbed him like a tree.

'So what's all this got to do with the snow?' Tom asked. Beau braced himself for the next crazy part of the tale.

'The snow is causing memory loss. Think about it!' Beau raised his voice over the negative muttering that had started to grow. 'Have you ever seen this much snow fall in one night? Especially when last night, in our memories, there was none at all? Not to mention that there shouldn't be any snow in *July*, anyway!' No one answered him and even Tom began to nod.

'It's just a bit of freak weather! That's all!' shouted a mother from the crowd.

'It *is* freak weather! Maybe the freakiest weather the earth has ever seen. But the reason we woke up this morning waist deep in snow is because it has snowed every night for the past five days and has been building up. When the snow falls, it erases twenty-four hours' worth of our memories and we wake up only remembering the weather on the sixteenth.' Everyone took a moment to ponder Beau's theory, which Luna took as a good sign.

'If I may …' she began as she slowly walked up the aisle towards Tom and Mrs Tucker, holding out her notebook at arm's length. 'Here.' Luna showed them the entries, the same date on every page and her apparent obliviousness in her writing. They both exchanged concerned looks over the pages.

'How do we know this isn't just a huge elaborate hoax?' asked Tom, still flipping from entry to entry. Heads bobbed up and down in the crowd, nodding their agreement.

'Well, you may not know me and so you have no reason to take my word for it but … you do know Beau. So it depends on whether you trust him?' Tom and Mrs Tucker looked up at Beau on the stage, who did a little half shrug.

'This is ludicrous.' Mrs Tucker folded her arms but her voice lacked the same firm authority it had when they had arrived. She looked from Luna to Beau and back again over and over, trying to make sense of everything.

'All right, all right.' Tom pinched the bridge of his nose, his child now sprawled out on the floor face down, his arms outstretched and clasped around his father's ankle, quietly singing the alphabet. 'Supposing this is all true and those videos haven't been tampered with and you didn't just write all this down ten minutes before you got here . . . what do you propose we do?'

'There are no trains today!' said Mrs Tucker.

'I know. There haven't been any trains for a while.'

'How did you figure all of this out?'

'Someone I know walked the tracks yesterday morning and went back out to them before the snow fell. He watched the snow fall onto the island, and only on the island, from a distance.'

'He walked the tracks?' gasped Mrs Tucker. 'But they're miles long!'

'At least we know that's an option for those brave enough to take it.'

'Where is this person now? Why aren't they here to vouch for your story?'

'He isn't the most . . . agreeable person. He even deleted the video he took from the tracks.'

'Convenient.' Mrs Tucker scoffed.

'Look. I'm not one for making up stories. Well . . . I'm an author, but what I mean is I'm not one for lying.'

'We don't even know you and you're asking us to walk the icy and potentially very dangerous tracks to the mainland? You're asking us to evacuate our homes?'

'What about our children?' A mother stood with her little girl in her arms, her legs wrapped around her waist.

'I wouldn't make it!' said an elderly man who raised his walking stick.

'I know, I know. I'm sorry. We've come to you all with a problem without a solution. We don't know the best way off the island.' Beau said. 'It would help if you were willing to use your boats to help ferry people off the island. Who has a boat and is willing to help?' Several people raised their hands and nodded their agreement.

'How come so many people have boats?' Luna whispered to Beau out of the side of her mouth.

'This is where people come to retire and do crazy things like buy boats they'll never use. Also, it's Ondingside. Everything here is about ten times cheaper than the mainland. Besides, it's handy to have a boat when you live on an island,' he whispered back.

'Boats would be a huge help to those who can't walk the tracks.' Luna spoke to the crowd.

'Even if you don't believe us, just go and visit family or friends on the mainland for a day or two. If we're wrong, you've seen family. But if we are right and something bizarre is going on … you can buy one of my coffees as a thank-you,' said Beau.

'I do just need to ask, though,' Luna said, massaging the wrinkles out of her forehead. 'Surely some of you must have noticed something isn't right here? It can't just be the two of us?' Silence followed but as Luna looked at everyone's faces in turn she could see realisation dawning on some and others averting their gaze with a hint of embarrassment. Someone stood up near the back of the crowd. It was a woman in her mid to late forties with an abundance of long, dark wavy hair that tumbled down to her waist. She was holding the hand of a man who was frantically whispering up at her to sit down.

'My boyfriend proposed to me today.'

'Congratulations,' Luna smiled, suddenly feeling the absence of her own engagement ring. Despite knowing her engagement, her wedding and marriage to Noel weren't meant to be, she couldn't help feeling like that companionship, that feeling of being a team, was missing from her life. Luna couldn't believe she was admitting it to herself but she knew she'd been shutting herself out for too long.

'But the thing is . . .' the woman said, looking down at her fiancé who finally conceded and nodded for her to continue, 'I woke up wearing the ring before he'd proposed and neither of us knew how it got there.'

Luna thought for a moment.

'He must have proposed yesterday,' she said. 'Or even a few days ago, which is why it was already on your finger before he popped the question.' She looked up at Beau who shook his head in disbelief but smiled at her. Seems like they really were right.

'This is such a minor thing but . . . my boy and I were growing cress,' said a man, 'y'know, for a school experiment. We only started the experiment yesterday, well, that I thought was yesterday, and I remember there being only seeds. When we woke up this morning it was like a mini forest! Thought we'd cracked the code for fastest growing cress but ... your theory makes much more sense ...' One by one the entire class and their parents muttered, 'That happened to us too!', 'Me too!' And 'I thought it was magic cress!'

'Come to think of it, I thought our fridge had emptied pretty quickly ...' said Tom. 'I blamed our son for finding and eating all the chocolate in the house but then found the wrappers in my glove compartment ... must have been me. Sorry, Aiden.' He bent to ruffle his son's hair.

'Pssst.' Another man stood. His daughter was sitting on the chair next to him playing with a teddy bear. He lowered his voice and leant over to Luna. 'I woke up this morning and my daughter found that our rabbit was missing,' he whispered. 'When I went out to search for it I noticed there was a strange indentation in the snow in our garden and what I uncovered looked like a patch of overturned soil. I went digging and ...' He looked back at his daughter who wasn't paying them any mind but even so, he slid his index finger across his neck. 'I found a little shoe box covered in unicorn stickers with the name "Tumbles" written across it in my daughter's writing. What was inside was definitely a few days old. There's no way it died today or even yesterday. I reckon that bloody dog next door got it.'

'Welles did no such thing!' A man stood in protest and something in Luna's mind started to sing in the distance as she looked at his face but there was nothing there, no memory she could grab on to.

'How would we know?' said Mrs Tucker.

'Well ... innocent until proven guilty, I say!' The man slumped to his seat and continued to grumble. Suddenly, everyone had a story. The room filled with tales of inexplicable appearances and disappearances and gaps in memories that everyone had put down to being old or forgetful because who would ever have thought that the reality was even possible, let alone a genuine explanation.

'Okay, okay, everyone! There's no need to panic.' Beau jumped down from the stage and joined Luna in the aisle.

'There is!' Mrs Tucker shrieked.

'There really isn't, Mrs Tucker. There are nearly four hundred of us and we have until midnight to get everyone off the island. That's just over six hours. Those of us able to walk the tracks will do so and the children and the elderly will be taken in the boats. Those of us who get to the mainland first will alert help. We will make it. But we have to get going. Now.'

'We'll go home and pack our bags as quickly as we can,' said Tom, lifting his little boy from the floor. 'Those with boats, get ready to sail and as soon as people start arriving and your boat is full, just go. Once you reach the mainland, sail back and pick up more of us. I reckon two boatloads each will get everyone to safety.'

'It's a load of old codswallop, that's what it is!' said a voice.

'You're a couple of troublemakers!' said another.

'We don't want to cause any more trouble than has

already been caused,' Beau reassured. 'It's your choice. If you choose not to come, we've done all we can to convince you. But better safe than sorry, in my opinion.'

'Me too,' said Tom, holding his son close and tight. 'I'd rather leave for a couple of days and see what happens than stay here for another day if something genuinely isn't right.' The majority of the crowd agreed and began to move. Some jumped up on stage to wrangle their rainbow-clad children from behind the curtain. 'I have a boat,' Tom said to Luna and Beau. 'I'll make sure I stay until the last possible moment to board any stragglers. Midnight, you said?'

'That's what we think.'

'Then my last trip will leave at fifteen minutes to. Eleven-forty-five,' he said and held out a hand which both Luna and Beau shook gratefully in return. Luna could feel the electric urgency of the crowd but she was sufficiently pleased that they'd managed to avoid complete commotion and chaos. However, there was something niggling in the back of Luna's mind.

'That actually went pretty well!' Beau said, snaking a hand around her hip.

'I agree but ... I dunno, something doesn't feel right.' She looked over the heads of the adults as they lifted their kids on their hips or loaded them into pushchairs.

What about our children?

'Beau ... the woman who works in the second-hand bookshop. Wendy. Where is she? Have you seen her here?' As she said it, Beau's face changed from one of pride to one of panic. Luna could remember talking about having met and made friends with Wendy in the CCTV footage. She remembered watching her hands mime a large belly once when she said her name in the video. 'Was Wendy ... pregnant?'

Twenty-Three

A New Arrival

Now the lack of commotion irritated Luna as she and Beau ran to Wendy's bookshop. The non-urgency with which people got in their cars and strolled away from the town hall, waving to friends and family as they went, whilst Luna was filled with a squirming itch that she couldn't scratch, made her want to scream.

'Wendy!' Beau beat his fist repeatedly on the door when they arrived. 'WENDY!' He stood back from the door and looked for an alternative way in and that's when they heard it. In the silence and the stillness of the empty street, Wendy broke it with a strangled wail from inside the shop. Beau continued to thump the door.

'She won't be able to answer the door, Beau, there's no use in knocking! We'll have to break it down.' Luna lifted one of the hanging baskets from a hook outside the front of the shop. It had a pointy end that would be perfect for smashing through the window.

'Wait!' Beau yelped as Luna raised the basket above her head, ready to crash it against the glass. He dug around in his pocket and pulled out a keyring adorned with at least fifteen keys. He rattled through them until he plucked out the shiniest and most unused.

'She gave me a spare key for emergencies. I think this counts and I doubt she'd thank us for destroying the front of her shop.' Beau wiggled the key in the lock. It was stiff but it finally turned and as the door opened the wailing was considerably louder. They clattered into the shop over plant pots and piles of books.

'Wendy! Where are you?!'

'Uuuuppp heeeeerrrreeeee!' Wendy howled, her voice coming from up the stairs behind the curtain to the left of the counter. Luna darted up the stairs with Beau hot on her heels. The landing was small but the door to the bedroom and the bathroom were wide open and there was a wet trail soaked into the carpet from one room to the other.

'Her waters have broken. Looks like this baby is well and truly on the way.' In the bedroom, Wendy was on her knees, her elbows pushing deep into the mattress, her fists clenched into tight white balls.

'We need to get her off the island,' said Beau standing over her, his arms held out in front of him wanting to be helpful but having no idea exactly how.

'So she can give birth in a boat or on the train tracks? We don't have a choice now. She'll need to have the baby here and then we need to get her off the island safely and comfortably.' Luna bent down next to Wendy and rubbed her back in circular motions like she'd seen people do to pregnant ladies in movies.

'What if she's in labour until past midnight?'

'I don't know, Beau!' Luna hissed. 'I just don't think we can risk moving her. Whatever happens, we're going to need help. Unless you're capable of delivering a baby?'

'I've watched *One Born Every Minute* but I'm not sure that qualifies me,' he shrugged.

'No, it bloody doesn't!' Wendy yelled with her eyes squeezed shut.

'Wendy, do you have anyone we can call?' Luna asked as softly as she could. 'A midwife, maybe?'

'If Wendy does have a midwife, the phones don't work and she may be on her way to the boats right now!'

'AHHHH!' Wendy wrangled the entire duvet into a ball in her arms.

'I know, I know, he's really annoying me too,' Luna cooed. Wendy continued to wail and it was a wonder that either Luna or Beau heard the clanging of the bell downstairs.

'Who's going book shopping whilst the entire island is evacuating?' Beau asked as he backed away from screaming Wendy and down the stairs to see who was in the shop. Luna could just about hear muffled voices and then footsteps over Wendy's panting and moaning until Beau entered the room followed by Maggie carrying a large black and blue bag.

'Well here's three people I didn't expect to be in a room together. Especially at the end of the world,' she said, plonking the bag down on the bed next to her.

'It's not the end of the world, Maggie, it's just ... it's ...' Beau looked to Luna for a little help.

'Think of it as a trip abroad?' she shrugged, quickly turning back to Wendy.

'It's the end of the world as I know it, Beau! No more living on the island? I've only left twice before in my life. This isn't how any of us imagined spending the evening.'

'It'll only be for a little while, I'm sure,' Luna said reassuringly, but she wondered how long it would really be until everyone could return to Ondingside. There was no off switch for the snow and as it had been snowing every night for a while now, it showed no signs of stopping itself.

'How did you know Wendy needed you?' Luna asked.

'When I didn't see her at the play, I guessed something wasn't quite right and thought I'd check in before I hopped on a boat. Good job I did! Now let's see if we can't get this little one out before we all forget what's going on, eh?' Maggie started pulling items from her bag that were foreign to Luna.

'You believe us, then?' Luna said, wincing as Wendy squeezed a little harder.

'I've been taking notes during Wendy's pregnancy.

Much like you, I couldn't figure out why I had five pages of notes for the same day. What was even more worrying was that the notes were showing signs of Wendy getting progressively closer to giving birth. Glad I came when I did! Looks like it's time!'

'You think?' Wendy mumbled into the sheets.

'None of that sass, my girl! I could easily get on a boat right now and leave you here on the floor.'

'Don't you even dare . . .' Wendy hissed.

'We'll let you take it from here.'

'We'll just be downstairs though, Wendy. If you need anything just let us know.' Beau widened his eyes at Luna as she bundled him out of the room and downstairs out of earshot.

'I'm not leaving her, Beau.'

'You don't even really know her. Why do you feel like you owe her your friendship?'

'Because . . . well, I sort of do know her. I *should* know her, at least. The me that met her really liked her and if I still had all of those memories, I'd want to stay. Besides, *you* know her! Why don't you want to stay?'

'I only kind of know her. We weren't bessie mates! We work next door to each other and I always thought she was a sandwich short of a picnic! I don't owe her my memory! Besides, Maggie is taking care of her! She'll be fine! They both will.' Beau tried to put his hands on Luna's shoulders but she pulled away, almost toppling backwards over a very large plant pot.

'Beau, I'm staying,' she said firmly and finally. 'I can't leave not knowing if both of them are completely safe. She'll probably have the baby in the next hour or so, anyway! Then we can all get her onto Tom's boat safely.' Beau checked his watch. It was nearing half six.

'Fine.' He sighed. 'I guess, I'll just ... wait here whilst you go to the inn and pack your things. Once you're back, I'll go and pack mine. Hopefully by then there will be one more person in this house and we can all leave together.' She held out a hand for him and he took it in both of his and kissed the back of her fingers.

'*Together*.' She smiled.

Twenty-Four

Forgetting

The wind outside had picked up and was howling so loudly that Luna's ears were ringing by the time she reached the inn. Trees had been bending so far in the gale they almost touched the ground and several car alarms leapt into action as Luna had run past them in the streets. It continued to whistle through the cracks in the inn as she raced up to her room for the last time. How Luna hadn't noticed how much laundry she'd collected for what she thought was just one day, she didn't know. She also found a grey teddy bear that she had no recollection of but she packed him in her case next to her toiletries all the same. She opened all the desk drawers and found a selection of pens and receipts scattered about, all dated with the correct dates. She was astounded by her own oblivious ignorance and knew she would spend the rest of her life waking up and checking every possible source she could for the correct date and time. Luna also found a collection of little white cards, each bearing various quotes on them. Something in her mind flashed like several lightbulbs all flickering in quick succession but there was no memory attached. She slid the cards into a compartment in her rucksack for later inspection. Luna was saddened that she'd spent so long in one place and yet it still felt foreign and unexplored. She wondered if, when she returned back to the mainland, when time began to pass once more, she would ever remember her time in Ondingside. Would she think of it fondly as somewhere familiar or would it feel like a distant memory that would continue to fade in her mind? Knowing you'd spent much longer in one place than you thought, and should have more of an attachment than your memory was letting you have, was a difficult thing to process so Luna put off thinking about it all until she was safe and could properly mourn the memories she had lost.

The inn was empty. There was a note pinned to the front desk that read:

Dear Guests,
  I have left and should hopefully
be on a hike across the railway
tracks by the time you read this.

What an adventure! The doors will remain unlocked so that everyone can retrieve their belongings and evacuate. Hopefully, I'll be back soon and will reopen the inn ASAP, with a fully functioning memory.

Au Revoir, for now.

Mrs McArthur

Luna was pleased Mrs McArthur had listened and believed her and Beau and their story but she was certain that after a little bit of research in her books and accounts, Mrs M would have found the evidence she'd needed. *It's funny what you miss when you're not looking for it,* she thought. As Luna wheeled her case over to the door, movement in the bar caught her eye.

'Jaxon? Are you serious?' He was slumped in his chair, snoring gently. She stormed over to him and gave him a shove and he snorted awake.

'Whhaaatt?' he groaned, repositioning himself and closing his eyes again.

'Everyone's leaving the island. You need to get your stuff and either walk back the way you came or get on one of the boats. In fact, strike that. You're walking. There are people far more deserving of spaces on the boats. So, come on. I can walk you to the waterfront.' Luna put a hand in the crook of his elbow and attempted to heave him out of his chair but he just wouldn't budge.

'Jaxon.' She whacked his arm. 'Come on.'

'I'm staying,' he grumbled.

'*Excuse* me?'

'I'm not going,' he sulked.

'What do you mean?' She shook her head.

'I. Am. Staying. Am I speaking a different language?' he said with his eyes still shut.

'I can hear what you're saying, I just don't understand. This place makes you forget.'

'And that's exactly what I need right now,' he huffed as he opened his eyes to look at her, the light making him squint.

'The booze not quite doing the trick?'

'Not even close.' Jaxon rubbed at his eyes with balled-up fists and yawned.

'The island only makes you forget the last twenty-four hours, Jaxon. Anything before that won't go away.'

'Well, I'm thinking: the longer I stay, maybe the more I'll forget? A fun little experiment for the lonely and sad.'

'That's not a tested theory. Is it really worth the risk?'

'I'm happy to be a guinea pig. Nothing to lose!' His face didn't move to match the strangled noise he'd made that was an attempted laugh.

'Jaxon, there will be people back at home who will miss you if you get stuck here.'

'Wrong again! My parents think I'm off wasting my life anyway, and haven't got in touch in forever. I don't have any money to carry on chasing storms and hurricanes and blizzards and my girlfriend left just before I came here so ...' Jaxon lifted the empty bottle and shook it near his ear. When he was sufficiently sure it was empty he threw it across the room where it shattered and cracked the glass in a picture frame on the wall. 'Nothing to lose!' he said, scraping his chair backwards and stumbling up and across to the bar where he attempted to fill a pint glass from the beer tap from the wrong side of the bar. As the glass filled, it gradually slipped out of his hand and smashed on the floor. Instead, he clambered up onto the bar, lay on his back and put his mouth over the tap. He reached up and pulled the lever and began to gulp.

'Wow.' Luna stared, half in awe and half in pity. 'Look. I'm going to the bookshop. I'll be there until probably the last minute tonight and I'm getting the last boat at eleven forty-five to make sure everyone who wants to get off the island is off the island. If you change your mind, that's where I'll be.' Luna turned away but heard the lever *thunk* back into place.

'Is your boyfriend going with you? Are the pair of heroes sailing off into the sunset?' he garbled. Luna paused in the doorway.

'Beau is coming with me, yes.'

'How romantic,' he said, positioning himself back under the faucet.

'What's your problem? Why can't you just be happy for people instead of seeing the world through the haze of your own misery?'

'Different people are dealt different hands, babe.'

'Yes, I know. That's not the issue, though, is it?' He didn't reply. 'Just because you've got unsupportive parents and your girlfriend left for whatever reason, that doesn't give you the right to try and make others miserable. No one *deserves* to be miserable. We should all be striving to be as happy as we can be and make life better for everyone else around us. It's bitter arseholes like you that think just because you've had a rough time, no one else deserves any goodness. Instead of trying to raise yourself up, you try and drag others down. I'd be angry at you if I didn't feel sorry for you.'

'This is you *not* being angry? Blimey. Don't feel sorry for me, feel sorry for Beau.'

'And what is the obsession you've got with me and Beau? We only met today ... technically.'

'Whatever's gone on between you in the last few days must have been pretty special. I see the way he looks at you.' Luna was taken aback by his sudden change in temperament.

'Well ... thanks. I guess.'

'Shame you're not that into him.'

'I'm sorry?'

'No need to be sorry. It's just sad, that's all.'

'What are you talking about?'

'He's completely besotted with you and you barely even know he's there.'

'I don't ... I don't think that's ...'

'It seems like with every day you've met again, he's fallen a little bit more in love with you, he's helped you become the person you've always wanted to be, but I bet as soon as you get back to the mainland, you're gonna run off with someone a little more in shape and a lot better-looking and leave poor Beau in the lurch.'

Luna watched his smug face as he resumed his alcoholic position underneath the beer nozzle. Calmly, Luna walked over to him and put a firm and strong hand on the lever and pushed it all the way down so the beer flowed full force out of the tap and directly into his mouth. He tried to act casual, like it was no big deal, but he couldn't swallow quick enough and it wasn't long before his eyes widened and began to water. He flailed and as he opened his mouth beer ran out over his face and neck and up his nose. Luna moved away as he spluttered and coughed.

'You could have killed me!' he whimpered, dizzy and swaying.

'What you think of me is none of my business. I know that's not who I am. I happen to like Beau. A lot,' she said, feeling her heart pound at the thought of soft and awkward Beau. The thought of how perfectly his cheek fit in her palm, the way he ruffled his own hair when he was nervous and the fact that he fought to not only be positive himself, but instil positivity and kindness in others when he himself still mourned the loss of an important person and a chapter in his life that he had longed for and never got to live. 'Actually ...' she giggled in spite of herself, 'I think it's more than that.' She looked at Jaxon, wiping beer from his stubbled face with his T-shirt, reeking of booze and cigarettes, and she wondered how long he'd felt like the world had owed him something. She wondered if that had come after any hardship he'd endured or whether that was something he had always felt. Either way, she pitied him. It seemed he would always find something to claim was against him as an excuse never to live the life he wanted to live because that was easier.

'The offer is still open. The last boat leaves just before midnight. I hope you come but if you don't, I hope you find whatever it is that you're looking for. Good luck, Jaxon.'

'You too ... holy shit. I don't know your name.'

'You'll forget it tomorrow, anyway.' She shrugged, smiled and without looking back, she left.

'Did I miss anything?' Luna asked as she set down her rucksack on a table in the back of the shop. Beau put down a copy of *Around The World in Eighty Days* that he'd seemingly raced through.

'Nope. A lot of wailing, expletives from both Wendy *and* Maggie but no baby yet.' Beau checked his watch before he stood and stretched. 'I better go and pack myself. I have no idea how to get everything from the shop off the island. I may have to make other arrangements when I get to the mainland.'

'Yeah, I mean … surely this is something that won't go on for ever, right?' They both fell silent. Luna certainly hadn't thought about what happened once they left. Who would need to be told? Who was the authority over Ondingside, or the weather for that matter? How could you stop the weather or what this weather in particular was causing? What happened to the residents of the island whilst it was being sorted? What happened if it was never sorted? Luna's mind was flooded with questions she'd never thought to ask and a panic rose in her body.

'I'm sure someone has the answer. Right now we just need to take it one step at a time and the first step is getting us all off this island.' As Beau passed her, he took her hand and leant in to kiss the top of her head. It was brief. So brief that Luna followed him to the door.

'You do know that I like you … a lot. Don't you?'

'I do now.'

'I really mean it, though.' Luna rocked onto her tiptoes and planted a kiss on his lips that she'd only meant to be quick but he caught her face in his hands and held her there. He pulled away and took a moment to look into her eyes.

'I'm looking forward to remembering today,' he whispered. 'I'll be back soon. Promise.' He kissed the top of her head once more and then he was gone.

Jaxon didn't purposely try to cause trouble. In fact, it came very naturally. Chaos felt like second nature and when it was absent from a room, the urge to cause it became overpowering. Stinking of stale beer, drunk and humiliated, Jaxon stepped out in the roaring wind and followed the whirr of Luna's rolling case and followed her bright white-blonde hair like a star in the sky. He stalked from a safe distance, enjoying the way her hips gently swayed with each step she took. He hovered around the corner as Luna entered the old bookshop and he stayed hidden until Beau appeared in the street a few minutes later and entered his own coffee shop next door. It was then that Jaxon made his move. Adrenaline began to sober him up as he ducked under the window of the bookshop, and stayed crouched until he couldn't see Beau any more. He pushed on the door of the coffee shop gently and slowly and only so much so that he could slip through without ringing the bell. The door behind the counter was open and Jaxon could hear the sound of Beau rustling around upstairs. He stumbled into a chair which squeaked against the floor and the rustling ceased and was replaced with quickening footsteps and, panicked, Jaxon ducked in front of the counter.

Beau looked around and saw no one but noticed the door was only rested against the door frame – he was certain he'd fully closed it behind him when he'd entered the shop. He straightened a chair as he went to close it properly but as he turned back around, he came face to face with Jaxon and got a whiff of his breath just before Jaxon's fist connected with his jaw. Beau's head was thrust into door frame and, unconscious, he sank to the floor in a heap. It took Jaxon a good ten minutes to haul Beau's dead weight across the shop, around the counter and through the back door where his keys still dangled in the lock. Dizzy and swaying, Jaxon shut the door which hit Beau's head and bent his neck up at a funny angle. He turned the key in the lock and rattled the handle to ensure it wouldn't budge. He left the shop, locked the outside door and pocketed the keys. His knuckles throbbed but he smiled all the same as he revelled in the delicious chaos he had caused.

Twenty-Five

Departing

The clock slowly ticked closer and closer to midnight and panic began to worm its way into Luna's mind. It made her skin prickle and she couldn't sit still. Beau had left at seven-thirty and three hours later he still hadn't returned. She'd gone outside and checked the front of the shop but it was firmly locked and she assumed he had business elsewhere on the island he needed to attend to. However, she thought it was odd he hadn't said anything to her, especially if he had any inkling that he might take this long. She had no reason to suspect that something might be amiss but something about the situation caused her stomach to tie itself in knots and she couldn't put her finger on why. With large chunks of her memory missing, this was a feeling she was starting to get used to. At ten-fifty-nine, Wendy let out a scream so loud and so long that Luna thought it would never end. The silence that followed seemed even longer until it was broken by the sound of a delicate, tinkling cry. Luna barrelled up the stairs but paused at the bedroom door. Who was she to barge in on this special moment between a freshly born baby and a new mother? Then again, could Wendy use a friend? Luna knocked lightly on the door and pushed it open only an inch.

'Come in! Come in!' Wendy whispered over the head of her child that was bundled against her chest. Maggie was red-faced and sweaty as she waddled in and out of the room.

'It's a girl! A teeny, tiny, little baby girl!' Wendy grinned as tears slipped down the bridge of her nose and onto the pink head of her daughter.

'Oh, Wendy. Congratulations.' Luna had never been this close to the scene of a birth before, as someone who hadn't quite found the maternal instinct, but Wendy had enough for maybe a hundred people. The love poured off her in waves and Luna found herself crying as she watched the woman cradle and hush her little girl, any thoughts of blizzards, time and escape completely lost to that singular moment. Then she thought of Beau. 'Wendy, has Maggie explained what's happening?'

'I thought I'd leave the explaining to you,' Maggie whispered. 'Not sure I totally understand myself. I'd only confuse her!'

'She said something about having to leave once the baby was born but ... well ...' Wendy looked back down into the face of her newborn.

'Yes, I suppose you've had more pressing matters to attend to. I know you're tired and I know this isn't ideal but we need to get you and your daughter off the island before midnight.'

'What? Why? I couldn't possibly. Not tonight. Maybe tomorrow.'

'I'm afraid it has to be tonight, Wendy,' Maggie said as she re-entered the room.

Luna tried her best to explain to Wendy and although she wasn't sure she quite understood in her tired state, she trusted the advice of her midwife and old friend and for some reason she also trusted Luna. Luna tried her best to pack Wendy's possessions in an old suitcase she had stored under the bed whilst Maggie delivered the placenta and cut the cord.

'Don't forget to pack the book I'm reading! It's downstairs on the counter.' Luna heaved the case down the stairs to get it out of the room whilst Maggie cleaned Wendy up and prepared her as best she could for the boat trip. Luna went to the counter and she recognised the book before she'd even turned it over to read the title. *Cloud Walking.* One of her own creations.

'What are the chances?' she laughed to herself as she picked it up but her breath caught when she opened the front cover and found her own signature scrawled on the inside page. By eleven-fifteen, the three of them were locking up the shop and carefully loading into Wendy's car to get them to the waterfront. Beau's shop was still dark and locked. She looked up and down the street but there was no sign of him and the wind was almost ripping the car door out of her hand. So, reluctantly, Luna ducked inside the car.

'Let's go,' she said, swallowing hard and fighting off the tears. *People always leave,* said a voice in her head. *Why ever did you think he would be any different?*

One single boat was rocking violently in the dock as they pulled up in Wendy's car. Maggie hummed most of the way, which unnerved Luna. She never trusted anyone who whistled or hummed with seemingly no reason. She assumed that everyone had something on their mind to occupy their thoughts and couldn't fathom someone's mind being so empty that it had to be filled by arbitrary tunes. Outside, bushes and trees violently rustled and bent in the wind that blasted them from all directions. Jaxon was right and tonight did seem to be the pinnacle of the blizzard. She'd not seen or heard gales quite like it before and it struck a fear in her that buzzed underneath her skin. As they approached the waterfront, the lights from the mainland were distant and twinkling dimly but they filled Luna with an urgent and overwhelming sense of hope. They were all so close to moving on, to having the future they'd all been robbed of, but Luna felt Beau's absence heavily in her chest. The thing that weighed on her heart the most was not having an explanation for his sudden disappearance. When he'd left her he'd kissed her so tenderly. It had been filled with a promise of a future *together*, regardless of what it held for them both. If he'd changed his mind, she just wanted to know why and didn't think it was beyond the realms of reason to think that she deserved some kind of an explanation, at the very least.

'Are you the last ones leaving?' Tom appeared on the dock, holding his hat on his head and immediately taking Luna's case from her hands.

'We are. I thought Beau would be coming with us but I've not seen him in hours.'

'Really? That doesn't seem like him. Usually does what he says he's going to, if only to prove someone wrong,' Tom chuckled as he wheeled the case down the dock with both hands, the wind trying to wrestle it from him.

'Guess he changed his mind,' she called after him and although Tom had already stopped listening, she couldn't seem to stop the flow of her consciousness from streaming out of her mouth. 'Maybe he had other plans. Maybe he really still is on his way and I'm just being paranoid and untrusting. He's never given me a reason not to trust him before ... I just ... ' she breathed through the wave of sadness, 'I just don't know.' She shrugged with a forced smile and turned her attention to helping Wendy out of the car to busy her sorrowful mind. Wendy's daughter was tucked up neatly in a blanket like a little snoozing burrito, oblivious to the severe weather conditions, and Wendy wouldn't even let go of her to get out of the car. She wiggled her aching hips forward until her feet touched the ground and Luna awkwardly helped as much as she could until she was on her own two feet. Luna still kept an arm around her to steady her.

'Does she have a name yet?' Luna tiptoed to look at the little girl's scrunched-up face. Even freshly born, she looked like her mother. She had the same button nose with a wide bridge and a prominent cupid's bow.

'I can't think of one,' Wendy said sadly. 'My mother didn't believe in giving those with new lives the names of people who had already lived theirs. Too much pressure. No one wants to constantly feel like they've got something to live up to.' They spoke gazing down at the child's face, completely mesmerised.

'She sounds like a wise woman.' Luna smiled down at the child.

'Any suggestions?' Wendy asked hopefully.

'I've only ever named characters.' Luna shrugged.

'You write?' Wendy's eyes brightened.

'I try.'

'Well, then you're the perfect person to pick a name!'

'I've never had to name an actual human who has to live with whatever ridiculousness I've thrust upon them,' Luna said. 'But, if it helps, I always like to give my characters names that fit their lives and situations. Like in my book *Cloud Walking,* for instance. I called the protagonist Misty because nothing ever seemed clear to her.' Luna shrugged and Wendy lifted her head, her eyes suddenly transfixed upon Luna instead of her daughter.

'You wrote *Cloud Walking*? You're Elle J. Lark?' Wendy breathed. Luna heard those words in her mind and she was sure she heard them echo back from a tucked away memory.

'I feel like maybe we've done this before ...' she said.

'Yes, I feel like maybe we have.' Luna watched Wendy's eyes through her thick glasses flit around her face like a moth dancing around a bright light. They filled with tears which quickly spilled over and onto the blanket that swathed the baby.

'And just like that my little girl has a name.' Wendy's lips fought themselves into a smile despite her face crumpling into tears.

'Really?' Luna squeezed Wendy's shoulders against her and Wendy took a deep breath to steady her voice to say her daughter's name with clarity.

'Tomorrow,' she said, instantly bursting into tears again. 'Since the snow started falling it's the one thing on this island none of us got. Except for me. I got a Tomorrow. And she's the most beautiful thing in the world,' Wendy sniffed.

'It's perfect.' Luna choked on her words and tried to hide her tears by leaning forward and planting a kiss on

Tomorrow's wrinkled forehead. Then she kissed Wendy's cheek. The days she must have spent in Wendy's company hadn't lingered in her mind but they'd certainly lingered in her heart and she hoped that Wendy could feel their friendship as strongly as she could, even if neither of them could remember it.

'When we get off this island and I actually remember you in the morning, can we keep in touch?' Luna asked.

'Really?'

'*Please.*'

'Oh ...' Wendy's hot tears fell faster and instead of answering vocally, she finally took one arm away from cradling her daughter and wrapped it around Luna's neck and Luna embraced them both. The three of them stood cradling each other, strong against the wind as it tried to knock them down like bowling pins. The sound of footsteps crunching through the snow broke their tearful moment as Luna's head snapped up, hoping to see Beau's smiling face coming out of the darkness. Her hope shattered as she took in Jaxon, instead, in all his beer-stained glory.

'Wendy?' Jaxon's voice cracked. Luna felt Wendy's heart begin to race before she pulled away from her.

'No. No, no, no, no ...' Wendy took one look at Jaxon's face and began to waddle away from him. As Jaxon ran to her, Luna took her place firmly between them.

'Don't come any closer. She's got a newborn in her arms and now is not the time for any drunken dramatics,'

Luna snarled but she could see now that Jaxon's cheeks were wet with tears that were falling hot and fast.

'Wendy, please talk to me,' he begged, any trace of a bad boy long gone.

'You left.' Luna was surprised to hear Wendy sobbing too behind her. 'You left and you didn't come back.'

'Things were ... complicated. I couldn't ... I didn't know ...'

'How could you know? I had no address, no number – it all happened so fast that I never even knew your name. I had no way of telling you.' She peered over Luna's shoulder. 'Besides, by the looks of you, we're better off just the two of us.'

'Is she ...' He gestured to the bundle in Wendy's arms.

'Yes,' Wendy snapped. 'Of course she's yours.' Jaxon took a moment to let that sink in, his face crumpling, but despite his broken, vulnerable state, Luna kept her hands up just in case he were to lunge for Wendy and the baby.

'Had I known this was ... that you were ... that there was ...' He sighed, desperately scrambling to find the right words. 'Wendy, I would have come back had I known, I swear.' He stepped towards her and Luna took a step towards him.

'Then you would have come back for the wrong reasons. You would have come back out of guilt and obligation. Not for me. Or for her.' Wendy buried her face in the blanket wrapped around her little girl and Luna could hear her let out a controlled emotional howl. Luna had

369

no idea she was hurting so greatly and certainly hadn't known it was because of Jaxon.

'It's a girl?'

Wendy nodded but Jaxon couldn't see past Luna.

'It's a girl,' Luna confirmed. 'Her name is Tomorrow.' A smile split through the sadness for a brief moment.

'Can I see her?' he asked, his arms already reaching out for his daughter.

'Luna, please keep him away from me.' Wendy sniffed back her sadness and replaced it with venom.

'Are you sure?' Luna whispered over her shoulder.

'He made his choice,' Wendy said, loud and clear. 'I've made mine.' She walked as quickly as she could down the dock to where Tom was waiting for them. Luna waited until she was out of earshot.

'Come with us?' Luna put her hands on Jaxon's chest as he went to run for her. 'You can't stay on the island anyway and at least then you'll have the boat ride to try and talk to her. Or there's always tomorrow and the day after that and the day after that but if you stay here, there's only today.' Jaxon turned his head and looked her in the eyes. 'She's tired and obviously upset but ... I don't think you're anywhere near as bad as she thinks you are and I reckon with a bit of work ... a lot of work ... you would make an amazing father to that little girl.' Jaxon bowed his head, hiding his tears from her. 'Come with us.' For a moment, Luna thought she'd convinced him. She had hoped at the very least that he would just get in the boat with them so they could all leave Ondingside behind them. Then his face turned stony and emotionless and his cold hard stare sent a shiver through her bones.

'I've told you. I'm staying here. You heard her. I made my choice.'

'And I really can't convince you otherwise?' she asked, pulling her hands away from him, letting him stumble forwards. He shook his head.

'Then I'm sorry. For how things have turned out for you. I hope you figure things out, one way or another.' Luna took one last look at the sad and sorry state that Jaxon had become before turning towards where her loyalty laid.

'Lover boy didn't show, then?' Jaxon called after her. One last desperate attempt at distance, at pushing away those who were trying to help. She slowed her pace but didn't turn around. 'I'm not surprised.'

'What's that supposed to mean?' Luna called over her shoulder, not wanting Jaxon to see how her face was already starting to crumple.

'I saw him leaving this coffee shop a few hours ago. Seemed to be heading straight here.'

'Well, he must be on the mainland waiting for me.'

'Seemed more like he was trying to get away from you, if you ask me.'

'I'm not asking you.'

'I'm just saying ...' he drawled and as Luna spun to

face him she couldn't understand how, at a time like this, his lips were still contorted into a smirk.

'Well, don't, Jaxon.' Her eyes welled and she watched something change in Jaxon. His face relaxed and it seemed he understood that he'd pushed just that bit too hard. It was no longer a game Luna could play or even tolerate and he was bordering on the cruel. 'Just . . . don't.' And he didn't.

The cold air was finding a way through her coat and her clothes no matter how tightly she held herself. Maggie, Wendy and Tomorrow had taken their seats in the tiny cabin but Luna couldn't stand the idea of being cooped up and trapped. She thought that Wendy and Tomorrow could probably do with a little bit of space, anyway.

'Is Beau not coming?' Tom asked as he helped her step from the dock onto the boat as it wobbled underneath her. She looked up at Jaxon's silhouette as he lit a cigarette, his breath mixed with smoke pluming out around him. He was very much alone and although the wind was loud and fierce she was certain she couldn't hear any footsteps. She breathed in the icy air and breathed out a painful 'No, he's not.'

'Are you sure? He's the one who made us all leave the island and—'

'I know. I do know. But is he here?' Luna snapped. 'He knew what time the boat was leaving and he hasn't come. We have two minutes to get far enough away from the island before the snow starts to fall and we have a mother and a baby to think about. Beau has made his decision. It's time to go.' Luna turned her back on the dock, on Ondingside and on Beau and sat down in her slightly damp seat. Tom himself gave the docks a quick scan and when he was sufficiently saddened to see that Beau really wasn't coming with them, he started the engine. The boat began to slowly pull away, as if reluctant to leave its home. Luna reached into her pocket and pulled out her phone which still told her it was the sixteenth but that the time was eleven fifty-nine.

'Can we go any faster, Tom? Midnight is about to hit,' Luna shouted. Tom lifted a thumbs-up from his driver's seat. It was then that the wind ceased its blowing and its roaring, the sea calmed its thrashing and waving and the only sound they could hear was the engine of the boat.

Epilogue

Luna

July 2020

Luna sat in a blue, neatly pressed jumpsuit that was more expensive than her brother's first car. She felt like she was unable to move in it properly for fear of creasing or pulling the fabric in some way that would ruin it for ever. Her hair and make-up had been done by a professional hired for the event and for once she actually felt like an author, instead of a woman who wrote silly little stories that people pitied enough to publish. An audience had gathered in a large bookshop in central London just to hear her talk about her book and to ask their most pressing questions.

'We have just enough time to take one more question from the crowd and then Elle J. Lark will be signing your books at the back of the store in the romantic fiction section.' Her publicist, Sophie Briggs, had decided to chair the event herself in order to have full control over the evening. She knew how close this story was to Luna's heart and her kind yet no-nonsense manner often coaxed people into asking the right kinds of questions but if they didn't, Sophie could assuage the situation.

No one had expected Luna's new novel to take off in quite the way it had; however, no one had expected it less than Luna. Her other books had sold well but none of them had ever exploded onto any kind of scene and Luna had enjoyed the anonymity it had given her. She'd struggled for inspiration and ideas in the lead-up to her deadline but she never thought something would happen to her that was stranger than the fiction she read let alone wrote herself. Inspiration comes easy when your life takes an exciting and supernatural turn. It took her five months to craft the story she had lived into a story she could tell. With lots of minor tweaks (and some major ones) she immortalised her time in Ondingside but more importantly, she had immortalised her time with Beau.

Beau had never appeared again once she'd arrived on the mainland. Either he'd changed his mind and found a way off the island without her or something had kept him on the island, in which case any memory of her was lost. She didn't even know where he was or where she could find him and so she wrote about him instead. She captured their story so she could finally close their book for good. Luna had had to change their names and appearances and although the factual story had been splashed over national news, no one knew what a vital part she had played. To most, her book was simply a work of fiction based on a true event. Beau would certainly never remember that he was part of her story were he to happen upon the book but even so, she felt like it was the best way she could immortalise what they had.

A flurry of hands shot into the air and flapped like salmon. Her publicist pointed and smiled at a woman near the back who had been desperately trying to get their attention all evening.

'I just wanted to know . . .' she said as she stood, 'why didn't Hazel try to find David? When it was all over?' Sophie shifted uncomfortably in her chair. Luna had asked herself this very same question over and over again but always came to the same conclusion.

'What do you do when the person you think you may have fallen for will wake up tomorrow with no memory of you at all? The balance between them would never have been the same. Her always a step ahead, him always a step behind. He had a life without her prior to when she arrived and she had one after because she had met him. In the end, she felt that they were probably better off apart. He could live his life as he had done before she had arrived on the island and caused mayhem and she could live hers better off for having known him.'

'But he may not have got off the island . . .' the woman

said, feebly. Luna felt her smile falter for a moment. She looked down at her hands in her lap as her fingers tightened around each other.

'The way I see it, either he got off the island or he didn't. So either he forgot her or he wanted to. Neither leaves our Hazel in a very happy place.'

'Do *you* think he got off the island?' the woman asked, adjusting her glasses.

'I'm sorry, I think that's all the questions we've got time for . . . ' Sophie stood, her left eye starting to twitch.

'It's all right,' Luna whispered, giving Sophie a nod. 'What do *you* think?' Luna asked the woman, whose cheeks flushed pink.

'Me? Well, I . . . ' She thought for a moment and it seemed the entire crowd took the same time to think of what their own answer would be, how they wanted the story to end. 'I think something happened and he was trapped on the island. *He loved her.* He wouldn't have let her go. Not without a fight.' The words sliced through Luna and it took a few seconds before she could find her voice again.

'That's what I like to think, too.' Luna smiled with shining eyes. 'Hazel couldn't bring herself to turn his world upside down again when he had a shot at living normally without the chaos of what had happened. Now it's time for them both to start living. Thank you, everyone.' Luna gave the crowd a small wave and rose from her seat as they erupted into applause but she barely heard them over the loudness of her thoughts.

'I'm so sorry. Next time we'll vet questions before they're asked.'

'No, no! Don't be silly, Sophie! It was a good question and I wouldn't have answered it if I didn't want to. It's all just still a bit ... raw.'

'Totally get it. Do you want to take a little break before you start signing?'

'No. No, I think we rip off the plaster. Let's just plough through.'

'YOU WERE SO MARVELLOUS!' Wendy burst past the security guard with Tomorrow wrapped around her waist like a little koala bear and threw her arms around Luna, trails of orange fabric wafting out behind her.

'Thank you, Wendy,' Luna laughed, taking Tomorrow from her and kissing her cheek until Tomorrow giggled the giggle that Luna couldn't get enough of.

'Oof, that last question. I'm proud of you for getting through that; you answered it perfectly.'

'Yeah?' Luna asked and Wendy responded by making a circle with her thumb and forefinger and a wink.

'Cup of tea for the table?' Sophie asked.

'Actually, a coffee would be great.'

'The events manager said there was a great little place that opened up a few months ago right across the road, so I'll get someone to nip out for you.'

'No, no! We'll go!' said Wendy. 'It'll be nice to get outside in the fresh, London pollution. Flat white?'

'Thank you.' She squeezed Wendy's hand as they

breezed back past the bewildered security guard. 'Let's do this.' Sophie led Luna through the back of the shop and out onto the shop floor where a table had been set up in amongst the bookshelves. The first few people in the queue gave her a little wave, which she returned. The hard part was over. Luna had found whilst touring the book that the Q&As were the hardest because you never knew what any given person was going to ask and whether you'd be able to think of an answer quickly enough. Now all she was required to do was spell everyone's name correctly.

One by one, people approached her table and Luna found her rhythm. She often found she asked the same set of ten questions in rotation and people often had the same answers. A signature and a selfie were the most requested; however, some surprised her with a gift or an odd request for a video to a relative or a friend who couldn't make it, which came at intervals when Luna was happy for a little deviation from the routine. Her audience was mainly women aged between sixteen and thirty and so she was always pleasantly surprised to see anyone other in the queue. A pen rolled off her desk just as someone was thanking her for her signature and so she was scrambling around by her feet when the next person approached the table. The deeper, more masculine voice caught her off guard but then recognition set in and she hit her head on the table as she snapped up straight.

'Ouch!' she yelped, unable to play it cool.

'Yeah, ouch. That looked painful. Are you okay?' His

round face hadn't changed in the year they'd been apart. His brown eyes hadn't lost their shine and his smile was still plump and kind. It took all she had to fight the tears that threatened to burst through the floodgates. Beau was exactly as she'd left him, only dressed a little smarter.

'Yeah, I'm ... I'm fine,' she breathed.

'I brought you a coffee,' he said as he placed a takeaway coffee cup on the table, the letters 'FW' written in his handwriting on the side. 'For some reason I felt like you were a flat white drinker.'

'Yes ... I am. Th-thank you.'

'I ... um ...' He wrung his hands. *Is he nervous? Am I making him nervous?* she wondered. 'I actually recognised you. From the photo in the back of the book.'

Luna felt her heart lunge for him. Did he *know* her? Like she knew him?

'Oh?' Her voice cracked.

'Yeah. This is going to sound completely mad but ... I think you took one of my pub quizzes, almost two years ago now. Won it, in fact! And then you—'

'Yes, I remember what came next.' She held up a hand to stop him relaying the details yet again. 'Of all the things to remember ...' she muttered but he must have heard.

'You got every question right!' he chuckled. 'How could I forget you?' Luna felt everything around her slow down as she truly absorbed the impact of his words. *How could I forget you?*

'It's easily done.' She tried to swallow but her mouth was dry. She sipped her new coffee.

'I actually used to live in Ondingside. I was part of that whole freak-weather thing too. Pretty crazy, huh?'

'Yeah ... crazy ... ' she parroted. 'So, what's your story then?' Luna busied herself with opening his book to the correct page, not able to look at his kind face for too long without her heart aching.

'I wish I knew!' he chuckled. 'I owned a coffee shop on the island and ... well, it's a bit embarrassing but – all I remember was waking up and finding myself locked in my own office! Took ages for anyone to hear me screaming the place down. Luckily, I'm told that when the first lot of boats reached the mainland, they sent for help and the whole island was thoroughly searched for stragglers.'

'I see,' Luna said, glancing up.

'So, I moved here permanently.' He shrugged, cheerfully. 'Opened up a coffee shop across the road. Seems business here is much better than it was back home. I'd always been too scared to take the plunge but now I'm here! So, I hope you like the coffee.'

'Yes ... thank you ... '

'You must have hit your head pretty hard. You've gone very pale. Can I get someone for you? Or maybe some water, instead?'

'No! No ... I'm fine.' She looked at him properly now. Every day she'd thought about seeing his face and she had thought of a thousand things she might say but now that he was stood within reach, all words seemed to escape her.

'Well . . .' He rocked back onto his heels, not knowing what to say in response to her gawping stare. 'Could you sign my book?'

'Of course! Of course!' she said, her voice high and squeaky as she almost knocked the book from his hand. She began to write 'Dear Beau' when she realised she hadn't asked for his name yet. She angled the book away from him so he couldn't see what she had written.

'What was your name?' she said glancing up, feeling a pang of longing each time she saw his face.

'Beau,' he smiled. 'B. E. A. U. I read the book the day it came out. I don't really read much but I'd heard a lot about it on TV and for some reason, I just knew I had to see what the fuss was about.'

'Oh yeah? And . . . and what did you think?'

'Well, I'm here, aren't I?' he laughed. 'It's incredible! Truly. Like I said, I haven't read a lot of books but your writing has a way of making me feel like . . . like it actually happened to me, y'know?' Luna really struggled to keep her expression intact. 'Maybe I'm being crazy.' He shrugged and ruffled the back of his hair in exactly the way she remembered.

'No . . . no, it's not crazy. I'm glad it made you feel that way. And I'm so glad that you . . . ' she sniffed, 'that you liked the story.'

'Are you okay? Is it your head?'

'I'm sorry,' she laughed, letting a few tears pour out. 'It's just lovely to hear that my writing has had an impact. If even just a small one.'

'More than just a small one! This book is what brought me and my ex-girlfriend back together!' Luna felt her insides hollow out and a coldness replace any warmth that had once been there. 'We hadn't spoken in years but she heard what had happened on the news. Assumed because I hadn't got in touch, I was okay and still didn't want to speak to her. Then she read your book and kept thinking, what if what happened to David had happened to me and I was somehow still stuck on the island with no way of escape. Well, she picked up the phone and we've never looked back.' He grinned. Luna felt like a hole had been punched through her chest to rip out her heart which was now being slowly steamrolled in front of her.

Luna had wondered if she'd ever see Beau again. Before now, she had been happy not knowing where Beau had ended up. Not knowing whether he made it off the island and not being directly faced with the future she could have had. Now that he was here, completely unfazed by their reunion and talking of the happy life he was now living, with someone else, somewhere else, she had another decision to make. It was make or break time. She could so easily let this set her back. She could so readily fall into a pit of dark, desperate despair and mourn the life she never got to live and the loss of the man she once knew, who was so very nearly hers. Or, Luna could continue living the life she actually had. She could continue writing and helping Wendy raise Tomorrow as her adopted auntie. Luna could even, if she let herself, find love. Luna held the cover of the book open and stared at the page in front of her.

In The Time We Lost

By

Elle J. Lark

She smiled a genuine half happy, half broken smile as she drew an arrow, pointing to her printed pseudonym, that snaked down to the empty space below where she began to write:

I just thought you should know,

Tears splattered onto the page, slightly smudging the ink but finally, she wrote ...

My name is Luna.

Acknowledgements

Thank you so much to all who helped make this story come to life. Hannah Boursnell and Viola Hayden, you guys put up with ridiculous questions and crazy ideas and work around the craziest of schedules. Thank you for your patience! Stephanie Melrose, publicist extra-ordinaire, please come forth! You're a dream! Thalia Proctor, you are an actual queen. Brionee Fenlon, thanks so much for all you've done behind the scenes! Bekki Guyatt and Helen Crawford-White, you never cease to amaze me with your beautiful book covers. This one is my favourite! Hannah Ferguson, you never cease to amaze me with your guidance and support. I can't thank you enough!

To all at Curtis Brown for being marvellous, support-ive and brilliantly bonkers, I love you all to Broadway and back!

Thanks to my parents for always being there at the drop of a hat. You're both mad and I couldn't love you more. Tom, Gi, Buzz, Buddy and Max. SUPERFAM! You five bring me constant joy and inspiration! Nan and

Grandad, you've both got a better memory than I do and always remember the little things. Love you both so much. Oliver, thank you for being patient and understanding and for making me laugh when stress is getting the better of me. Poomkin.

To my friends! Scott Paige, Mollie Melia Redgrave, Alex Banks, Emma Kingston, Jonny and Lucy Vickers, Paul Bradshaw, Rob Houchen, Celinde Schoenmaker, Richard Fleeshman, Becky Lock, Sophie Isaacs, Louise Jones, Ryan Hutchings, Louise Pentland and Adam Hattan. I'm scared to think of who I'd be without you all!

Finally, to you reading this book. Whether you've been here from the start or this book is the first you've heard of me, thank you for supporting me and my work. You have no idea what it means to me.

Xxx

Carrie Hope Fletcher is an actress, singer, author and vlogger. Carrie's first book, *All I Know Now*, was a number one *Sunday Times* bestseller and her debut novel, *On the Other Side*, also went straight to number one. *When the Curtain Falls* was Carrie's fourth consecutive *Sunday Times* bestseller.

Carrie played the role of Eponine in *Les Misérables* at the Queen's Theatre in London's West End for almost three years. She has since starred in and received awards for a number of productions including *The War of the Worlds*, *The Addams Family*, and *Heathers: The Musical*. Carrie will soon rejoin *Les Misérables*, this time playing Fantine, in a new concert version at the Gielgud Theatre.

Carrie lives just outside of London with numerous fictional friends that she keeps on bookshelves, just in case. Her debut album, also called *When the Curtain Falls*, was released in 2018.

Join us at

For competitions galore,
exclusive interviews with our lovely
Sphere authors, chat about
all the latest books
and much, much more.

Follow us on Twitter at
@littlebookcafe

Subscribe to our newsletter and
Like us at /thelittlebookcafe

Read. Love. Share.